The Day Trip

by Stephen Cheshire

Published by Pen It! Publications, LLC in the U.S.A.
812-371-4128 www.penitpublications.com
ISBN: 978-1-952011-15-3
Edited by Rachel Hale
Cover Design by Donna Cook

Acknowledgments

A special word of thanks to New College Nottingham, in Nottinghamshire, UK. You were the only academic campus in the United Kingdom to allow me to undertake a Foundation Degree in Aviation. All of the other academic campuses said, "No".

So I am so grateful that you had faith in me. So many thanks to you guys!

Contents

Introduction

There are approximately one hundred billion stars in our Milky Way Galaxy. That is quite a lot. What is beyond the galaxy? Another time? Other forms of life? The likeness of parallel universes and life on other planets is discussed quite a bit in scientific circles. How could we travel through outer space? Aliens from another universe would have to do a lot of searching to find this unique planet we call home. But if they did find us, why would an alien species invade? Overpopulation of their home planet? Lack of resources perhaps? Anything we have and they want could encourage them to attack. In this case, the Armazoids had little interest in our resources or respect for human civilization as we know it. Their reason for coming to Earth could be construed as our planet being in the wrong place at the wrong time. One spaceship carrying vital information simply strayed from its course back to its mother ship and crash landed in Russia, and in its search for the crashed ship, another descended on the small island of Manhattan in New York State. Just as in human wars, the casualties can seem trivial when the stakes are high. To the Armazoids, it was just too bad that so many New Yorkers got in their way. What they did not anticipate was a little pack of every day youths taking a day trip into the Big Apple and their strong will to survive. For all their advances, they couldn't counteract heroism—it just doesn't compute.

The Armazoids are all different sizes, their stumpy bodies covered with a light green skin. Like us, they have two eyes and a heart—nothing special. Their intelligence is average. However, they are years ahead with technology. For example, they can change their size at will; they are short or tall depending upon the circumstances. Their laser guns have a stealth range and deadly charge. It would take years of study by the world's leading scientists to even begin to understand the technology the Armazoids possess, and when under attack victims just gawk in awe.

Chapter 1

$\mathbf{A}$ green, five-foot- six tall Armazoid named Gremlon stared out the front of his dropship window. He was an average interstellar pilot away from home on a ship mainly used for troop transport. Moderate sized and dull, the ship had two atomic engines at the back capable of propelling them through universe quicker than the blink of our eye. They were on Planet Sygonia, which is approximately eight point nine trillion light years from Planet Earth—very far away.

"Where are they?" Gremlon snapped. "They should have called in by now."

The situation was tense. Comlon, his co-pilot, looked onto the radio stand on the avionics compartment of the ship waiting for the call. Ibregorg, the only other crewman aboard, looked pointlessly into the foliage for anything that could appear and pose a threat to their position. The dense shrubs surrounding the ship made it hard to see into the distance.

"This is Strike Force One calling Armazon three-one-six."

Gremlon jumped to attention and saw Comlon sit straighter in his chair.

"That's them," Gremlon yelped. "Answer it!"

"Go ahead, Strike Force One," Comlon stated. "What is your status and estimated time of arrival?"

There was a short pause.

"ETA four minutes, Armazon three-one-six."

3

"Power up!" Gremlon said. "We are out of here."

Comlon fired up the atomic engines, and three minutes later watched as the strike force team came from the huge shrubs and bushes, chased by the tribal inhabitants of Sygonia. The gangplank was down—all the troops had to do was run fast and get on board. Alas, they were being shot down one by one by the vengeful Sygonians.

Gremlon watched as the sprinting group slowly dwindled as they got closer and closer to the awaiting dropship, the foliage around them swaying with the force from the engines. He stared in disbelief. Colleagues he had known for years were perishing right in front of him. Nowhere in the universe had they come up against such an invincible force of creatures. Apparently, the Armazoids couldn't contend with their tribal nature and ability to unite and strategize.

"Come on!" Gremlon gasped. "Come on!"

Only one Armazoid from the strike force remained. He sprinted out towards the safety of the dropship, grasping the weapon he did not have time to recharge and use. Gremlon watched as this last remaining member of the strike team was shot in the back. The body froze, as the blood from his body ran out of his back. Eyes wide open, staring at the Armazoid Dropship, he slammed into the ground, knees first.

Gremlon started running towards him.

"Cover me!" he shouted over his shoulder.

"What?" Comlon gasped. "We haven't got time."

Comlon watched as Gremlon dived out the back of the ship. Comlon had his back and opened fire onto the incoming Sygonians—there was no comrades left standing that he could possibly hit—while Gremlon dove onto the ground near the soldier.

The soldier was panting from pain. His voice almost a whisper, he said, "It is in my pouch."

Gremlon knew he wasn't going to make it. He pulled a small disk out the pouch of his dying comrade. He looked down as the green blood ran out of the body. He didn't have the time to say goodbye, which added to the anger he felt.

"*Gremlon!*" Comlon screamed at the top of his voice.

Gremlon leapt up, sprinting back to open hanger of the dropship. He and Comlon shut the hanger door and ran to the control room. The atomic engines were at full power and ready to roll. Gremlon grabbed onto the stick in front of him, lifting the ship of the ground. He pushed the two power throttles forward.

"Hold on!" he screamed. The nose of the dropship leveled out as it reached cruising altitude. He looked down at the blips on the radar, showing several dots following their own. The Sygonian ships were chasing after them.

"Get the burners on," Gremlon yelled. "They are right behind us!"

"Won't be a minute," Comlon replied. "They're still powering up."

Gremlon looked down onto the computer screen. The rays from the chasing Sygonian ships fired onto them as they powered away from the planet. He tried to dodge them.

"Ready!" Comlon yelled.

But before he could activate them, one of the rays hit the engines. There was a small explosion at the back, but the dropship continued to move upwards. Gremlon looked down at his screen as the afterburners continued to fire up. Finally, a blue ray zoomed from the back, blasting the ship forward—luckily they were still working. The Sygonian

5

spaceships could only watch as the Armazoids craft disappeared into the depths of space.

Gremlon lay back in his seat as the silver light of the stars passed the main front window.

"That was close," he said, relieved. "You guys okay?"

The two Armazoids nodded, stunned by the sudden fire fight they had just got into. They were lucky to be alive.

"Let's assess the damage," Gremlon ordered. "To see if we can make it back to base with this data."

Comlon and Ibregorg stood up to take stock of the state of their ship. Gremlon stayed on the helm but looked up when his two crew-men came back quickly.

"It should be okay until we get back to the ship," Comlon said. "Hopefully."

He sat down in the co-pilot seat of the dropship and looked out as they sped through the galaxy. He noticed a huge yellow star in the center of their present galaxy.

"How far have we travelled?" he asked.

"About seven point nine trillion," Gremlon replied.

"All that for this!" Comlon said remorsefully, gesturing to the small disk with the valuable data in Gremlon's hand. "I knew Iennae and Blapau for years. It should have been me on that raid."

"Hey," Gremlon snapped, looking Comlon straight in the eyes.

Comlon looked at Gremlon, his eyes wide.

"Don't you ever let me hear you say that again," Gremlon yelled. "Those two signed up to defend our motherland, our home, our Armazon. Their deaths will not be in vain, I can promise you that!"

The back of the dropship went unusually quiet. Suddenly, an explosion from the back rocked the ship. The nose of the ship lowered. Gremlon grabbed onto the stick, pulling back. It was a struggle, but it pulled out. Alarms were screaming at him to act.

"Now what?" Comlon asked.

Gremlon looked up at his computer. He watched as the left atomic engine started to shut down. They would never be able to make it to the mothership. Light smoke started entering the cabin of the ship. There was a sudden surge. He continued looking at his computer as both the engines flared up.

"Declare an emergency," Gremlon said.

The ship started to slow down as Comlon switched on the radio.

On the main ship still light years from them, Circo, the leader of the first attack force, stood in the control room, trillions of miles away.

"This is Comlon," the radio mumbled.

Circo stormed over to it. The signal was weak.

"Comlon, this is Circo. Can you hear me?" he asked. There was a short break.

"Yes, only just," Comlon replied. "We have been hit and are unable to reach base."

"Comlon—" started Circo. The radio went completely dead.

***

Gremlon looked up as the smoke filling the cockpit grew thicker. The radio was dead, and the ship had sustained too much damage. He scanned the radar, looking for a place or a planet to ditch the craft. Sparks flew out of the radio. But something caught Gremlon's eye as the ship banked to the left. He saw a medium-sized planet coming into view. He stared through the windshield at the lumps of blue and a funny looking green color that covered the planet. It was their only option.

"There," he yelled. "There!"

"I heard you the first time," Comlon replied.

Gremlon was pointing at Planet Earth. He looked at the curious planet as it grew in their view screens. He turned the ship and headed directly towards it. Sparks continued to rain down from the ceiling as the instruments and system gauges started to fail one after the other. The planet filled their view as they continued to slow down with the loss of engine power. The nose of the ship heated up as they entered the planet's atmosphere. Gremlon pulled the control stick back, straining the craft's hydraulic system to try to slow the descent. The two other Armazoids could only sit and watch as the flames sped over the ship, adding to the heat from the burning engines, and the craft gently rocked from side to side. The orange flames and plasma trails disappeared from the ship. Dense, jet-black smoke poured from the back of the engine. Comlon looked out of the window as they continued quickly dropping from the sky.

"What is this place?" Gremlon demanded.

"I, I don't know," Comlon replied.

"How high are we?" Gremlon asked.

"We are just over five thousand feet above it. We've got maybe two minutes of glide time before we crash," Comlon replied.

Something else caught Gremlon's eyes. He looked to his left to see two black jets pulling up next to them as they continued descending towards the ground.

"What the hell are they?" Gremlon asked.

The two other Armazoids walked up to the window and looked out as the ground continued to get closer and closer.

One of the black jets pulled in front of the dropship, gently rocking its wings. Gremlon followed the black jet over the land. He looked out to see a long strip in front of them, approaching as they passed through five thousand feet.

"Sit down," Gremlon ordered. "This is going to be rough this landing."

The two other Armazoids sat down as Gremlon reached out and pulled down the landing gear lever. The landing gear came down as the airstrip came closer and closer to them. The wind drag it created helped slow the ship for the landing. The two black jets continued accompanying them towards the threshold of the runway as they descended. Gremlon grasped hold of the control stick and pulled the nose up as the back gear slammed into the ground. The black fumes continued piling out of the aircraft. The speed brakes opened on the top of the wings as the nose gear touched down onto the runway of the huge military airstrip. The end of the runway was getting near, and the dropship had started to slow down, but they were still going too fast. Gremlon felt the nose wheel start to creak. He held on tight as it touched down, skidding along the rest of the runway. The scraping echoed around the cabin as the ship. Luckily it helped to slow them down to a stop.

The onlookers at a military base in Yenisei in northern Russia, around 300 miles from the Siberian border, gawked as the alien spacecraft stood on the runway, nose gear collapsed. No signs of life could be seen.

Gremlon slowly lifted his head up and peeked out of the window, which already had a dusting of snow settling on it. He didn't know what to expect. The life forms slowly started walking towards them, armed well.

"What the hell are those things?" he asked in a shocked and confused voice.

Comlon walked to the front of the ship. Still shaken from the crash, he stared at the gray uniforms and wide hats. The weather outside was freezing, and snow started to obstruct the view of the beings moving toward them.

Gremlon pulled himself together. "Prepare to disembark—now!" Gremlon ordered.

As the Armazoids prepared to leave the ship, the life forms completely surrounded them. Gremlon looked down at his computer. He pushed the tiny emergency button, which signaled their location to the mother ship light years away from their current position. He also took the time to assess the area outside him via his computer readouts. They reported very high levels of carbon dioxide and very low temperatures.

"Suits," he ordered. "Carbon dioxide out there and lots of it."

"We're going out there?" Comlon asked in a shocked voice

"Got a better idea?" Gremlon replied, looking into his eyes

The group got into their suits, looking at one another apprehensively as they prepared to go outside.

"Hide the data," Gremlon ordered, waving the disk in Comlon's face.

"What?" Comlon asked.

"Just do it."

Comlon took the disk and hid it in a flap under the floor. They armed themselves, ready to fight to the death.

Gremlon looked at his two comrades as he pulled the red lever. The bay doors slowly hissed open. The smoke poured in from the outside. It was extremely cold.

"Here goes," Gremlon said.

Gremlon walked out first, uncertain of what to do first. There was another group of natives approaching dressed all in white.

"What do we do?" Comlon frantically whispered to Gremlon, clearly panicking.

Gremlon didn't say a word.

"Now!" Comlon yelled.

"Wait," Gremlon shrieked, trying to prevent the fight.

Comlon fired onto the men, followed closely by Ibregorg. Their purple rays zapped through the air, mostly slamming harmlessly into the snow, but one hit a man dressed in gray. The men in gray began to run and shout, finding cover and firing back at the Armazoids.

"Shit," Gremlon yelled as he dove behind the ship's cargo door.

He watched from his position of relative safety as Comlon and Ibregorg, his only two remaining crewmen, fell to the ground, riddled with bullets. He knew he would have to surrender, but the fate of Planet Armazon rested in his hands and on that disk.

Gremlon dropped his weapon onto the floor. He stood up slowly, looking at the people as they walked slowly towards him, clutching their weapons. Two of the men placed him in a strong plastic bag. Gremlon felt his body being tightly compressed as he was lifted and placed on a metal table. He struggled to get out, but the straps were too tight. He trembled as he wondered where on earth he was going.

11

***

Volkov Radoslav, the Russian Premier, woke to a banging on his door. His eyes slowly opened to the heavy knocks. His head burned from the warmth of the heaters. He sat up slowly and rubbed his eyes. He got out of the bed and walked across the red carpet toward the front door of his room. He found himself looking at his assistant, Stanislav.

"Sorry to wake you, sir, but there has been an incident," Stanislav said quietly.

Volkov paused for a long moment before speaking. "Okay. A minute please."

He dressed slowly, wondering what on earth had happened for him to be woken up so early in the morning. The sun had started to come up over the horizon of Moscow. Volkov walked out of his bedroom and down to his office. He sat down as three of his military top generals waited to speak to him. He looked at his white coffee cup on his desk as he sat down and noticed the lack of steam.

"Okay, bring me up to speed on the situation," Volkov demanded.

One of the generals stepped forward. "Sir," he said quietly, "an alien spacecraft has crashed at our Yenisei air base."

Volkov didn't say a word. He wondered if he was still asleep and if this was just a dream running through his head.

"An alien spacecraft," he repeated.

"Yes, sir. Crash-landed a few hours ago. We only just got the message."

There was a silence in his office. He looked up at the clock.

"Did anyone see what damaged the ship?" he asked.

"No, sir," his general said. "It flew in from the north already smoking and crashed at our air force base there. We managed to guide it in."

"Did any living thing emerge from the craft?" Volkov asked.

"Yes sir," The general replied. "Three of them."

"Did they offer any resistance?" Volkov asked.

"Yes. Two were shot and we have one at Area 52," the general said.

"Has he tried any type of communication with you?" Volkov asked.

"No, sir," his general replied, "but we are working at it."

"Okay," Volkov said. "I want a media blackout on this. No one is to know—only us."

"Understood, sir."

Chapter 2

Three months later.

If you asked Bradley Harrison to write about himself and what was important to him, this is what he would say:

We used to be the typical boys, running around with toy guns, shooting at enemies and, of course, not to forget the aliens. You know what I mean. So we had the practice. Who was to know that one day all that pissing around would have been needed on a normal day like today.

My name is Bradley. Bradley Harrison. I'm your average, everyday teenager. Love women and have my mind on one thing only. You guessed it: gun clubs and martial arts. Of course, you know what else I mean. I was born on the 2nd August 1999. So nearly eighteen. Let me introduce you to some of my friends, and to make things better, the enemies too, who are going to have a different view of me after today.

Meet Kevin, my longest running and most loyal friend. I have known him since kindergarten. He has a great brother called Will who has joined the US Army. Then we have Max. Nice guy, the best sniper shooting at the local gun club. He has had more bull's eyes than I have had hot dinners. And of course, we leave the best man till last. Meet Eric. Yes, Eric. Mind you, Eric did help us out a lot when the Armazoids were invading, but he isn't the sharpest tool in the toolbox. But we all love him very much.

Now to the others. Kate is my childhood sweetheart, and Lisa is Kevin's. To this very day we are trying to get in their pants. I didn't just say that, did I? But haven't had much luck since—well, you get what I mean.

Now to the fun people. Ms. Hogan, our form tutor, has had it in for me ever since I started high school. I don't know it's one of those things, but she has a little sidekick named Colin. If I said boo to a goose, he would tell her. So, there you have it.

However, a normal day trip to the Big Apple is going to change the way they viewed life as they saw it. The day before the big day began in the afternoon in New Haven City. The day slowly came to an end. The sun shone down on the busy city as Bradley stared out of the classroom window at the golden statue of the high school founder. The reflection of the sun glistened in his eyes. The hanging baskets by the main entrance blew in the afternoon breeze as the sun beamed down on the busy city. They are into the summer season now. Mr. Knightsbridge, Bradley's physics teacher, stood at the front of the classroom, absently feeling the pens in his front shirt pocket. He was in front of a digital computer board that displayed a huge map of New York City. That was all Bradley was thinking about—the trip tomorrow. The bell rang as the clock struck three. Home time. The group slowly got up as the bell continued ringing, lumping folders into their bags.

"Okay, New York, here we come. I am sure it is going to be the best field trip we have been on this year, so half past eight, bang on, please," Mr. Knightsbridge said. "Oh yeah, and don't forget your homework for next Monday. I want to see at least two thousand words on what effects an electromagnetic pulse has and how it could wipe out a country."

Bradley looked disappointed as he knew the whole of his weekend after New York was going to be spent writing about the EMP. "It goes bang and anything electric is fried," he muttered, walking towards the room door.

"I'll need just a bit more, Bradley, my friend," Mr. Knightsbridge replied.

Bradley looked over at Kevin, who was throwing his new gray rucksack over his shoulder.

"We going straight to the club?" Kevin asked.

"Yep. I told Eric and Max to meet us after school," Bradley replied.

"Safe," Kevin replied.

Bradley and Kevin slowly walked through the busy corridors. He heard the old physics room door closing. Mr. Knightsbridge's jingling keys could be heard over the lockers being slammed shut by students eager to get home. There was still one day before the weekend. Bradley and Kevin strolled towards the exit of the school. They walked out of the main entrance and were blasted by the hot, humid—still a relief after being inside half of the afternoon.

"New York tomorrow," Kevin eagerly said.

"Yep. But sadly it's a day with Ms. Hogan," Bradley replied. "What's the bet she puts us all in different groups like when we went to Washington."

"That most possibly could be true," Kevin replied. "You know what she is like."

They saw Max and Eric standing at the bottom of the stairs by the entrance of the school, ready to leave. Their bags were slung over their shoulders, weighed down with schoolwork and folders.

"Hey guys," said Kevin.

"Hi," Max said, clearly relieved to be out of school. "Are we shooting tonight?"

"Yep," Bradley replied. "I am." Now that they had been outside for more than five minutes, the sun was getting too hot. He noticed Kate and Lisa getting into their friend's car to go home. Bradley pointed over at them. "Here, watch this," he said to his friends. He took a deep breath as he turned toward the two blond girls.

"Alright, short skirt, wanna go out?" Bradley yelled. "I'm free tonight."

He watched as Kate looked over her shoulder at him.

"Get real, freak," she yelled.

Bradley made a rude gesture and smirked. Kate looked at him in disgust. Bradley and his friends laughed as they continued down the sidewalk.

"Hell, it's hot."

"Yep, most probably the same in New York tomorrow," Kevin replied. "All day long."

"Lovely. A whole day without coursework," Bradley replied.

"Have you got your science project done on the EMP?" Max asked Bradley.

"Nah, almost done though," Bradley replied. "You?"

"Yep, all done," Max bragged. "The weekend is mine"

"Nerd," Bradley joked. "I mean, big deal. It pulses out, all electricity fried. Merry Christmas." He made a left turn and walked onto a quiet street, absentmindedly looking at the cars as they drove past.

"Have you heard from Queen's Gate College yet, Kev?" Bradley asked, trying to make the trip home quicker.

"No, not yet. I'll let you know when I do," Kevin replied. "You?"

"Same," Bradley replied. "I'm debating whether to join the police or the military."

"Me, I'm applying for the NYPD," Kevin said. "Just think—patrolling the streets. They say it's a different story every day."

"Suppose it would be a laugh," Bradley said. "Why not go in the army with your bro? How is he doing, by the way?"

"I did think about that," Kevin replied. "He is doing well—starting training soon."

The group approached a crossroads.

"Okay, shall we meet at my house same time as usual? Four?" Bradley asked.

The group nodded as they set off in different directions. The sun was slowly starting to descend, still very hot. The trees moved gently in the breeze as the leaves dropped onto the road. Bradley turned up the swept path, barely noticing the well-kept flowerbeds.

"Hey Mom," he yelled over the closing door.

"Oh hi, Bradley. How was your day at school?" she asked him from the kitchen.

"Fine. Glad it's over," Bradley replied, walking in to lean on the granite countertop.

"Did you have Ms. Hogan?" she asked.

"No. Not today. But sadly I have her all day tomorrow when I am in the Empire State," Bradley said, rubbing his hands together. "Might have some fun with her."

"Oh dear! Never mind. You will be finished there in just under a year's time and then you can go to college," his

19

mom said. "It's a lot better and you won't have Ms. Hogan there."

"Yeah, I suppose that is a benefit," Bradley replied. "Right, I have got to get ready. Kung fu isn't on this afternoon, so I am going straight to the club with the guys."

Bradley ran up the well-vacuumed stairs towards his bedroom and pushed the door open. His window was wide open and a soft breeze was blowing in; the room was relatively cool. He got out of his school clothes and chucked them down on the floor, getting dressed in clean clothes and looked for his small string bag. He finally found it hanging up behind his door. His mom had obviously hung it there when she had cleaned his room out.

"Women!" he said, smiling.

Bradley walked out of his room. He rubbed his knuckles on the string straps of his bag as he went down the stairs.

"Right, I'm off," Bradley called. "Time to kick some ass."

"Oh, see ya, Bradley. Be good," his mom yelled.

"I will," he replied. "I always am."

Bradley walked out the front door of his house. He pulled it shut as he stepped down on to the newly laid pathway. He turned to see his friends already waiting for him.

"Come on, let's go," Bradley said.

Bradley, Kevin, Max and Eric slowly walked along the busy street. Bradley looked down the street as the city came into view.

"So, we're kung fuing this afternoon, aren't we?" Kevin asked.

"No. The lesson is off—Alex is ill. But that means more time on the shooting range. I can't be bothered to head to the gym," Bradley replied.

"Me, neither," Max replied. "Got a long day tomorrow, bros."

They continued along the road as they approached the High Street Gun Club. Bradley looked up at the huge magnum weapon on the top of the old building. He pushed the door open and slowly walked in. He could smell the gunpowder as Barry, the shop manager, stood behind the counter and polished his twin-barrel shotgun.

"Hey, Brad," he said. "How's it going?"

"Hi Barry. I see the old Winchester is looking good," Bradley replied.

"Yep, it's my pride and joy. I was out last Saturday with the wife, clay pigeon shooting," Barry replied. "You popping a few rounds?"

"I'd love to," Eric said. "Hard day at school."

"Me, too," Max replied.

Barry looked up at the clock as the shooters already on the range slowly returned to the shop through the metal door after their round.

"Right. In you go, boys. Have fun." Barry stated. "As I always say—be safe. You know the drill."

"When can I have a go on that?" Eric asked pointing at the Winchester pump.

Barry and Bradley both stared at Eric, who was staring at the shotgun.

"Never," Barry replied.

"Oh." Eric sighed. "Why not?"

"You know why," Barry replied with a dangerous look into his eyes.

The boys walked to the table at the back of the range where the weapons were stacked up, each going toward their preferred gun. Bradley leaned down and picked up a handgun from the table. The magazine was poised next to it. Bradley slipped the magazine into the slot below, cocking the top back and forward. The golden bullets were loaded into the chambers and the gray door was locked into place. Reaching into his bag, Bradley brought out earmuffs and gray, plastic goggles, which he quickly put on. He stared through the sight and flicked off the safety catch. A cardboard cutout dropped out from the ceiling above. He squeezed the trigger and launched the first round through the air. The golden bullet slammed into the cardboard cutout at the end of the range.

"Bull's-eye," Bradley yelled. He continued shooting at the targets, Eric shooting to his right.

"You miss all the time," Bradley remarked.

"No, I don't," Eric replied. Then he shrugged and grinned. "Well, I try my best."

"Max," Bradley called, "whoever gets the most bulls pays for drinks tomorrow after we return from New York."

"You got it," Max said.

Max and Bradley watched as the cardboard cutouts dropped out one after the other. The boys took shots, feeling the vibrations run through their ears.

"Missed!" Eric said. "Blast, missed again."

"I didn't," Max said, smirking at Bradley.

The boys finished shooting and walked back to the table to put their guns back down onto the table.

"Damn that felt good," Max said.

"So I won that one," Bradley said.

Max raised his eyebrows, shocked. He turned his head, looking at the cardboard cutouts that were in Bradley's area. They all had shots in the middle.

"Wait till the sniper tournament," Max said.

"I will," Bradley replied, smiling. "So you owe me tomorrow."

"Yeah, yeah" Max said non committally.

Bradley looked Max in the eye.

"Okay, I'll buy you a drink tomorrow," Max sullenly said.

Bradley brightened and turned toward the others. "Right. I need to get home. I am very tired. Didn't sleep well last night."

"Me too," Kevin replied. "Need to be ready for the trip tomorrow."

They slowly walked to the exit of the club. The strain of schoolwork slowly lifted off their backs as the prospect of New York came closer. Bradley looked across the busy street to see Kate and Lisa walking out of a clothing store.

"Look," he said to the group, then he yelled, "Hello again!" to the two girls.

The two girls continued walking, glancing at Bradley as they held onto the small bags full of their purchases after the afternoon shopping spree.

"What did you buy?" Bradley called. "Come on show me."

Kate and Lisa looked away from Bradley, trying to ignore him.

"Seems like she really likes you," Eric said in a sarcastic voice.

Bradley didn't answer. He watched as the two girls slowly walked away, heading for home.

"I'm off," Kevin said. "I'll see you lot in the morning."

"Me, too," Bradley replied. "I'll see you lot tomorrow."

Bradley walked home consumed in thoughts of the Big Apple. As he turned up the walk to his front door, he could smell the lasagna his mom had prepared for dinner. His mouth watered.

Inside, he saw his dad staring at the newspaper as he sat at the dining table. Condensation ran down the glass of water beside him.

"Hey Dad," Bradley said.

Mr. Harrison lowered the paper.

"Hey Brad."

"Nothing in the papers today?"

"Just the usual rubbish."

Bradley nodded as he put his bag down onto the floor, then slipped his shoes off next to it. He walked into the kitchen as his dad reopened the paper.

"Did you have fun?" his mom queried. She knows what the answer is.

"Yep," Bradley said as he sat down on a chair. "Kicked Max's ass again."

"You always beat him," his mom replied proudly.

His dad looked up again.

"So, New York tomorrow?" his dad asked, changing the atmosphere. "You got enough spending money?"

"Yes," Bradley replied. "Can't wait. I think it's going to be an exciting day tomorrow."

"I'm sure it will be," his dad replied. "That's where I met your mom."

Bradley had heard the story about a thousand times. "I've heard the story, Dad," Bradley replied, putting his head into his arms.

His mom walked over to the dining table with dinner and sat down, Bradley right behind her. The lasagna was cooked to perfection and all ready to be eaten, steaming and bubbling hot.

"Smells good," Mr. Harrison said, praising her.

"Well," Mrs. Harrison said, "tuck in, you work hard for this family."

Bradley smiled. He looked up at the clock. Six o'clock on the dot hit. There wasn't much on television this time of the day. He picked up the knife and fork as his mom put a hot serving onto his plate. He immediately started into it. Bradley felt the food roll down the back of his throat. It was a godsend after the long day in school. Going to the gun club made him hungrier.

"So what are you doing tomorrow in New York?" his mom asked.

"Sightseeing," he replied.

"What sights?" his dad asked.

"I am not too sure," Bradley replied. "God knows what Ms. Hogan has lined up for us."

"Do you still get grief from her?" Mr. Harrison could not understand what the woman's problem was.

"Yes," Bradley replied, shrugging.

Mr. Harrison placed his knife and fork onto his plate.

"Do I need to pop into that school again?"

"Nah," Bradley replied. "Leave it. Mind you, I instigate it."

Mr. Harrison looked at Bradley. He wiped food from the corners of his lips with his napkin, studying his son.

***

Bradley looked up at the clock: nine o'clock. Dinner was finished, the sun had gone down, and the stars were starting to come out. It had cooled down as well.

"Right, I'm off to bed," he said. "Busy day tomorrow."

His dad looked up at him as he walked towards the door. "If I don't see you in the morning, have a great time." his dad said.

"Thanks, Dad. Don't be late for work."

"I'm never late," his dad replied. "You know me."

Bradley walked up the stairs, stopping quickly in the bathroom to brush his teeth before heading to his bedroom to hurriedly put on pajamas. He pulled the duvet back and fell onto the bed face first.

He sighed contentedly. "Oh man."

He checked to make sure his alarm clock was set for seven and closed his eyes, thinking of the day ahead.

Chapter 3

Manhattan, New York City—where tourists wander as cargo ships head into the Atlantic for destinations all over the planet. The horn from the ships echoed as the evening sun shone red on the Hudson River. Tugboats chugged up the dirty old river, their wakes interfering with the reflection of the sunlight. The neon lights on the skyscrapers in Times Square started to switch on and light up the evening sky. Smartly dressed businesspeople in their suits and carrying their briefcases left their offices as the evening cleaners started their night shifts. The smell of toilet disinfectant permeated the air as the old ladies sprayed the windows and wiped them down with their yellow shammy cloths. Afternoon taxi drivers went home after their long shifts, the moon slowly rising above them to beam down on the city. The last flights from the airport took off in front of the moon, leaving trails of ghostly fumes. The North Star began to twinkle as an owl in Central Park hooted, scanning the ground for any mice. A cool evening breeze started to blow. A road sign squeaked and leaves blew into the lake in the center of the park. An old park warden swept up the rubbish, the sound off his brush scrubbing against the new path echoing. Mice ran off as he hauled the wheelbarrow along the short-cut grass. He looked up into the clear night sky as the stars continued to gleam down onto the planet and the city.

***

Circo looked out of the front of the huge ship as the rest of the Armazoids scanned the surrounding computers for Gremlon's ship tracker. He listened to his people speaking to one another as the craft gently drifted through the universe, skimming past the other planets not even known yet to mankind. He suddenly jumped at a sudden beep coming from behind. He turned and looked at the small digital screen in the bridge where a little white light was gently flickering on and off.

"Talk!" Circo demanded. "Now!"

"Yes," one of the Armazoids replied. "The signal is very weak I only just got the figures of the location; we can do it."

Circo looked down at the digital board. "Where is that?" he asked.

"It's about three point seven billion miles from here," the Armazoid replied. "It's a very weak signal. We haven't got long before we could lose it."

"Turn to that heading," Circo demanded. "Let's get there—the fate of our planet could rest in that data."

The two pilots of the Armazoid ship slowly turned the craft and headed towards Earth. They zoomed past all the other cosmic scenery and looked anxiously for the planet. Circo squinted his eyes as the green and blue planet slowly started to appear.

"Are we landing sir?" one Armazoid asked.

"Yes," Circo said instantly. "Yes, we are. For the sake of Armazon we have to."

The craft slowed as the two Armazoid pilots looked down onto their computers. They studied at the radar screen as it looked for a suitable landing spot within the planet.

"Are we changing size, sir?" one pilot asked.

"Yes," Circo replied. "No one is to know of our being here."

He walked back as Planet Earth slowly filled the viewport.

"Sir, we have just intercepted some sort of space station and it is taking pictures of us."

"Destroy it," Circo commanded. "And switch on jammers, so no one knows where here."

Circo looked out of his spacecraft as one of the smaller laser launchers rolled out and pointed towards the Hubble Telescope. The power started to surge up behind the machine, getting to maximum for firing through the air. Circo watched as the ray slammed into and ripped through the outdated electronic object. It spiraled toward the blue planet, heating up to a bright orange when it entered the atmosphere.

"Piece of junk," Circo said.

In a moment they had passed the wreckage, and now sparks flew as the huge spaceship slowly entered the excessive heat of the atmosphere.

"Excellent," Circo said, rubbing his hands together. He watched as the rest of his troops prepared to land the ship on the planet without being spotted. He squinted his eyes as their ship thundered through Earth's atmosphere.

An alarm started beeping, indicating a problem with their communications antennae. The Armazoids in the front looked down onto the planet as their ship slowly started to glow a light green color. The craft slowly shrank in size as they descended over the dark blue ocean. Now the size of a remote-control car, the shrunken Armazoid pilots studied their monitors they zoomed over the densely populated area, unobservable to the passing life forms below.

Circo ordered the ship toward a wide green expanse—Central Park in Manhattan. The nose pointed down as Central Park got bigger and bigger. There were few people around. The ship flew over the lake and headed for a small cave in the shrubs and landscape. The engines powered back as the Armazoids slowly flew in, still keeping a low profile. While Circo watched the huge sets of landing gear come down, the crewman approached and reported the antennae was completely dysfunctional and would take quite a while to repair. The jolt of the ship's landing matched Circo's bad temper as he shooed the Armazoid away. The atomic engines began to shut down one after the other.

Circo turned to the rest of the crew on the bridge. "No one is to leave without my permission," he ordered. "How safe are we here?"

"The computer reports that it is quite safe," replied a co-pilot.

Circo looked out the front of the ship into the shallow underground cave.

"Okay, I want a vehicle to take me around to control room one," he ordered. "Now, hurry up!"

Within a few minutes, one of the Armazoid vehicles pulled up outside the main entrance to the bridge to the ship. Circo walked down the steps escorted by his armed guards. He stepped into the shiny, white vehicle. It pulled away from the entrance to the bridge. Circo watched as the lights from his now-shrunken ship passed overhead.

He stepped out of the vehicle as they pulled up outside the entrance to the smaller control room, walked up a short set of steps and pushed a green button next to the door to the smaller control room. Circo tapped his foot impatiently as the airlock slowly opened. Three Armazoids were waiting for him the main table, looking down at the map of the planet.

"Any luck in locating Gremlon?" he asked before sitting down.

"No sir," Araphon said, standing up.

"Sit," Circo ordered. "Now!"

Araphon looked at Circo calmly and sat back down.

"Can we trace that signal?" he asked.

"No sir," Adamlon said to Circo. "The signal was too weak at the time—we were lucky enough to locate this planet."

"Who is in charge of this dump then?" Circo asked.

"We don't know yet, sir. We're trying to locate its leader," Araphon replied.

"Get in contact," he ordered. "If not, we take things further, can we still contact with the main communication down?"

"Yes sir" Araphon replied "I'm using a backup for the local area"

Circo's eyes rested on the map of Earth for a moment before looking up again. "Okay, we're going to explore the planet we are on while we discreetly find out who or what we are dealing with"

Circo had to think. He couldn't communicate with the home planet because of the damaged communications antenna.

"What's the main language of this planet?" Circo asked.

31

"It seems there is not one unified language for the planet, according to the computer." Araphon said. "But this region speaks the language English."

"Ok, get this language English programmed into every Armazoid on this ship."

"Yes sir!" Araphon said.

"Any news on the antenna?" Circo demanded.

"Yes sir," Araphon replied "If we stay on schedule, tomorrow evening this earths time, it will be fixed."

Circo smiled at the positive turn in events. "Then if these things haven't given us what we want, we can take it further. I also want a full report on this planet's defense system."

"Sir," the three replied in unison.

***

Two Armazoid soldiers stepped off their shiny transport as it pulled up by the elevator that would take them to the surface of the ship. They knew they would need to be careful when they returned to their normal size when out of the ship. The Armazoids switched on the electric filters on their suits.

"Okay, let's do this," one of them said.

They stood before the elevator and waited as its shutter door slowly started to roll up. They walked onto the huge metal plate and turned to face the now-closing shutter seal them in. The two stood in their suits, listening to the filter on their backs working as they breathed in the pure oxygen from the ship.

"Here we go," one said. "Let's see what this place is like then."

They stared up as the large elevator slowly took them to the surface. It clanked to a stop at the top of the ship, which was near the top of the crater caused during landing. Holding onto their weapons, the two Armazoids slowly walked over the top of the ship to a bridge that had been set up to span the distance from the ship to the top of the crater. They could see very little of the new planet from inside their ship's chosen refuge—the cave blocked both stars and city lights. Their headlamps illuminated dangling roots above and moist soil beneath.

The two Armazoids arrived at the cave's entrance after the ten-minute run. In the open again, they looked at one another and nodded. Their eyes sparkled and their slimy bodies started to glow a light green. The ground slowly got further away as they grew back to their original size. They looked at one another and pulled out their ray guns.

The moon shone down onto the bright city, its light drowning out the twinkling of the stars. The leaves rustled in the breeze as the Armazoids cautiously moved away from their ship, scanning Central Park and staying out of sight. Through the clump of bushes, they saw a life form, covered in newspaper and lying on a bench. It stunk of alcohol. The Armazoids crept over carefully, keeping their distance.

"What the hell is that?" one said.

"I have no idea. But let's take him."

As they studied the male, they didn't find him a threat. One slowly placed his hands over his mouth. The man's bloodshot eyes popped open.

"What the hell?" he yelled at the top of his voice. "Who are you people? Communists!"

Nobody heard or cared. Drunken yelling was not uncommon this time of night. Despite his larger size, the

Armazoids picked the drunk up and set him on his feet, pushing him towards a cave entrance.

"Come on," one soldier insisted. "Move it!"

"Help," the drunk shrieked and looked around in shock as the two Armazoids dragged him in front of the cave and shrunk him. "What is this? Who are you people? Help!"

The two Armazoids laughed as they approached the bridge leading to the ship. They walked across toward the large elevator, ready to take the human down into the ship. The drunk looked around in disbelief as the brakes clunked off one after the other. The lift lowered into the ship as the two aliens held onto the man.

"Get away, you communists," he yelled. "I dealt with you people in 'Nam, I can do it again! Trust me on that."

The lights from each floor swept over the two Armazoids and the hobo as they approached the floor below them. The brakes came on and the shutter door opened. The hobo looked around the ship in amazement at the shiny glossy floor as the rest of the Armazoids looked at him. The pure oxygen from the ship made him high as the two Armazoids bundled him into the back of one of their vehicles.

"This is a violation of my rights," the hobo yelled, and then he giggled. "Did you hear me? I have rights as much as you do, you know."

The Armazoids continued to laugh as they sped through the ship towards the labs. The lights zoomed past the window, almost hypnotizing the man, who continued yelling as the vehicle pulled up outside the labs. The two Armazoids stepped out of the vehicle and walked around to the back. They swung the door open, pulling the man out as Circo arrived at the labs in another vehicle.

"What have we here?" Circo asked.

"This is a violation of my rights," the hobo yelled again in a loud voice.

"God, you stink," Circo remarked as he looked down at him again. "I want a full analysis of...of this thing as soon as possible."

The two Armazoids strapped the man onto a gurney and walked over to their computer. The hobo continued shouting incoherently.

"I have rightttssssss," he shrieked again. "Do you know what they are?"

The two Armazoids continued giggling at the man as the experiments went on into the night.

Chapter 4

A crow landed on the tree branch outside Bradley's bedroom window. It looked through the glass pane at him as his shiny alarm clock showed a minute to seven o'clock. The cool morning breeze blew gently through the bird's feathers as it cawed and looked around the beautifully maintained garden, trying to find the glint of something shiny and accessible.

Bradley slowly opened his eyes to the croak of the crow and shut them. The sun beamed through the blue curtains as Bradley's alarm clock started to beep. The crow shot off the branch, knocking leaves onto the ground as the beeping continued. Bradley again opened his eyes slowly, looking at the flashing alarm clock as the crow headed off into the distance. It beeped on and off, echoing in his ears. He tried to block it out, but then slowly rolled his hand out from under the soft quilt, switching it off as he felt his eyes wanting to close again. His small eyes stung from the long night's sleep and his black hair was ruffled up into a fuzzy ball.

"Shit," he mumbled.

Bradley clumsily got out of bed, looking at the casual clothes his mom had set out for the big day ahead of him. He felt his legs go slightly wobbly as the blood rushed from his head, and he put his hand to the wall. The shower was running in the bathroom opposite his room, so he waited outside the bathroom until his mom walked out wrapped in a towel.

"Oh morning, Bradley," she said to him. "We are excited!"

"Oh yes," he replied, walking into the shower and closing the door.

Steam filled the bathroom. The green tiles that climbed halfway up the walls had tiny drops of water running down them. The sun beamed in, adding to the muggy atmosphere. Bradley showered and returned to his room, slowly getting dressed as he looked out the window on what looked like the start of another hot day. He put his small string bag onto his back as he picked up his cash-filled wallet. He ambled down the stairs to see his dad running out of the kitchen.

"Are you okay, Dad?"

"Yes," was the brisk reply. "Running late!"

Bradley watched as papers were piled into the briefcase, which was unceremoniously shut with some documents sticking out. Bradley turned into the front room and looked at his mom sitting down at the dining table and slowly eating her toast. She was dressed and ready for the day. He sat down, pulling at the tiny bits of toast as he looked up at the clock on the wall. The radio on the table was softly playing classical music.

"You look tired," she said.

"A bit. Can't wait. I've never been to New York," Bradley replied.

"I have. I used to work there," his mom said.

"Oh really?" Bradley mumbled under his breath.

"It was an office, right in the city center. I met your dad when I was on a coffee break. I will never forget that day. I walked into the coffee shop a few minutes' walk from where I worked, and there he was—just standing there. Spiked hair and in a suit."

Bradley smiled as he looked up at the clock again: 7:30. "Okay, I gotta go now," he said, putting the piece of toast into his mouth and standing up before his mom could go off on one.

"Hope you have a nice day," she said, watching the crumbs roll off his mouth onto the clean table.

"Thanks, see you tonight."

He walked over and opened the front door, the morning sun warming his face. He hesitated by the front door when he heard the radio news come on. The young reporter took a deep breath.

"Good morning. New Haven news at seven thirty. It has been confirmed by the United States government that the Hubble Telescope has crashed into the Atlantic Ocean last night. Investigators are currently on their way to the location of the crashed vehicle. The cause has not yet been confirmed."

Bradley shrugged and stepped onto the welcome mat, firmly closing the front door beside him. He walked down the sidewalk toward the school. "What on earth brought the Hubble down?" he asked himself.

He looked down the sidewalk as a young female jogger headed toward him, headphones on and bass audible. He smiled, following her with his eyes as she jogged past in her bright pink, silky shorts. Bradley smiled again as he continued down the empty sidewalk.

Reaching the school a few minutes later, he saw the brown gates wide open to welcome the students. He walked in slowly, looking at the huge statue of the school's founder as it cast its shadow over the newly laid flowerbed. He took a deep breath and slowly walked to his classroom, following several students in his class. In the doorway, he glanced around until he saw Kevin, Max, and Eric sitting at a table, string bags on and ready to roll.

"Morning," he said, pulling out a plastic chair. The other guys nodded in greeting. Bradley took a small Red Bull from his bag, listening to the hiss after he cracked it open before taking a sip. He looked toward the doorway of the classroom.

Ms. Hogan walked in. Her plump, short frame was dressed in a purple skirt and blouse, and she was holding a huge plastic box full of schoolwork and homework from the day before. She slammed it down onto her desk, breathing heavily from the exertion of carrying the load.

"Morning, people. Ready for the day?" she asked.

"Not with you," Bradley mumbled. Ms. Hogan whipped her head toward him.

"Sorry, Bradley," Ms. Hogan said. "You got something to say?"

Bradley tried not to smirk. "No, Miss," he answered innocently.

Ms. Hogan turned away and began to take roll call when Colin Coxendale walked up to her.

"Hello Ms. Hogan," he quickly said.

"Oh, hi Colin," she replied, smiling. "How are you, my dear?"

"I heard what Bradley said," he said in an undertone. "After you asked the class if they were reading to go, he said, 'Not with you, Miss.'"

"Oh," Ms. Hogan said, nodding understandingly. "I feel the same about him."

Colin went and sat down as Ms. Hogan continued with the register.

Bradley and the group waited at the back of the classroom waiting to go.

"Is kung fu on tonight?" Bradley asked.

Eric said, "Um, I don't think so. Alex is still ill."

Kevin rolled his eyes. "I got a call from him last night. It's on."

"Oh, good," Eric said. "Sorry."

Through the window they saw a massive passenger bus pull into the front parking lot. It seemed like the same one that had taken them to DC earlier that year, especially when the same driver stepped out.

Ms. Hogan saw the bus arrive and checked her watch. "Okay class, let's go." They slowly followed her out of the classroom and along the narrow corridors.

"How long does it take to get to New York?" Bradley asked Kevin.

"About an hour and a half, depending on traffic," he replied. His parents had taken him there for a week last summer.

The group walked out into the parking lot and lined up in front of the bus door. The bus driver, dressed in his shaggy shirt and wrinkly red tie, stood outside, waiting to welcome them on board. Bradley climbed on and sat next to Kevin with Max and Eric behind them. The engine rumbled, rattling the windows, and the air conditioner blew the cold air onto his hair. He glanced at his cell phone: 8:15.

The last of the students clambered on the bus, and the driver stamped out his cigarette with ratty black shoes and followed. The birds in the trees nearby flew out as the driver put the bus into drive and pushed on the gas, slowly pulling toward the brown front gates as Ms. Hogan put her purple jacket into the overhead locker.

The bus pulled onto the main road and headed toward the highway leading toward New York State. Bradley looked out of the window at the passing motorists. The driver pushed the accelerator down, picking up speed until he merged smoothly with traffic on the busy highway. Bradley lay back in his seat and relaxed as the sun beamed in through the window. The driver looked lazily through the windshield, thinking he could still feel the taste of the morning tea at the back of his throat and tongue.

***

Circo looked out the front of his transport as he was driven to one of the control rooms on the ship. As it grinded to a stop, an attendant opened the side door and he stepped out, feeling his ray gun dangle by his side. The ship's lights beamed down on him as he walked up the steps to a set of double doors with a red button to the side. He pushed the small button in, allowing it to read his fingerprint, and the two doors silently slid back.

Circo walked over to Araphon and Adamlon, who stood around a digital table screen.

"Bring me up to speed. What have you found out on this place?"

Araphon took a deep breath and changed the table screen to show a map of a skinny island labeled *Manhattan*.

"Okay sir," he said. "As you know, we have landed at a place called Earth, and it is inhabited by a species called human beings. The region we are currently in is called the United States of America." He cleared his throat. "From my research, I have learned that these people are ill prepared for an alien invasion of any kind. Their technology is centuries behind ours."

Circo smiled. "Excellent. Any news of Gremlon's tracker?"

"No sir," Adamlon replied. "We are still looking for that."

"Any luck making contact with these humans?" he asked.

"Beyond the pathetic thing we picked up last night, we have been unable to communicate with the humans," Adamlon replied "We will keep trying."

Circo shook his head impatiently. "It is obvious these humans are ignoring us, so we must resort to an invasion in order to find Gremlon."

"Sir?"

"The fate of Armazon rests on that ship."

"I agree, sir," Araphon replied. He pressed on a green section in the center of the island. Circo watched as it the map zoomed in and a new name flashed: *Central Park*.

"This is our location," Araphon said.

Circo waved his hand dismissively. "I don't care where we are—I need Gremlon's ship! Tell me about the planet's defense system."

Araphon looked up and smiled. "A joke," he replied. "Our tanks could rip theirs to pieces. Of course, their weapons can kill us, but ours are so much more powerful that we just need to avoid close-range combat because their weapons can pierce our suits, which evens out the deadliness of our weapons and theirs."

"Excellent," Circo said. "This is turning out to be easier than I thought. Do we have enough manpower?"

Araphon laughed. "We have more than enough troops to take out this part of the island. Would you like me to ask the armory to prepare all the tanks and fighters ready for deployment?"

"No," Circo said. "Save that for later. I want to get a message across to these people first."

Adamlon stood up. "We are still looking for the planet's leader," he said. "Are you going to invade if we communicate?"

"Before," Circo said.

"Why's that, sir?" Araphon asked.

Circo stood up and looked around the control room. "Because I want to get the message across to these people that Armazoids do not mess around, and we want that data back."

He took one last look down on Central Park, knowing that taking over the planet was going to be a very easy job.

Chapter 5

The bus pulled past the end of Newark Airport's main runway, the lumbering jets seeming graceful in the air. Bradley looked over at the long line of yellow taxis that seemed to stretch to the city skyline. The ride had gone by fast. The bus slowed down in the heavy traffic as they arrived at the bus station. Bradley admired the huge skyscrapers and skylines as they headed north into Manhattan.

He reflexively reached for his cell phone to check for any texts or social media updates as the bus pulled into a slot at the station. The windows on the bus stopped vibrating as the engine was turned off. The bus is silent. Bradley got up, reaching down to hoist up his drooping pants. He checked for his wallet in his string bag, then slung the bag over his shoulder, content that his cash was where he had left it.

The group met on the lawn of the station as the smell of the bacon sandwiches from the depot's food court wafted out and into the atmosphere around them. Bradley, Max, Kevin, and Eric stood by Mr. Knightsbridge waiting for Ms. Hogan and the other teachers to take them to the tram for the trip into the city.

Ms. Hogan walked up beside Mr. Knightsbridge and turned to the assemble students. "Okay, class, here we go. And make sure to stick together." The group walked up the sidewalk toward the tram station. "Oh, before we go on, have you all got my cell number?" she asked.

"Yes. We're okay," Mr. Knightsbridge said.

The driver of the tram rang the bell as he pulled into the station, slowly pulling the control lever back to idle. The doors slid open, and the last few passengers stepped out and hurried to catch their next bus.

The group boarded the tram. Bradley sat down near the driver's cab. Everything was in perfect order and running smoothly, and that made Bradley feel restless. He pulled out his cell as he placed his feet up on the seat in front of him. The digital clock at the front of the tram showed ten o'clock. The driver positioned himself in his seat. The doors slowly locked into place and the driver carefully pushed the control stick forward.

Bored, Bradley read the notices attached to the tram's wall.

"City Runlink operates the world's newest and upgraded trams. If there is a sudden loss of power, the tram will not roll. Emergency brakes will stop the tram and prevent injury. These trams are wheelchair friendly and carry up to five times more people than the original ones. New destinations will be opening soon. You can feel safe when traveling with City Runlink"

Bradley looked away from the board and through the driver's cab. He imagined the different dangerous scenarios in his head that would require decisive action. The tram whizzed along its tracks past the yellow taxis as they drove into the busy city. He closed his eyes, relaxing until the tram pulled into their destination.

The doors slowly slid open as the brakes hissed on locking the wheels into place. The group stepped off the tram. Bradley looked up at the skyscrapers lining the sky as the sun beamed on them on the hot summer's day. Ms. Hogan pulled the schedule for the day out of her bag.

"Museum of Art," she said. "I cannot wait. Oh, and the library!"

"Oh my God," Bradley mumbled to Kevin.

"That shit," Kevin replied. "We are in the Big Apple and they are going to look at old paintings and bunch of books about what Uncle Sam takes from us each and every year." He stopped talking when he saw Colin looking at him.

Ms. Hogan was addressing the group. "Class, have a good day. Remember you have my cell number if you get lost." Then she turned to Mr. Knightsbridge. "Do you want to go to that coffee shop before we head to the big sites?"

"Yeah, why not?" he replied.

The group began heading in different directions with their assigned teachers. Mr. Knightsbridge followed Ms. Hogan up the busy roads, scanning the streets for pickpockets. He thought back to the days when he was a student studying at the New York University for his teaching degree and all the great times he had when he was younger.

They approached a small cafe opposite Central Park. Bradley and his friends picked a table and sat down, looking around at the park and the people playing happily. Ms. Hogan placed her brown leather handbag on the sidewalk as she pulled her chair out from a table near Bradley's.

"My goodness, it's warm today," she said.

"Yep, it's lovely. Just what we need," Mr. Knightsbridge replied as he sat back in his chair. "Better than the rain, and not to mention the snow, we had earlier this year."

47

"Suppose that's true," Ms. Hogan replied. "I spoke to Amber Richards yesterday." She and Mr. Knightsbridge rambled on, talking about various students

Bradley looked over his shoulder, listening to Ms. Hogan and Mr. Knightsbridge talking. He turned to Kevin.

"You going out tonight?" Bradley asked.

"Yep, downtown New Haven. Star Bright Club—the best," Kevin said.

"Yeah, and I'm going to get totally wasted." Max laughed.

"How can you?" Bradley asked. "You're only seventeen."

"I have my ways," Max replied.

"Do you know the door man?" Bradley said.

"Yep. John knows my mother," said Max.

"Oh, is that how you get into the club? He knows your single mom?" Eric grinned slyly.

Max smiled as he shook his head in mock disbelief.

"Eric, you have got one sick imagination," Bradley said.

"You can talk," Eric replied.

"Excuse me?"

"Remember Sports Day?" Eric asked. "We were getting changed and you found that hole leading into the girl's locker rooms."

"Oh yeah," Bradley replied. He smiled, looking over his shoulder at the three girls who had just sat down at a nearby table. They turned up their noses at his leering glance.

The Brazilian waiter returned with Ms. Hogan's drink and suddenly struck up a conversation. The boys listened in, grinning.

"Are you okay, Ms Hogan? It is very warm today," Rico asked.

"Yes, I'm fine, thank you," Ms. Hogan replied.

Rico cleared his throat. "So tell me, Ms. Hogan, do you have any family?"

Ms. Hogan's face slowly turned a light red.

Bradley covered his mouth to hide his laughter. "Look at her!" he whispered to his friends.

"Er, no I haven't," she quietly answered.

The waiter smiled broadly and bowed to her, then turned back toward the shop. Ms. Hogan got up and headed toward the ladies' room as Bradley called the waiter over.

"Hey, dude, listen. Do you really like her?" Bradley asked.

"Em, yes. I really like her," the waiter said. "She's a very, very nice lady."

"Where are you from?" Bradley asked.

"I'm from Brazil."

"Did you know some of the prettiest and sexiest women come from there?" Bradley asked. "When I have enough money, I'll be down there as soon as I can. You too, huh, Kev?"

"Oh yes," Kevin agreed fervently. He could barely keep a straight face.

The waiter looked flustered. "Em, no, I don't know. Sorry." He walked back into the café. Bradley placed his hands behind his head and smiled at Kevin. Then he caught Colin staring at him with his mouth open wide. Bradley rolled his eyes as Colin stood up at the sight of Ms. Hogan returning to her table.

Suddenly, a hobo staggered out of the park. Two police officers got out of a parked police car to see what would happen. The old man clutched his whiskey bottle and yelled, "Help! Help me please!"

The word 'help' seemed to hang in the air.

"Oh, for God's sake," one officer said to the other. "Now what is wrong with him?"

"Is there a problem, sir?" the other officer asked.

"It's coming—the invasion," the hobo yelled. "The apocalypse! It is coming, run for your lives!"

The two officers looked at each other.

"It's coming. Everyone run while you can," the man shrieked at the top of his voice.

"Okay sir," the officer said. "I think you should just calm down. What have you been drinking?"

"The end is coming. I saw it!" the hobo yelled, walking up to the officer. He lowered his voice as he got closer to the officer. "They tied me to a bed." He looked straight at the officers. Bradley had to strain to hear his next words. "They molested me."

The officers stepped back as the strong smell of whiskey on the man's breath wafted over them. A group of young Chinese students stood laughing at the man as he walked around in a circle holding the old bottle of whiskey.

"Jesus!" the officer exclaimed, waving his hand to disperse the smell. The officers continued watching the drunk as he walked around in circles, warning all passersby of the imminent invasion. Bradley giggled as he leaned back in the chair, still watching the two officers dealing with the man.

***

The two Armazoids came out of the ship and slowly sneaked through Central Park after returning to their normal size. They were ready to explore some more of the city and planned on heading out a bit further.

They crept through the green terrain, slowly approaching a manhole. They scanned the area around them. When the coast was clear, they darted to the manhole, dragging off the metal lid and hesitating only briefly before climbing down the grungy metal rungs and putting the lid back in place. Two businessmen turned a corner and walked over the manhole, oblivious to the aliens beneath them.

The Armazoids flicked on their headlamps and looked around at the steaming walls as the water ran down them. They slowly crept through the long tunnels, looking around.

"What is this place?" one asked.

The other shrugged and pulled out his tiny computer and looked at it. He looked at the red lines indicating which way was safe to go. "This way," he said.

They moved along the hot sewer in the intense heat. The steam heated up their suits as they trekked along. They looked up a short while later to see another metal ladder leading up to the surface. They looked at one another and slowly climbed up. The lead soldier lifted the lid slightly to look out onto a pretty rundown area. Two drunks staggered along into an alley, not knowing the time of day. Judging it safe, the aliens climbed out of the manhole just in view of the two men as they rested against the alley's dirty walls. They stared down at the drunks as they lay on the pavement, trying to take swigs from the empty alcohol bottle.

"God! Look at these things," one Armazoid said. "We should just leave this shit hole and never return."

The two Armazoids walked toward the docks. A ship's horn hooted in the distance as two rusty cranes lumped containers onto a freighter. With no humans visible, the aliens walked wherever they liked, looking around but unable to find anything to report back to Circo.

The sound of a horn blasted in their ears. They turned just in time to see an oil truck speeding towards them. The horn blared as the driver rammed his brake down and turned the wheel sharply, skidding away from the two Armazoids. The huge tanker started to roll onto its side as the driver kept the brake and clutch down to the full, struggling to stop the runaway vehicle. Sparks flew everywhere. With a final *kerchunk*, the truck righted itself on all eighteen wheels.

The driver kicked the truck door open and climbed out onto the road, throwing up into the dirty alleyway. When he looked up again, the Armazoids had their laser guns pointed at him. The driver, eyes wide, slowly put his hands up, then made a dash for the open manhole. He almost fell down the slippery metal rungs in his haste to escape the strange creatures. The two Armazoids followed him down.

"Get away," the man yelled at them and ran off into the sewage system, still being chased by the Armazoids.

***

The two officers had finally decided the hobo was no threat when their radio suddenly blared: *"Attention, crashed truck on Twelfth Street by the docks, all units in the vicinity, please report."*

The two officers gave on last look at the hobo and got in their patrol car.

"Any problem, call 9-1-1," one policeman ordered the onlookers through his open window.

The police sped off toward the crash scene. They knew they were close when the saw the cloud of black smoke and a group of grubby dockworkers. One officer stepped out of the car and walked over to the cab but saw no one inside it. Thick smoke was coming from under the hood.

"Did anyone see what happened?" he yelled.

"No," one younger man said. "We heard squealing breaks and a loud crash and came running."

"Okay. Can you step back, please?" the officer asked. "If this thing blows…"

The workers started to slowly back away from the truck as the other officer walked over to the open manhole. He felt the hot steam blow up into his face.

A voice rang out from the storm drains. "Get away!"

"What the hell?" the officer went. "Let's get down there."

"No, we should call in SWAT," the other officer said.

"No time," the other officer said as he climbed down the metal rungs.

The other officer watched as the rest of the New York emergency services rolled up to the emergency scene, including two fire trucks. Then three officers went down the old rusty ladder into the sewer. They soon caught up with the first officer, and together, they trekked toward the man's screams, their flashlights illuminating the humid, noxious air. The ground vibrated from a nearby subway, and when the vibration stopped, they realized they couldn't hear the screams anymore.

The officers continued through the tunnels, hearts pounding. In one hand each clung to a handgun, steam settling on the metal work, and in the other, the flashlight. Suddenly one beam of light illuminated a body. One officer stepped forward to check while the other three tried to set up a perimeter, their beams frantically bobbing everywhere.

The body was clearly the truck driver, and as the officer knelt down to feel for his pulse, he saw blood dribbling from a neck wound. The pulse stopped almost as soon as he found it. Visible through cracks in the walls, the thundering trains echoed around the thin tunnels.

"We have to perform CP—" The officer was interrupted by a small snarl that came from his right.

As one, the officers slowly turned as their lights into an alcove that they had missed in their earlier search. The beams illuminated the two Armazoids standing and staring at them. For a moment, the officers were frozen in disbelief as one Armazoid reached into his back pocket, pulling out what even the humans recognized as a grenade. While the officers dove for cover deeper into the tunnel, the Armazoid threw the grenade through a crack in a wall onto the tracks of an oncoming train.

The grenade exploded as the old train passed over it. The driver gasped as he was swung off his old metal seat. The glass along the old carriages shattered into it as the screams echoed over the thundering train. The old carriage turned onto its side, and the driver crashed against the doors as the train screeched to a halt, completely off the track but just in view of the 28th Street station. The station workers, alerted by the horrendous explosion, looked down the tunnel at the train barely visible in the thick, black smoke. One employee ran over to the red plunger, slamming it in. The alarms wailed as passengers from the wrecked train slowly materialized out of the smoke, disoriented and injured.

"Everybody out!" a station employee yelled as he jumped down on the tracks and ran toward the train. He found the driver lying on the ground, staring into open space, blood still dripping blood a head wound. A fire flared from under the train as a few people staggered out of the carriages toward the platform, crying frantically as they tried to locate the exit. After closing the driver's eyes, the employee calmly directed the passengers toward the escalators that would carry them above ground.

"You okay?" he asked a woman. She didn't say a word as she slowly staggered along the platform towards the stairs, arms folded. The NYPD officers ran into the station, covering their mouths as the dead driver sat in his own gore. The congealed blood gleamed.

Fire trucks, sirens wailing, pulled up outside the station as paramedics and EMTs helped people out of the station and toward the waiting ambulances.

***

Bradley and his group meandered along a busy road toward an outdoor shopping center. Ms. Hogan stopped to watch a TV in a store window that was showing a camera view of the 28th Street station. She squinted her eyes against the glare. When she didn't move on, Mr. Knightsbridge came closer, and the other students huddled in. They could just barely hear the young reporter.

"I'm standing outside 28th Street Station where a subway train has just exploded. There is at least one confirmed death and the trains leading to the station have been re-routed. Police and fire service officials are on the scene. Fire has engulfed one of the carriages and they are struggling to get everyone out of the station."

"Dear God," Mr. Knightsbridge said.

"Come on, let's move on," Ms. Hogan said brusquely. "Accidents happen in the big city, and we aren't near this one."

The group started walking on again. Bradley and Kevin found themselves in the fortunate position of walking behind Kate and Lisa.

"Look at that ass," Kevin mumbled.

Kate looked at Lisa with disgust, and they both rolled their eyes, though they didn't walk away. Colin sidled up to them, seeming to appear from nowhere.

"Ignore him, girls," Colin said.

"Oh, I will," Lisa said. "You ignore them, too."

"I do," Colin replied.

Bradley laughed quietly as the group turned the corner and walked towards the shopping center. He looked up at the huge retailers lining the street. A couple girls his age walked out of a massive Forever 21 holding their bags of the latest fashions.

"More hotties," Max said.

"Will I ever find love?" Eric asked wistfully.

"I doubt it, Eric," Max joked.

"Why?" Eric asked. "You never know."

"Don't ask," Bradley joked. The group had reached the outdoor shopping area, the streets closed to cars and bustling with vendors and pedestrians. Ms. Hogan dismissed her group to explore for an hour.

Bradley sat down on a bench as the group went off in all directions. He spotted a game shop down a side street and pointed it out to his friends. "I'm going in there," he said. "You coming?"

"Yeah, I am," Kevin replied. Max and Eric waved as they walked to a sweets stall, ice cream on their minds.

The air conditioning hit Kevin and Bradley like a sheet of cold air as they walked into the game shop. A young Mexican watched their entry from behind the counter. The two teenagers immediately started perusing the shelves.

"Oh, look, Fight Buster Three!" Kevin exclaimed.

After looking around for fifteen minutes and not seeing anything he really wanted, Bradley got distracted by Kate and Lisa talking with Ms. Hogan near the game shop window. He couldn't hear them, but Colin suddenly came up and joined them. Ms. Hogan tapped her watch and then waved to the three students as they walked away together. Bradley shook his head in disbelief and tugged Kevin out of the shop. They found Max and Eric, and the four wandered aimlessly around until the hour was up.

When the group had reconvened, Bradley stayed near the back and followed along as they headed toward the subway station. Some of the students were nervous after the subway explosion, but Ms. Hogan was quick to reassure them. Bradley wasn't worried, and he mimicked a panicky girl who was talking with Ms. Hogan. His friends laughed, and Ms. Hogan shot him a look. He rolled his eyes.

In the subway, Bradley couldn't help but get caught up in the life of the city around him. A busker sat cross-legged on the side of the platform, playing his saxophone and trying to collect money to earn his living. The wind from passing trains ruffled his hair and blew newspapers into a cyclone. On the train, a smartly dressed man's tie swung to the motion of the swaying train, and the smell of Thai food came from a young Asian eating from a take-out box.

The train slowly pulled into the station, and Bradley and the group stepped off and headed up the stairs into the heat of the day. Ms. Hogan and some students who wanted to go to the museum went to the left, while Bradley and his friends and a few others followed Mr. Knightsbridge.

"This city is magnificent," Mr. Knightsbridge remarked.

"Were you born here, sir?" Kevin asked.

"I was born in New Jersey, near Newark actually, but I went to school here," Mr. Knightsbridge replied. "By school, I mean college."

"I can't believe how big and alive it is!" Bradley said.

"Oh, yes. It never stops. I don't think anything less than the apocalypse would bring this place to a stop," Mr. Knightsbridge replied with a smile.

Chapter 6

Circo stood up after a brief rest in his quarters at the back of the bridge. The first phase of the invasion was about to begin. Attempting to contact the Earth with the local communication antennae had failed, but he was sure the humans would want to talk after he had taken over this Manhattan region.

He briskly walked over to his staff as they worked at a small video camera that would broadcast his image and words to the rest of the ship. He took a deep breath and sat down in front of it.

"Ready?" he asked quietly. One staff member nodded, and they all backed out of the shot.

"To my fellow Armazoids," he said. "The time has come to begin the takeover of this land. If you encounter any of these humans, annihilate them. The survival of our home planet and people depend upon this invasion."

The Armazoids, already armed and briefed by their commanders, gave a cheer that could be heard all the way on the bridge. The first wave of Armazoids headed towards the elevator, prepared to invade New York City. As the large elevators slowly rolled to the top of the craft, humans passed the small cave, unaware of what was about to happen. The Armazoids walked out of the underground cave and glowed green as they returned to their normal size.

A middle-aged woman was sitting down on an old wooden bench reading tattered magazine. Her eyes opened wide as two green Armazoids walked out of the undergrowth by the path. Their heads swiveled until they saw her. She dropped her coffee onto her outdated gray pant suit as she stared at their gleaming white teeth. One of the Armazoids pounced on her and sliced her neck with its laser, her blood spattering the bunch and running into the mucky gutter.

As the Armazoid dropped the woman and calmly walked away, accompanied by the other Armazoid, chaos broke out. People ran in all different directions away from the aliens. They ran out of park exits into the street, oblivious to the cars screeching to avoid them and the pileups they caused. One car ran into a hydrant, which immediately spewed forth a fountain of water that showered park-fleers and car-crash victims alike. The Armazoids opened fire.

A young police officer, dressed in his smart navy-blue uniform, watched in horror as people fell to the ground, blood gushing from their wounds into the storm drains. He swiped his handgun from its holster as his radio went berserk with help calls from fellow officers.

"Come on, run!" he yelled. He aimed at the Armazoids as they shot at every moving human. They were heading in his direction. He pulled the trigger and watched as the golden casings fell from the weapon and hit the ground. He thought about his newborn daughter, only a few days old. The officer looked at his gun as the coupling flung back. He reached into his pocket and pulled out a full magazine of cartridges, ready to start firing again.

But he was out of time. With return fire, the Armazoids had started charging toward him. The young man shut his eyes as he felt the laser slice his neck. He struggled to stay upright as his handgun fell onto the blood-spattered sidewalk. The officer fell slowly, his blood pouring down his neatly ironed uniform. He listened to the echoing drips of his blood as it trickled down a drainage grate. A moment later, he was dead, the white puffy clouds above oblivious to the killing.

**

Ms. Hogan led her students from a side shop onto a scene of chaos. The group froze on the sidewalk, the students still inside pushing to see what was happening.

Ms. Hogan grabbed one woman who was running by. "What the hell is going on?" she asked her, shaking her shoulders. "I mean-"

"I'd run if I were you!" She replied

People continued to run by, the woman wrenched herself from Ms. Hogan's desperate grasp. Then the explosions began. Several of the girls screamed as fireballs could be seen in the air above the trees lining the streets.

Ms. Hogan stared as a streetlight fell into the street, hitting a car and causing people to leap clumsily over it in their attempt to get away from the chaos. The yellow bulb sparked into the street. She felt her cell phone vibrating in her pocket. She pulled it out and saw Lisa on the screen.

"Hello," she yelled over the screaming people.

"Oh, hello. It's Lisa. Ms. Hogan, are you okay? What is going on?" She sounded panicked.

"Calm down," Ms. Hogan ordered, trying not to panic herself. "What is going on where you are?" She listened to the sound of her fast breathing and the screaming people in the background as the signal started to crackle and fuzz as the cell lines were overloaded. Too many people were trying to get through to loved ones.

"We were in this store and these things just came out of nowhere. We are on our way to the police station at—oh, I don't know! The main police station!"

"It's okay, Lisa. What things are you talking about?" Ms. Hogan asked. No sooner had the words left her mouth then she saw, not more than two blocks away, a group of Armazoids walking slowly toward them, lasering everything in sight. "You know what, we'll just meet you at the station, okay? The main police station." She hung up without waiting for a good-bye.

Students had tried to get back in the shop, but the shopkeeper had locked the door and was looking fearfully from behind the curtains. Now many were hiding beneath the tables of a nearby outdoor cafe. She ran over and joined them, unable to think of how she and Mr. Knightsbridge— who had started shrieking like a little girl at the first explosion—would get all these students to the station.

Water continued to gush from busted fire hydrants, and only one streetlamp hadn't fallen. Screeching cars and collisions could be heard near and far. Suddenly, sirens got very close, and an NYPD SWAT van zoomed past them and skidded to a halt a block from the advancing Armazoids. Two armed officers stepped out of the van holding loaded MP5 machine guns. They pulled out two yellow barriers from the back while the remaining officers piled out of the van and covered them. The barriers were spread across the narrow side street.

One officer approached the cowering students. "You," the officer yelled, pointing at Ms. Hogan. "Where you heading to?" he demanded.

Ms. Hogan blanked momentarily, and then stammered, her voice a full octave higher than normal, "Uh, uh, the police station! The main police station!"

The police officer helped her get up from underneath the table and gave her a little shake. "Ma'am, head straight down this street for about three blocks. Our main police headquarters is there. Do you understand?"

"What's going on?" she yelled.

"Just go!" The officer turned back to the barricade. If this woman wanted to stick around when these aliens and their lasers got here, that was her problem.

Ms. Hogan's students didn't hesitate. They ran, tripping and fighting through the hordes of people, in the direction the officer had indicated. Max tripped over something and found himself lying on top of an unconscious man. He scrambled up and ran on, Ms. Hogan screaming, "Don't look! Keep going!" behind him. News helicopters circled above, looking down onto the city through their cameras, trying to figure out what the hell was going on.

The group made it to the police station. Armed officers helped injured people into the station. Ms. Hogan ushered her students through the swinging glass doors, one of many panicky adults. She struggled to count her students, finally realizing she was short two.

In the crowded lobby, she struggled to regain her breath. An officer caught her attention and ushered her and the students into a large back office. The students sank gratefully to the ground in the relative quiet of the room, too shocked to speak. Several were quietly crying.

The office seemed to be a holding area for other's seeking refuge from...whatever had overtaken the city. Ms. Hogan sat down on a plastic bench and looked at all the frightened people. She looked at two calm senior citizens as they sat down with bags of groceries in each hand.

"You okay?" the old man asked her kindly.

"Yes, I, I, I'm fine," she replied. "What is going on?"

The man shrugged helplessly. "We don't know, darling. We were happily walking through the farmers' market doing our weekly grocery shopping when suddenly these green things just came out of nowhere and started attacking people. Haven't seen anything like it before, and I grew up in the city."

"How did you get here?" Ms. Hogan asked.

"We were helped by two officers," the man's wife said "They just pulled over and offered to help us to the station"

"I've lost two of my group," Ms. Hogan said. "And I've got to find them." She pulled out her cell phone and tried to dial, but another glance at the screen showed she had no signal.

"Oh God," the lady mumbled. "I hope you do."

***

Two students, visiting from Japan, stood in front of a noodle stand in Chinatown with their music players, breathing in the aroma of the cooking noodles and vegetables. The old man, his apron stained, was busy behind the counter. One student turned when he heard screams in the distance. He saw people in the distance running.

He hit his friend on the arm and gestured to the panicking people. The screams seemed to be getting louder by the second. Suddenly, row upon row of Armazoids appeared, marching down the street, lasers firing continuously.

The students screamed and abandoned their lunch, running away from the aliens. Cars skidded to a stop as the people ran across the busy streets. Sirens wailed as two patrol cars arrive, narrowly swerving around a collision of two yellow taxies. The officers parked their cars across the street in front of the oncoming aliens. Three officers jumped out and assumed defensive positions behind the vehicles.

More patrol cars skidded to a stop at the entrance to Chinatown. The two officers opened their doors and got out from their car, drawing their weapons. They were in a good position to shoot the Armazoids if the people would just move!

"Get out of the way!" one officer yelled, running forward. "Take cover!" He held on to his pump action shotgun, looking through the sight as two Armazoids ran toward him. He squeezed the trigger. The Armazoid fell onto the ground and his green blood spattered everywhere. The officers continued firing at the oncoming Armazoids. People continued running in all directions, slowing the officers ability to pick targets. The first officer watched the top of his handgun ping back—empty magazine.

He reached into his side pouch to pull out his last magazine, but something caught his eye. Three Armazoids stood behind him, their weapons trained on his head. It seemed like the chaos around him froze. Suddenly heavy gunfire burst through the air, and the Armazoids twitched as AK47 rifle bullets ripped through their suits, killing them instantly. They slowly fell to the ground, looks of surprise on their alien faces. The officer swung his head around and looked at two young men holding AK47 assault rifles, their faces covered. The officer slowly got up. The two men turned around and headed into the alleyway behind them.

"Wait," the officer yelled. *"Where did you get those?"*

But the two men disappeared into the darkness of the alleyway, not to be seen again.

"Come on," another officer called. "We need to treat the wounded."

The officers rejoined his unit in helping people through the city to safe zones.

***

Bradley looked around as they walked down a quiet street toward the north of Manhattan. He looked down at his watch. "Twelve-fifty," he said quietly.

"What's up, Bradley?" Mr. Knightsbridge asked. "Bored? We have got the museum to go to next."

"No," Bradley replied. "Just thinking about college."

"Have you applied yet?" Mr. Knightsbridge asked.

"Just Queen's Gate College," Bradley said.

"You should keep your options open," Mr. Knightsbridge advised. "Places can get really hard to get into these days with people turning to education." He paused. "You ever thought of studying here?"

"I haven't, no," Bradley replied.

"Well, what do you want to study?" Mr. Knightsbridge asked.

"I wouldn't mind joining the army," Bradley said. "Then maybe the police."

"Hear, hear," Kevin agreed.

A disturbingly loud rumble was heard in the distance. It seemed to go on and on.

"What was that?" Bradley said, looking around.

Mr. Knightsbridge froze for a few seconds. "There's always a lot of construction in the summer," he answered hesitantly. "I'm sure it's nothing."

"I suppose," Bradley replied.

They saw a big group of people gathered outside a TV store that was broadcasting the news on its many screens. Bradley pushed to the front of the group to see what everyone was gawking at. He saw a young news reporter standing outside Grand Central Station. She lifted the microphone to her mouth as the TV screen started to flicker. They could only just about hear the TV set.

"I'm standing outside Grand Central Station where people are trying to flee the city due to this, well, invasion," she said and paused.

"What the…" Bradley said, confused and alarmed.

***

A middle-aged officer stood in Grand Central Station as the people shoved and pushed, trying to get onto the double-decker trains. He was supposed to be maintaining order, but what could he do against such hordes of people? He clenched his shotgun as the driver started up the engines. The smoke from the exhaust puffed out as the doors slowly closed and locked into place. The officer watched and held on to his shotgun as the people were pushed against the doors. A train slowly pulled out of the station away from the city. A second train slowly pulled into the station, and again people mobbed it to get on.

The officer glanced back at the main glass doors. That suddenly shattered under a sudden surge in pressure from the people behind.

"What the—" the officer muttered. Then he saw a group of Armazoids coming, herding the people into the departure area of the train station. Two officers that had been helping inside fell to the floor and were trampled by the panicked people.

"Oh shit!" one officer yelled. He pumped his shotgun. He knelt down on the clean platform looking at the hordes of people as they charged towards them and the train. He struggled to get a clear view of one of the Armazoids. He was concerned about hitting an innocent person. "Get out of the way!" he yelled.

He squeezed the trigger, and the cartridge flew out and smashed into one of the pursuing Armazoids. The Armazoid fell onto the floor, his green blood spattering the station floor as a tanker train moved through the station. There were just too many of these aliens! The officer stared as another Armazoid dove for him. As he fell back under the bulky green monstrosity, he pulled the trigger on his shotgun. The bullet exited from the weapon, whistling through the sky and hitting an oil tank on the passing train. The rusted metal sparked and oil fumes rushed out from inside the tank. The people at the station dropped to the ground as a huge fireball ripped through the tanker. The explosion ripped through the station, incinerating a mass of Armazoids before they could escape.

***

The TV that had been relaying the details of the disaster at Grand Central Station suddenly turned to static. The sound made Bradley jump, and the TV screen faded.

"What a good film," Eric said, impressed. "Wonder what it's called."

Mr. Knightsbridge hustled the students down the sidewalk.

"It's just a film," he mumbled to himself. "It's just a film."

Bradley looked over his shoulder as the sound of police sirens got louder and louder. Three New York patrol cars and van shot past them, skidding around the corner.

"What's going on?" Eric asked.

Mr. Knightsbridge felt his heart start to pound as the sound of shooting came from around the corner. "I think we should head back," he stammered. "Back to the subway." He turned around.

"Nah, let's have a look," Bradley said. "The police just went around that corner, I'm sure it's fine."

With Bradley at the head, the group slowly walked around the corner. His mouth dropped open in shock. The three patrol cars had formed a barrier in the road, and the officers were crouching behind them, shooting at an army of, well, aliens! Mr. Knightsbridge looked at a car crashed up on the sidewalk with smoke pouring from the running engine, driver's door wide and blood splatted on the leather seats.

Max suddenly yelled, "This way!" Bradley turned toward him and saw that Max was gesturing toward a casino, its doors wide open. The casino's manager was beckoning to them urgently.

Bradley followed the group as they ran up the concrete stairs into the casino. The manager slammed the glass doors shut and locked them in. An armed security guard ran up to the entrance, sidearm ready to be used if the need arose. In the shocked silence, Mr. Knightsbridge's phone started ringing in his pocket. He ripped it out of his pocket.

"Hello," he said in a shaken voice.

"Oh God, Alan, you're alive," Ms. Hogan said, though she was hard to hear through the bad connection and the sirens on both ends of the call. "I've been trying to get through to you for ages—the signal just came back! Are you okay?"

"We're fine, just about. Where are you?" Mr. Knightsbridge said to her.

Ms. Hogan struggled to hear and think over the panic and confusion in the police station. "We're at the main police station, about a mile and a half from Grand Central. I think we should be able to make our way out via there and back to New Haven."

Mr. Knightsbridge was shaking his head. "No point, we just saw Grand Central explode. Is there another way? Can we meet you at the police station?"

"You can," said Ms. Hogan tentatively, "but I think they are going to evacuate the building soon, so you better move it."

"Don't worry," Mr. Knightsbridge said. "We'll be there soon." He hung up.

Mr. Knightsbridge looked at the small group.

"Okay, we have got to get out of here," he urged. "Ms. Hogan is at the main police station about a mile and a half from Grand Central."

"Where's Grand Central?" Eric asked.

"It's about—" He stopped suddenly, looking behind the boys in horror. The boys turned around to the glass doors

Three Armazoids were staring in at them. Bradley clenched his fist, desperate to use it.

"Just you try it, you rat bags," he muttered.

The Armazoids walked away from the glass door. The security guard breathed a sigh of relief as they walked away. The tension in the room lightened, and Mr. Knightsbridge gave a weak chuckle.

"See? Stand up to them and they walk away," Eric said.

This statement was followed by the cacophonous sound of smash glass as the three Armazoids charged into the doors. They dived onto the security guard, who had no chance. His gun slipped from his lifeless fingers and bounced off the blood-soaked carpet, landing near Bradley.

Before he could think about what he was doing, Bradley dove for the gun, picking it up and sliding well away from the aliens on the lush carpet. The casino was a madhouse, but he ran back to his friends and Mr. Knightsbridge. "Come on," he urged.

The group followed him around the side of the casino, trying to keep out of sight of the attacking Armazoids. They came to a small set of stairs. Bradley looked down, checking to see if the coast was clear. "Move it, I'll cover you," he whispered. Kevin took point, and the group crept down the steps as the casino slowly started to go quiet. The screams slowly faded away into nothing as they went deeper into the casino. Bradley clung to the firearm, carefully walking backward to ensure no aliens snuck up on them.

The multi-colored lights continued shining down on their heads as they slowly crept along through the quiet casino. It felt different, seeing empty blackjack and poker stands and no one working them. As they neared a back exit,

Kevin held up his hand to halt them. *Two*, he mouthed, and held up two fingers.

Bradley nodded and moved to the front—he was the only one with a weapon. He took a deep breath then swung around the corner, sighting on the two aliens who stood there. Bradley squeezed the trigger, launching the bullets into the Armazoids.

"Oh, that felt good." He smiled.

The group sprinted past the fallen Armazoids and through the casino, up the carpeted stairs towards the rear fire exit. On the way past a bar, Mr. Knightsbridge grabbed a glass half full of dark liquid. He gulped it down, but it didn't seem to ease his nerves. He was as white as a sheet.

"Come on," Bradley ordered. "We'll save that till later when we are out of here."

"If we do get out of here," Mr. Knightsbridge said despairingly.

"We will," Bradley replied.

Bradley looked at the back exit to the casino. Coast was clear. He motioned for the group to run past him out the exit. They ran out onto a street full of panicky people. Two yellow taxis had crashed into each other. Bodies were lying everywhere and fires raged through the buildings.

"Jesus Christ!" Bradley said, holding on to the sidearm. He didn't have a clue about who or what to shoot at first.

Mr. Knightsbridge regained some of his composure. "Right, follow me," he ordered.

Bradley gave Kevin a look. "Someone got his balls back," he said under his breath.

The boys followed their teacher down the small flight of steps onto the sidewalk. He crept along slowly, try to hear around the screams and vehicle collisions for any immediate danger. Water gushed up from destroyed fire hydrants. Mr. Knightsbridge felt his heart pounding as the fear of death overtook him, but Bradley calmly followed on behind. The breeze picked up as the NYPD helicopters circled above. The police sirens were moving further away, though not too far.

"This way," Bradley ordered. He ran in front of Mr. Knightsbridge, and then ducked down, looking over the hood of a vehicle as Armazoids attacked innocent people a couple blocks away. As he scanned the wrecked cars around them, he saw a middle-aged woman hanging upside-down, held in by her seatbelt, in a green sedan that had turned over. Its top was smashed inward, the windows half their normal size under the weight of the car. He could just see her red skirt and a business bag inside the car. She had been on her way to a business meeting.

"Come on," Max said, seeing where Bradley was looking. "She's dead."

The woman overheard them speaking and slowly opened her eyes, coughing up small drops of blood. She felt the blood pounding in her head. Police sirens wailed through her ears into her brain. She took a deep breath and felt her chest push out against the strong material of the seat belt. "Help!" she yelled. "Help me, please!" She feebly struggled to open her door.

"Shit!" Bradley gasped. "Come on."

"Bradley, no," Mr. Knightsbridge yelled. "Come on, we have got to get out of here."

"We can't just leave her," Kevin said. "What would you want in her situation?"

Mr. Knightsbridge shook his head as Bradley led Kevin, Max and Eric over to the car. Then he followed close behind. Bradley dove to the ground to get a better view of the woman. The engine was smoking.

"You okay, miss?" he asked.

Blood was running down her face and mixing with her straight white-blonde hair. "I, I, I'm okay," the woman gasped. "Get me out, please!"

"Okay, stay calm," Bradley said to her. He got up and ran to the other side of the door, carefully army-crawling in the broken window. He winced as glass dug into his forearms and legs, but he had to release the woman's seatbelt if she was going to get out. The smell of gas was overpowering.

"Kevin," Bradley yelled.

Kevin leaned down and looked into the car. "What's up?" he asked.

Bradley took a deep breath. "Remember that smashed up fire truck? Go and get me something like the jaws of life," Bradley ordered.

"Got it," Kevin said and left.

"And an extinguisher!" Bradley yelled as Kevin ran across the road towards the fire truck. "Just in case."

Kevin ran inside the truck, but called out, "Eric, watch out!"

"For what?" he replied.

Kevin rolled his eyes as he searched every compartment he could find in the truck. "I don't know, the green things?"

"Oh, right," Eric replied. He walked around the truck to get a better view of where the Armazoids were attacking people a few streets away.

Kevin finally found what he was looking for and hauled the jaws of life and extinguisher over to Bradley, who was now standing outside the driver's door assessing where he should cut without harming the woman. As Kevin passed over the jaws of life, he heard Eric scream. He whirled around to see two of the Armazoids coming towards him from the fire truck.

"Shit!" Kevin gasped. He pulled out the tiny plastic pin and activated the extinguisher. He pulled the silver hook and blasted the Armazoids away from him. As they were blinded by the foam, Kevin delivered two beautiful head kicks, knocking them out cold.

Bradley looked at Kevin and then the extinguisher. "Not what I had in mind," he said, "but there we go."

Thicker smoke started to billow from the hood of the sedan, and the woman began to wail. "Shit!" Bradley gasped. "Kevin, spray now."

Kevin sprayed the car engine, struggling to find the source of the smoke. Bradley started cutting through the material—it wasn't easy. "Come on," he started to groan.

The thick black smoke started to fill the car, the lady finding it harder and harder to breath. Finally, the last of the material was cut. Bradley pried off the door and took the woman's outstretch hands, helping her to avoid the sharp metal edges of the car frame.

Kevin watched Bradley help the lady until he saw some flames licking the inside of the engine compartment.

"Bradley, we gotta move." He sniffed the air, the gas smell thick in the smoke. "This car is gonna blow!" He took the woman by the other elbow, and together, they ushered her out of harm's way, followed closely by Mr. Knightsbridge, Max, and Eric.

The fire slowly crept into the engine, igniting the gas and fumes. The green sedan was thrown up into the air from the explosion. Bradley fell forward as the explosion rocketed through the street blasting other car windows out. He looked up at Kevin, who was helping the woman stay standing. They all turned their heads around and looked at the burning car.

"Jesus Christ!" the woman said. "Thank you so much."

"No problem," Bradley said. He lay back down on the ground.

"Come on," Mr. Knightsbridge yelled. "We have to go."

The woman continued to look at Bradley. "Name's Amelia," she said.

"Hi Amelia," Bradley said. "Nice to meet you. We must go out for a drink sometime."

"Hello," Amelia replied, shaken up. "I think I am a bit too old for you."

"After today," Bradley said, "I think people will have a lot more on their minds than a younger man and an older woman dating."

Bradley saw movement behind Amelia and quickly rose to his knees, looking behind her at a group of Armazoids charging towards them. "Move it, people," he cried, shoving Amelia behind him. Mr. Knightsbridge and the other boys started running down the sidewalk, away from the aliens.

Bradley reached into his pocket and pulled out the security guard's handgun. He took aim and squeezed the trigger repeatedly. The Armazoids dropped to the floor one after the other as their suits were penetrated with a bull's eye to the heart. Then he stood up and jogged to catch up with his group. He continued scanning the streets in trying to be one step ahead. In an abandoned patrol car, he saw a loaded pump action shotgun.

Signaling the group to stop, he reached in and grabbed the gun while the others gratefully took a needed breather.

Mr. Knightsbridge leaned against the car, panting. Bradley pumped the shotgun lever, looking over the car hood for any movement. He felt the nerves in his hand twitch as the long metal and wood weapon pushed into the palm of his hand. Spotting movement to the right, he zeroed in on three Armazoids that had noticed them and split off from their main group. As they got closer, Bradley could see their gleaming white teeth in their smiling mouths. As soon as they were in range, Bradley took a shot. It whistled as it flew through the air, piercing the lead Armazoid in the forehead, spraying his green blood on his companions. The remaining two aliens looked at each other, then simultaneously reached for their ray guns holstered at their sides.

"Take cover!" Bradley yelled as he ducked down behind the patrol car. The rays zoomed overhead and smashed into a lamppost. Bradley quickly jumped back up, the stiff breeze blowing in his face as he sighted the one alien and then the other, getting off two clean kills before their ray guns had time to recharge.

"Move," Bradley ordered. He held onto the shotgun and peered over his shoulder, watching Mr. Knightsbridge slowly creep along the sidewalk.

"Oh, for God's sake," he moaned. Mr. Knightsbridge started coughing as he fell against the wall of a shop.

"You okay, sir?" Bradley asked.

"Yes," Mr. Knightsbridge replied. "I am not that young anymore."

While Mr. Knightsbridge recovered, Bradley scouted ahead a bit, making sure there were no surprises behind the wrecked cars. He whirled around when he heard Kevin's scream.

Too far away, he could only watch as an Armazoid leaped over a car and landed on Mr. Knightsbridge. Kevin took quick care of him with his kung fu, but Mr. Knightsbridge was hurt. Bradley ran back to them and put a bullet in the downed Armazoid's head. The Armazoids blood drained into the sewers as Bradley looked down at Mr. Knightsbridge. He helped him slowly get up. Over his teacher's soldier, he saw a bigger group of the green monsters coming in their direction.

"There's too many of them," Bradley yelled. He looked at Mr. Knightsbridge. If they stood any chance in survival, they would have to let him go. He gave Mr. Knightsbridge a push in the direction they had been heading.

"Go, go, go," he yelled.

"What?" Mr. Knightsbridge asked, clearly confused.

"Don't argue with me!" Bradley yelled. "Just go! Give Ms. Hogan my regards."

"Amelia, you go as well," Max ordered.

Bradley pushed Mr. Knightsbridge and Amelia up the small alley as he pumped the shotgun. He took aim and pulled the trigger blasting the lead Armazoid. He only hoped the teacher and woman were getting away.

Kevin looked over at Bradley as Mr. Knightsbridge and Amelia disappeared. "They're gone, dude," he said. "Why did you let him go?"

"Why not?" Bradley replied looking at him.

Bradley watched as the rest of the Armazoids charged for them. He turned away from them, hoping to run to a position that was more easily defended—they were way too open.

"Come on," he ordered. He crossed the road, looking both ways at the smashed-up vehicles as they piled into one another, people still screaming for help. There was nothing he could do. As they reached the other sidewalk at a dead run, he saw Eric trip and fall. With the Armazoids charging closer, he swerved and pulled Eric roughly to his feet. "Come on!"

Kevin, the fastest runner, had run ahead and was beckoning to them madly. Bradley pushed Eric in his direction, then turned to squeeze off his last two shells into the lead Armazoids. Their lifeless bodies fell, tripping their companions behind.

"In here," Kevin yelled as he pushed a set of wooden doors open. Bradley followed Eric into the restaurant, his eyes slowly adjusting to the dark room until he could see the small group of frightened people inside.

"Hey, you boys okay?" The waiter asked. "What's it like out there?"

Bradley didn't bother answering. He slammed the two doors shut and pulled two huge dining tables across to try and hold the door shut.

"Will that hold?" The waiter asked.

"Probably not," Bradley replied, catching his breath. "But there we are."

There was a short pause as the boys panted after their sprint and the others watched them in scared silence. Then the banging started. The Armazoids had arrived.

"Shit," Kevin gasped. "They are going to get in."

"What do we do?" Max asked.

The people in the restaurant gasped, some gasping, as the banging on the doors intensified.

"What do we do?" a voice said from the panicked people.

The Armazoids outside the entrance continued slamming into the wooden doors, determined to get in and slaughter everyone inside. Eric stepped forward.

"I've got it!" He yelled

Eric walked towards the door. The people in the restaurant looking at him.

"Stay back I've got a chainsaw!" He yelled, "Ram, nam, nam, ram, nam, nam, nam, nam, ram, nam!"

Bradley looked at Eric as Kevin and Max did the same thing. Not saying a word. The Armazoids stopped slamming into the door. They kneeled down and peered through looking at Eric as he stood there still holding the pretend chainsaw.

"Who is this joker?" The Armazoid asked.

Bradley looked at the people, just staring at Eric after what he just done.

"He watches a lot of movies." He said in one at the onlookers.

The Armazoids started attacking the door again.

Bradley took deep breaths as bits of muck rained down each time the Armazoids banged on the door. He handed Kevin the handgun he had picked up off the dead security guard before.

"What?" Kevin gasped.

Bradley didn't't answer. He walked into the kitchen to look for the fire exit. "Come on," he yelled when he found it. "Go! Get these people out of here."

"Wait. What about you?" Kevin asked.

"Don't worry," Bradley said. "I'll catch up. Now come on, go."

Kevin pushed the fire exit open and started ushering out the frightened people who had holed up in the old restaurant. Just as Kevin was shooing at the las tone, three Armazoids burst into the restaurant. They pushed the old tables that had been blocking the door out of the way.

Bradley was ready for them. He clenched his knuckles. "Bring it on," he yelled.

The three Armazoids charged towards Bradley. Bradley felt his heart pound as all the martial arts and fighting he had learned over the years were called into action. He took a deep breath and swung his leg round, slamming it into the lead Armazoid. The alien fell back into his companions, making them all fall in a painful heap.

Bradley knew he had to get out of there. He sprinted for the exit and down the sidewalk, not knowing how far behind the Armazoids were. Not many people were around as he continued along the sidewalk, his heart pounding in his chest. He took a chance and ran down a small side alley, skidding to a stop when he reached its end: a brick wall.

The Armazoids ran around the comer of the alley where they thought they had seen the human male. They looked around the alleyway, seeing nothing but cluttered garbage in the quiet shadows. The passageway ended in a brick wall.

"He's gone," one Armazoid said to the others. He shrugged. "Never mind. There's plenty more out there." The Armazoids looked around for a few seconds more, then ran out of the alley in search of easier prey.

Bradley heard their retreating footsteps but gave it a few minutes. Then he slowly lifted the cardboard box off of him. He felt his heart starting to slow down. He wiped tiny drops of sweat away from his face as he looked around the dark alley, trying to decide if he could scale the wall—he wanted to avoid the main streets. He took a running start and leaped up, scrabbling for the top of the wall until he miraculously found a good handhold. He pulled himself up and then launched himself over, landing gracefully in a roll that brought him up to a standing position. He couldn't hear any screaming and assumed this part of the city was mostly deserted at this point. Where would his group be? He felt his pulse slowing as he continued to wipe his forehead. "Jesus Christ," he mumbled.

***

Kevin ran down the alley behind the restaurant. It was lined with the back doors of other shops. Eric and Max were close behind. He looked at each door as they jogged past, waiting until he saw an open door.

"In here," he commanded. He went up the steps to a door that had been left slightly ajar. It led into a quiet, dark café. He slowly closed the door behind Eric and Max, trying not to make any noise that might draw attention to them. He stopped and looked around the small building. The coffee machine was still running, gently dripping onto the silver plate. The chairs were overturned from when people had run from the alien attack.

"What are we doing here?" Eric asked.

"Staying out of sight while we figure out what to do," Kevin replied. He crossed to the front of the café and slid the bolt across.

"Guys, stay down," Kevin ordered. He could see some movement on the street but didn't wait to see if it was people or the alien invaders.

Eric hit the ground, bumping into a cart holding dirty dishes and knocking a few onto himself. He froze.

Kevin rolled his eyes, but nobody seemed to notice the noise.

"Okay, now what?" Max asked.

"We wait here for a while," Kevin said.

"How long?" Eric asked, still afraid to move. His eyes were wide with fright.

"For as long as it takes," Kevin snapped. "Until we can think of what to do without getting killed."

Eric remained silent as he stayed down on the floor. The coffee smell from the hissing machines lingered around the small building. The shadows of two Armazoids fell across the coffee shop. Kevin leaned up against the wall, trembling as the shadows passed over the curtains to his right. Would they be able to smell the humans inside the building? Kevin didn't know how acute alien senses were. He could just see them for a moment in the gap between the curtains and the side of the window. They were looking all around, ray guns at the ready.

Kevin shook his head in disbelief. "What are they?" he whispered.

"They're aliens," Eric replied, just as quietly.

"I know that," Kevin replied, "but where are they from?"

"The thing is, where did they come from," Max said. "No ship, nothing. They just appeared out of nowhere."

"Beats me," Kevin said, "But before we start with the science fiction, let's try and get out of here...alive."

"I agree," Max replied.

The three friends stayed down on the ground. Kevin could see the two Armazoids had stopped by the door of their café. He looked toward the back exit they had come through, making sure the path to that escape was clear in case things got worse.

"Where the hell is Bradley?" Eric almost whimpered.

"He's okay," Kevin replied. "I know he is."

"But where is he?" Eric asked again.

Kevin let his breath out. "Eric, listen to me" he said. "He is okay, trust me. Keep quiet."

Eric looked up to see the two looming shadows of the aliens outside the café. He couldn't tell if they knew the group was inside. Then one of the Armazoids turned the shiny golden handle. The lock slowly pulled back. Kevin clenched his fist, ready to fight them. The door moved back and forth as the bolt held it closed. Kevin held his fist tightly closed. He felt relieved as the two aliens started to walk away from the door to the cafe.

Kevin looked back at Eric. His friend's face was white and panic stricken—he looked like he could bolt at any moment. He also saw a couple plates precariously perched on Eric's legs.

"Do not move," Kevin whispered. "Please, Eric, don't move." He slowly started walking toward Eric, planning to move the potentially noisy plates.

"What?" Eric asked

"Don't move," Kevin whispered again.

Eric didn't move as the pile of plates slowly started to slip over the top of his leg. Kevin closed his eyes tight as the plates fell to the ground and smashed with a loud noise. He swung his head forward, looking up at the two Armazoids as they looked through the blinds of the small café down onto the group.

"Shit!" he gasped. "Come on." He jumped up, grasping the handgun. He opened fire through the windows. They ran back into the alley, sprinting down it until they seemed to reach a warehouse district. They could hear the footfalls of the heavy Armazoids behind them. Kevin skidded to the right and saw an open warehouse entrance.

"This way," he yelled. He ran down the small side alley towards the back entrance of the huge building. He looked at the wide-open door ready to be run into. He skidded to a stop. "In here," he yelled. "Come on, come on, come on."

Kevin watched as the chasing Armazoids followed Eric towards the back door. He reached out and pulled it closed. The Armazoids slammed into the door as Kevin got his breath back.

"Shit!" he gasped.

Eric looked at Kevin. "What do we do?" Eric asked as he started to panic.

"Eric, calm down," Kevin said. "We should be safe in here for a while. They are tough doors."

The banging continued on the back door. The group ran up the narrow corridor into the warehouse. They looked at all the empty offices and rooms.

"What is this place?" Eric asked.

"A warehouse," Max replied.

"I know that," Eric replied. "I mean, what is stored here?"

The group turned the corner looking out over a long balcony. Piles of orange canisters filled the storage space below them.

"Damn, man," Kevin said. "Why did we have to come here?"

"What are they?" Eric asked.

Kevin slowly walked down the metal steps to the concrete floor. He walked up to the orange canisters and looked at the labels. "Gas," he said.

"Gas," Eric repeated. "Great. Just great...........what sort of gas?"

***

Bradley peeked his head around the corner as he walked out of the alleyway. He looked both ways down the dead street and then at the two motor bikes that stood smashed in the middle of the road, smoke seeping out of the engines. The old black crash helmets in the middle of the road were still rolling about in the gentle breeze. It was the only sound that could be heard besides the few cars that had crackling fires burning down in their blackened shells. He continued to look over his shoulder as he advanced out of the alleyway onto the sidewalk. He needed a weapon and he needed a place to hide.

He was trying to decide which shop to enter when he came upon a patrol car smashed into one of the streetlamps. He walked over to it, looking around cautiously, and pulled open the driver's door. Tepid coffee that had spilled on the black leather seats got on his hands and jeans as he crawled in, looking for a gun or nightstick. Not finding anything useful in the car, he pulled the red trunk lever and got out of the vehicle. He looked around briefly before ducking down and walking around to the trunk, which was now open. His eyes widened in surprise and he felt the adrenaline surging through his body as he saw an AK47 assault rifle lying there.

"What the..." he gasped.

Bradley reached in and pulled the weapon out, placing the leather strap over his head and checking the magazine. There was plenty of ammo. He took a deep breath, feeling like his luck had finally turned, and nearly choked on the fumes from the burning vehicles.

Now thoughts of finding shelter did not cross Bradley's mind. He casually walked along the sidewalks in search of the Armazoids, eager to use the weapon. He heard a sudden crash from the street ahead and dove behind an overturned car. Bradley took a shallow breath as the strong taste of gas went down the back of his throat. He peeked up to see a long line of the alien invaders running down the road in one direction.

Bradley looked out onto the main road. He moved along the sidewalk to the dead street leading to the industrial estate north of the city. He kept his head down and watched as the Armazoids ran towards a warehouse. "What are they doing?" he wondered aloud.

He came out of the alleyway onto the main road. He grasped his AK47 assault rifle, ready to use it if he had to. He watched the aliens attacked the main entrance to the warehouse. They slammed into the metal door, struggling to get in. The door was slowly starting to give way.

"I wonder…"

He ran up to the entrance of the huge building and looked into the security shack. Blood covered the swivel chair. Bradley turned his attention to the roof of the building. He looked up to see a metal ladder leading to the roof for maintenance of the air conditioners. He sprinted over to it, all the while keeping an eye on the Armazoids.

Bradley quickly climbed the ladder and walked onto the roof of the building. He came across a huge skylight. He leaned over carefully, trying not to cast a shadow down into the huge building but still trying to see in. He blinked. He could see Kevin leaning against a small wooden crate, watching the warehouse door that the aliens were ramming. Bradley shook his head as he caught sight of a coil of rope near his feet, left by the builders when they finished construction on the huge warehouse. A loud crack brought him back to the front door, where the Armazoids had finally gotten the huge shutter open.

"Shit, they're getting in," Eric yelled.

Kevin held onto the sidearm. He was too scared to shoot because of the gas canisters. He could only watch as the Armazoids charged forward.

"Shoot, Kevin," Max yelled.

Just then he looked up as the huge skylight glass shattered. The tiny shards of glass started raining down on them as the unravelling rope tumbled down towards the floor. The Armazoids walked in as Bradley's shadow fell on the floor of the warehouse.

"Down!" Kevin yelled.

Bradley took a deep breath as he looked down into the floor below him. The Armazoids didn't have a clue what the hell was going on. He started sliding down, the rope safely anchored to a pipe on the roof, his hand burning from the friction, his other hand still holding the AK47. Eric stood looking up with his mouth agape as Bradley opened fire on the aliens. The tiny golden bullets shot through them.

"Jesus Christ, Bradley," Eric yelled. "There's fucking gas around."

Bradley jumped when he was still a few feet from the ground, landing gracefully. He turned to the group. "MOVE!" he yelled.

Kevin, Eric, and Max ran to the back exit of the warehouse. Kevin kicked the gray bar of the door, forcing it open violently, and then he ran down the dark alley.

Bradley had stayed behind to clean up. He was watching the oncoming Armazoids. "Come on, then," he muttered. He curled his finger around the trigger and fired. The bullets spewed out, penetrating the large group of canisters. He turned and ran to within sight of the exit, then turned around and fired a last round at the metal piping. It sparked.

Bradley threw the AK47 down and ran as the gases throughout the building ignited and erupted. Bradley sprinted out of the building as the huge fireball chased after him. Even outside, the force slammed him to the ground. "Ouch," he moaned.

Kevin ran over after the explosions had finished. "Brad, where the hell you been?" he asked, smiling once he saw his fried was okay.

"Just around," Bradley replied as he got up off the floor and brushed off the bits of muck from his clothes. "You guys okay?"

"We're okay," Eric said.

"Good," Bradley replied. "What have I missed?"

"Not much," Max replied. Then he smiled.

Bradley looked down the alleyway. Garbage cans lined the walls, and old newspaper bits were blowing around them. His ears were still ringing after the explosion. He shook his head as he took another look down the alleyway. "Come on," he said. "Let's get out of here."

The group started walking up the alleyway away from the burning warehouse.

Chapter 7

The Williamsburg Bridge went up in flames instantly before his eyes. Lieutenant Kipling clambered into the Ft-17 tank holding on to his rifle as he stared across the empty Queensboro Bridge. He slowly turned his head to the left as the sun beamed down on his head. He looked over as a few puffs of smoke came out from under the bridge. The huge shockwave from the explosions rippled through the air, and the burning, twisted metal slammed into the Hudson River. The splashes were huge.

"May God have mercy on our souls." He said.

The atomic motors on his tank and three behind him roared to life, the tracks slowly starting to roll forward onto the Queensboro Bridge, one of the last remaining escape points for the island of Manhattan. Kipling looked behind as he looked out the top of the tank. He grasped his rifle as the end of the old bridge was near. The roads were clear ahead.

"Standby," Kipling said into the radio.

He ripped the machine gun lever back, looking at the golden bullets dangling beside him. He grasped the trigger, ready to squeeze it as the tank rolled out from the bridge. The roads were covered with smashed up vehicles. There was an eerie silence as Kipling raised his hands for the brigade to stop. Kipling looked around the dead quiet streets. The manic sounds from Queens, now behind them, disappeared as he continued to observe the streets around him. There wasn't a soul in sight.

The tanks slowly started turning to the left, heading up the street towards the police station, which was just over two miles away. Kipling's eyes twitched as they slammed through smashed up buses and trucks. But something caught his eye ahead of him. He raised his fist, stopping the tanks again.

He stepped down from the tank, holding onto his rifle. Kipling stared ahead at the dead corpse of a slender woman lying in the middle of the road. She was smartly dressed, with a pleated skirt down to her knees, long blonde hair curled around her face—must have been going to a family get together or a date. Kipling kneeled down next her. He placed his hands on the corpse, slowly turning her onto her back as two more of his troops ran over, scanning the area around them. Kipling stared down at her face. The blood had dried on her neck where one of the aliens has shot her. "Jesus," Kipling said.

One of the young troops looked down at her. "Damn, very nice," he said approvingly.

Kipling continued looking down at her. Her eyes were still wide open with shock.

"Where was she off to?" the soldier asked.

Kipling looked down at her as he felt his inner emotions start to turn.

"Let's see what she is made of, then," the soldier said, using his boot to start lifting her skirt.

"Hey," Kipling snapped. "Show some goddamn respect."

The soldier quickly lowered her skirt.

"Don't let me see you do that again," Kipling ordered.

"Sorry sir," the soldier replied.

Kipling looked over at the sidewalk. "Move her over there," he ordered. "Now."

Kipling closed her small eyes. Two soldiers started to move the woman's body. Kipling walked over to the tank and pulled out a small map, checking the location of the police station was—about a mile away. The two soldiers placed the young lady down on the sidewalk.

One soldier looked over at Kipling studying the map.

"Go on quickly while he isn't looking," he said.

"You heard what he said," the other soldier replied.

"Just do it."

The young soldier placed his rifle by his side as the tanks started up again, ready to roll. He was just lifting the young lady's skirt when he heard a sudden scuffle coming from the shop next to him.

"What was that?" his companion asked.

The two men peered into the dark shop as the lights had gone out.

"What is it?" the soldier asked again.

The two men slowly walked into the shop, glass crunching beneath their feet. The sound echoed around the empty shop. The two soldiers stared into back depths of the shop, trying to see clearly.

From outside the shop, Kipling looked up from the map to see the inside of a dark shop illuminated with the purple light he'd seen from the alien weapons. He heard a man screaming.

"Man down," he yelled, running to the shop. He arrived in the doorway just in time to see the other soldier gunned down.

"Shit!" he gasped. He ran back out to the tank, grabbing hold of the heavy machine gun and swinging it toward the shop as the two Armazoids sprinted out. Kipling squeezed the trigger. The two Armazoids fell to the ground. He stared down at their slimy bodies as the green blood ran out of their wounds onto the sidewalk, running against the young lady.

"Come on," Kipling yelled. "Let's roll."

The tanks started to pick up speed as Kipling brushed the loose golden shells onto the floor of the tank. His eyes were peeled as they moved along the road. He grasped the machine gun as he looked down at the map. The police station was nearing.

"I want all side roads blocked," he ordered over the radio. "Let's get a clear route back to the bridge. *Move it.*" Ahead, the police cars forming a barricade in front of the station slowly rolled back to make way for the tanks.

***

Ms. Hogan quickly got up from her seat in the police station office at the sound of military jets flying overhead. The drinks in the cups on the table rippled as the engines roared off into the distance. She felt very hot. She walked down the concrete steps looking down the street at the people standing about, all looking very scared. Many people were still crowding into the police station, having just arrived at a place of safety since this terrible day had started.

A distant rumble grew louder and louder, and the crowd started pointing. Ms. Hogan slipped on her glasses. It was not the sort of thing one saw every day. United States' military tanks rolled down the street, smashing into and running over crashed and stopped vehicles. Ms. Hogan stepped onto the sidewalk as the tanks pulled up in front of the police station. The noise from the engines was horrendous. The soldiers climbed out of their vehicles, arming up and looked around at the terrorized people. A young lieutenant walked up the concrete steps into the police station past Ms. Hogan. She turned around, watching them go, and she finally felt a little hope.

Lieutenant Kipling and two of the soldiers turned left once they entered the station. They headed up the stairs toward the office of the chief of police. From the other side of the closed glass door, they could see the chief, head in hands, listening to his radio. The sound of shooting and cars crashing from the radio was only slightly muffled by the closed door.

Kipling knocked twice, the chief turned his head and motioned them in. Kipling opened the door and strode in.

"Chief Irons?" Lieutenant Kipling asked.

"Yes," he replied. "Yes, that's me."

There was a short pause from both the men.

"Lieutenant John Kipling, sir. New York City and the surrounding areas and districts have been put under martial law, as you may be aware. Now we are going to need as many men as possible here, so can you get your officers back here?"

Irons got on the radio. He called his officers back to the station, knowing that not many of them would be returning.

"We also have put a call out for all emergency service personnel to report here," the lieutenant continued. "Everything—fire, ambulance, and all military."

Chief Irons walked to the window. He could see the line of tanks and people still flowing into the station. "How are you evacuating?"

95

"I've not had my orders yet, sir, but from what I know there is going to be only one way out." Kipling replied.

Irons was shocked. "What?" he gasped. "There are many bridges and tunnels you can use to aid this evacuation."

"I'm sorry, sir, but I cannot disclose that information as of yet," Kipling replied. "I will be keeping you informed of the situation as my men and I progress."

"What's the status on the subway?" Irons asked. "We lost contact with the subway control center a while ago."

The lieutenant took a deep breath. "I have been told that Grand Central Station has been destroyed."

Irons bowed his head.

"Once our people have cleared a route out of the city, we will begin evacuating them, but it is too dangerous right now," Kipling stated. "We will be in touch, Chief Irons." He smartly saluted and turned around, followed by his two men. They walked downstairs, through the station and out into the street. Two tanks were moving into position to guard the entrance to the station.

Kipling shook his head as more people came out of the subway station and surrounding streets toward the police station. He knew it was going to be filled up very quickly.

Chapter 8

Bradley led his friends up a back alley. He didn't have a plan and he didn't know what to think. He just knew they had to keep moving and stay out of sight, especially now that they didn't have a weapon.

Kevin tapped his shoulder. "Dude, where'd you pick up the AK?"

"Just found it," Bradley said.

"Just found it?" Max said, eyebrows raised.

"Yep," Bradley replied, smirking. "In the back of a patrol car."

"Lucky man," Max stated.

"Yep, I definitely found it more by luck than by judgment."

Max took a shallow breath. "What's the plan then?"

"To stay alive," Bradley replied. "That's about it for now, I think."

Movement on the ground caught his eye, and Bradley raised his fist up into the air, a signal to stop moving. He slowly pointed at the moving shadows that came between two buildings. Everyone froze, waiting. Slowly, the shadows moved away.

Bradley took a deep breath as he crept forward along the alley, motioning the other boys to stay put. He tried not to step on the cracked cement as the light from the main street beamed in. Bradley peeked around the corner of the alleyway. He looked out into the streets to see the Armazoids patrolling around together, wielding their weapons, ready to use them. Smoke poured out of the crashed vehicles. Glass lay scattered about on the ground. Bradley slowly moved back into the alleyway back to the bewildered group. He kneeled down on the ground and looked at Kevin. "Okay," he whispered. "Definitely aliens. Let's stay in the alley."

"Got it," Kevin said.

As the started creeping down the alley again, they heard footsteps from an intersecting road not far away. Each boy dove for cover behind piles of garbage or industrial-sized garbage cans.

Two Armazoids walked into the alleyway, talking to each other in their alien speech. They didn't seem very alert. As they passed, Bradley almost held his breath. He heard his heart pounding in his chest, and he crossed his fingers that none of the other guys would make a noise. Bradley watched as they walked away.

Bradley stayed still for another minute, until he was sure the aliens were gone. Then he stood up and gave the all-clear sign.

"Phew!" Kevin said, standing up from behind a garbage can. He joined Bradley in the alleyway, and Max and Eric soon followed.

The group started creeping along. Bradley felt that they probably wouldn't run into Armazoids again in the near future, so he ran ahead to scout out their path through the twisting alleyways. He didn't find any more of the aliens.

When he met up with his friends again, he could tell they were dragging.

"Okay, guys, take two," Bradley said. He kneeled down, thinking about their next move. It was very quiet.

"Hey," a voice suddenly whispered. Bradley looked up toward the back window of a shop. A middle-aged man was looking down at them. "You okay?" he asked. "Come inside. I'll let you in."

Bradley stood up and looked at Kevin. He shrugged his shoulders as the back door slowly started to open. The creak of the hinges seemed to go on and on, but finally the door was wide enough for the boys to enter. Bradley looked into the corridor, which was barely illuminated by a skylight in the store proper.

The man stuck out his hand. "Name's Roger," he said.

"Hi Roger," Eric said

"Name's Bradley," Bradley said. "What the hell is going on?"

Roger shook his head. "I don't have a clue. My cousin owns this shop and I'm just watching it while he's away on vacation. All of a sudden, people are screaming and running. I walked up to the entrance of the store to see those things attacking people left, right, and center." Roger shuddered. "It was horrible to watch."

Bradley walked out of the back hallway into the store proper. His eyes widened with amazement. There, in front of him, stood stack after stack after stack of weapons. They had walked right into a weapon store.

"How come you weren't raided for weapons?" Kevin asked as he walked over and started examining the merchandise.

"I put the shutters down straight away and got the door locked, but I don't think people even had the time," Rodger said. "They were just massacred."

Bradley peeked through the tiny holes in the shutter. He could just barely see two Armazoids walk down the other side of the street.

"What you boys in New York for? Vacation? Field trip?" Roger asked

"Just a field trip," Kevin said. "At least it *was* a field trip."

"Where's your schoolteacher?" Roger asked.

"He was getting in the way," Kevin replied.

"Oh," Roger replied folding his arms.

"So we let him go," Eric said.

Bradley turned around. "Have you got a TV?" he asked.

"Yes. Why?"

"I want to check the news."

Roger turned around and turned on the small television behind the counter. Bradley joined him, staring at the static while Roger fiddled with the old set. Finally, Roger stopped trying.

"Sorry, kid. It's a dodgy piece on the best days."

"Okay. Do you have any plans for survival?" Bradley asked.

"No, I'm just staying here as long as I can. What are you doing?"

"We should head off and get back to our people at the police station," Bradley said. "Where is that?"

"The main one?" Roger asked.

"Yes." Bradley said.

Roger pulled out a small pocket map from under the counter. He unfolded it and looked down onto the Manhattan area. "Let's plot a route," he said.

Bradley leaned over the counter and studied the map.

"Okay, we are here. The main police headquarters is here," Roger said. He circled the station as Bradley looked down onto the map.

"That's not far," Eric said.

"It's about three and a half miles from here, but I suggest you take the alleys and back routes all the way down to here," Roger said.

"Where's the bus station?" Bradley asked.

"The bus station is here," Roger said, circling the station with a red pen. "Why do you want that?"

"Our bus and our driver may be there. He could help with the evacuation," he replied.

"Cool," Roger said. "Okay, boys. Good luck in getting to your friends. Take what you want."

Bradley shook his head in disbelief. "Anything?" he asked.

"Yep, anything. This place will be gone soon if they start bombing the crap out of the island anyway," Roger said.

"That won't happen for a while," Kevin said.

"Don't bet on it," Roger said.

Bradley didn't want to get a long conversation.

"Right". We had better get armed and get out of here."

He turned around and walked into the shop. He looked at all the weapon utility belts, choosing one to strap to his body. He felt the tight straps cling to his leg as he placed the handguns in the pockets, all fully loaded and ready to be used. He continued round the shop, putting two a sub machine gun straps on each shoulder so that they crossed his chest and let a gun hang at each side. They were followed by the SPAS shot gun on his back, ready to be used in a crowded place.

Kevin turned the corner. He looked at the shelf to see some flick out batons all lined up, ready for purchase. "Wicked." He pulled a selection of the truncheons off the shelf. "Brad," he called. He chucked one into the air and Bradley reached up and caught it. He flicked it out, admiring the small weapon.

"Cool," Bradley said, smiling.

Bradley closed the weapon and put it into a pocket on his leg strap as he continued scanning the shop. He looked to his right to see a large, leather jacket. He pulled it down off the coat hook and placed it over all his weapons.

Kevin watched as he swung around walking towards the group as they stood by the entrance, similarly armed and ready to leave. "Ready when you are," he said.

Roger handed Bradley the map and a small silver gun.

"What's this?" Bradley asked.

"That's a flare gun," Roger said.

"Good idea." Bradley said. He tied the tiny weapon holder to the lower half of his leg. He locked it into place. "Thank you, Roger."

They shook hands and Kevin pushed the back door open slowly, anticipating the creaks. Instantly, sounds of glass smashing made them all whirl around to see glass falling from above in the store. Armazoids had broken in through the skylight.

"Go!" Roger yelled. "I'll hold them off!"

Bradley turned around. He slammed the backdoor shut. He could hear Roger yelling and shooting a semi-automatic machine gun.

"Come on," Bradley ordered. "Let's get the hell to that station."

102

The group ran down into the alleyway as the sound of the shooting from the shop faded into silence.

Chapter 9

Mr. Knightsbridge felt his stomach turning as thick saliva started to build up in the back of his throat and mouth from all the running he had done.

"You okay?" Amelia asked.

"Yeah," Mr. Knightsbridge said. "Just fine." He felt his heart thumping in his chest as they took a brief rest. He placed his hands on his hips and leaned his large body against a bent lamppost. His heart missed a beat as he looked around at the destroyed city. It felt different with only smashed up cars in the streets and no people bustling about on their business. There were no happy tourists photographing the landmarks around or businesspeople rushing to their next appointment. For once there weren't even any beggars.

They sat down on a bench of a covered bus stop that sported an ad for an alien invasion movie. He did not appreciate the irony.

"Are you okay?" he asked Amelia.

"Yes, I am, thanks," she replied. "Still a bit shaken up, though."

"We shouldn't be far now," Mr. Knightsbridge reassured her. With a sigh, they got to their feet and started walking again, constantly trying to look out for aliens and ignore the gore around them. It seemed death was lurking behind every corner.

They took another break at a bus stop with clear plastic walls and a dark roof.

"So what were you doing here in New York?" Amelia asked.

"Well," Mr. Knightsbridge said. "It was meant to be a field trip."

"Were those boys with you?" Amelia asked.

"Yes," he mumbled. "They were. You?"

"I'm on business from New Haven," Amelia replied.

"I'm from there," Mr. Knightsbridge replied. "How come I haven't seen you around?"

"It's quite a big city," Amelia replied, laughing a little.

Suddenly Mr. Knightsbridge closed his mouth. Through the plastic behind Amelia, he could see a single alien looking out of an alleyway at him.

"Oh shit!" he exclaimed.

The Armazoid snarled, running straight for them. Mr. Knightsbridge put his arm around Amelia and closed his eyes. He heard a sudden slam and opened his eyes again, looking at the Armazoid's squashed face on the plastic panel of the bus stop. The Armazoid slowly slid down the paneled plastic, falling down into the mucky street.

It started to shake its head as if clearing it. From the alley where Mr. Knightsbridge had first seen it, more Armazoids appeared. Mr. Knightsbridge pulled Amelia up with him and they started sprinting down the center of the destroyed road, dodging cars and fallen telephone poles.

"Come on, Amelia," he yelled.

He didn't have a clue where the police station was. He looked over his shoulder again at the chasing Armazoids—they were catching up. Mr. Knightsbridge felt the side of his large body start to clench as he came to a stop and the stitch in his side got worse. He pushed his hand into his side, feeling the pain radiate outward. He leaned against a lamppost as the Armazoids slowed and walked toward them.

Amelia cowered behind him. "This is it," she cried.

Mr. Knightsbridge held onto Amelia's hand as his heart banged in his chest. The sun beamed down on the Armazoids as they slowly swiped their ray guns from their side pouches. Mr. Knightsbridge closed his eyes as death looked at him, thinking about his short life.

The sound of gunfire from behind made him jump. He swung his head around to see three soldiers in the middle of the road wielding their rifles, gas masks covering their faces. Mr. Knightsbridge looked back to see three dead aliens on the ground. The tingling still rang through his ears.

"This way," the soldier commanded.

Mr. Knightsbridge released his breath from his exhausted lungs. "Come on," he said to Amelia.

The soldiers helped him along the deserted road towards a barricade. He squeezed through the yellow plastic barriers, looking over his shoulder as the young soldiers stepped back and scanned the roads ahead, guns drawn and ready to be used again.

Mr. Knightsbridge turned around and realized they had walked into a military zone. He stared at all the parked tanks guarding the main police headquarters as people ran about in different directions. "Jesus Christ," he said quietly.

"God! What a mess!" Amelia said.

Mr. Knightsbridge watched as two Humvees pulled up outside the entrance to the station and coach buses started turning up. The frantic people struggled to get a seat. Mr. Knightsbridge headed towards the police station entrance. Now that the adrenaline was leaving his body, he could barely make it up the concrete steps. He opened the door and instantly heard chorus of ringing phones at the main desk, ignored by a police staff that was running in all directions. He looked into one office and saw Ms. Hogan. She was standing, looking out of the side window onto the busy streets as the military vehicles continued rolling in. She slowly turned around, holding a small, half-puffed cigarette in her mouth. Her mouth opened in disbelief when she saw Mr. Knightsbridge, his shiny pink tie half undone and his jacket hanging damply from his huge body.

"Alan!" she yelled.

Mr. Knightsbridge watched Ms. Hogan run over and wrap her long, thin arms around him as he struggled to keep his balance.

"Thank God," she said, relieved. "You are okay? Are you injured?"

"No, I'm fine," Mr. Knightsbridge replied. "How are you?"

"We are okay," Ms. Hogan said.

"Where were you when this all happened?"

"We were about five minutes from here," Ms. Hogan said. "We were lucky."

"We were right at the other end of the city," Mr. Knightsbridge said. "You're sure you're okay?"

"I'm fine. Where are Bradley, Kevin, Max, and Eric?" she asked, looking behind him. "I want to make sure they are okay."

Mr. Knightsbridge looked past Ms. Hogan at the group of students looking expectantly at him. He could see the questions about their missing classmates in their eyes.

"Bradley—um, well, we had this little situation," Mr. Knightsbridge stuttered. "They left me and went ahead. They did! They just left me."

"Okay," Ms. Hogan said in a dull voice. Then she suddenly started, opening her eyes wide. *"What!"* she asked furiously.

"I lost them," Mr. Knightsbridge went on. "We were being attacked by one of those things and Bradley insisted that I just go."

He saw the anger in her eyes.

"You mean to say you have left four of my students out there in this, this, this invasion all by themselves? They are probably dead, and you left them." Her face started to turn the color of her purple suit.

"No, they're not," Mr. Knightsbridge whined. "He's a tough boy."

"What do you know about him?" Ms. Hogan yelled.

"A lot more than you," Mr. Knightsbridge replied shortly, getting angry himself. "All you ever do is throw your negative attitude towards him."

"What?" Ms. Hogan yelled.

Mr. Knightsbridge and Ms. Hogan glared at one another as Amelia walked up to them.

"And who is this?" Ms. Hogan asked.

"Oh, this is Amelia," Mr. Knightsbridge said.

"Hi," Amelia said gently.

"And where did you find her then?" Ms. Hogan groaned.

"Alleyway."

Amelia looked offended. "Excuse me, I'm not some street hooker. I'm in the city on business."

"I didn't say you were," Ms. Hogan said. She turned back and looked at Mr. Knightsbridge. Amelia walked closer to Ms. Hogan, arms folded, ready to ram her words back down her mouth.

"Bradley and Mr. Knightsbridge actually saved me from my vehicle, which overturned," Amelia said, "so I owe him and Bradley my life."

"Oh, good for you," Ms. Hogan replied. Amelia clenched her fist.

"Okay, calm down," Mr. Knightsbridge said.

Two girl students ran up to Ms. Hogan. "Ms. Hogan, we can't contact Kate or Lisa on their cell phones," one said.

"Oh my," Ms. Hogan cried, falling against the wall of the office.

"Where's Kate and Lisa? Who were they with?" Mr. Knightsbridge asked, folding his arms.

"They, they—I let them go off by themselves," Ms. Hogan said, looking up at Mr. Knightsbridge. "And Colin went as well."

"So you let two young school girls and Colin go around New York City by themselves. That's just great," Mr. Knightsbridge replied, voice rising. "Just great."

Ms. Hogan turned her back on him with a huff but then her shoulders slumped dejectedly. She put her hands over her face. "Where are they?" she whispered. "They must be alive."

Chapter 10

Bradley held onto the sidearm as the smells of the burning vehicles and death pervaded the air around him. He felt his heart pounding as he scanned the area and saw nothing but trashed vehicles and burning buildings.

"Bradley," Eric called. He was pointing toward a new police patrol Jeep smashed into one of the bus stops. "Could we drive it?" Eric asked. "Or anything else around here?"

"No, look at the streets. They're too blocked," Bradley said. "Let's see what's in here." He opened the Jeep door and slowly brushed aside the tiny shards of glass. He looked down at the vehicle radio and slowly reached in to switch it on. Nothing happened.

Bradley looked behind the box to see the wires pulled out and destroyed. "Okay, let's keep moving," he said. "Don't want any attention." He kept his eyes open as he slipped his weapon back into his side pouch continuing to look around the deserted street.

"Where is that station now?" Eric asked.

"About four miles this way," Bradley replied to him, gesturing down the road.

Up ahead, Kevin froze in the middle of the street, eyes wide at something Bradley couldn't see.

"Bradley," Kevin whispered urgently. He pointed at the crossroads half a block ahead, and Bradley moved slowly to his left until he could see two Armazoids standing there, unaware of the humans' presence.

Bradley felt a sudden rush of adrenaline in his system. "Okay, this way." He held onto his sidearm as he ducked down by a broken shop window, watching the two Armazoids. Eric crept up behind him. Without sparing him a glance, Bradley whispered, "Keep quiet, Eric. You don't know when they're going to move."

Eric nodded, taking his eyes off the road for a second, and stumbled over an empty coke can. It bounced loudly into the gutter. Eric froze. "Oh shit!" he gasped.

Bradley rolled his eyes as the Armazoids honed in on the noise and started moving in their direction. Bradley quickly swiped his handgun out of his pocket, aimed, and squeezed the trigger: two hits. The Armazoids fell, but behind them Bradley saw something much worse. A horde of Armazoids was running down the street towards them, yelling and brandishing their ray guns.

Bradley looked wildly around and spotted the entrance to a subway station. "Go, go, go," he yelled, gesturing to the stairs that led underground. "I'll cover you!" His friends dashed across the street while Bradley looked through his sight and took down Armazoids one by one.

"Bradley," Kevin yelled. "Come on!"

Bradley abandoned his position and ran for the subway, Kevin covering him from the subway entrance. Sparks rained down from an electric sign that dangled by its partially severed wires.

"Come on," Max yelled.

Bradley hurtled down the stairs, crushing a coke can beneath his thundering feet. He skidded to a stop at the bottom where Max and Eric were with Kate.

Kate turned to him, her liquid eyes emotional in the dim light.

"Kate!" he exclaimed.

Kevin ran down after him. "Where's Lisa?" Kevin asked before Bradley could say anything else. "Is she okay? Where is she, Kate? Tell me."

A door swung shut to their right, and the boys turned, weapons ready. Lisa held her hands up. "I'm fine," Lisa said, eyes wide. "Just using the bathroom."

Everyone sighed. Bradley laughed. "Calm down, Kev, the day isn't over yet my friend."

They heard a crash in the men's bathroom, but Kate and Lisa laughed. The boys looked at them, surprised. They turned their attention back to the bathroom as someone slowly appeared from the darkness. It was Colin.

"What?" Kevin gasped. "You?"

"Yes, me," Colin said. "What's going on?"

Bradley slowly walked up to Colin. "So flirting with these girls, are we?"

"Yes," Colin replied, smirking. "It's really quite fun."

Bradley shook his head.

Kevin placed his arms around Lisa's trembling shoulders, but she shrugged him off. "I'm fine," she said defiantly.

The thunder of feet announced the arrival of the aliens.

"Come on," Kevin ordered. "Lisa, you stick with me."

"Colin, stick with Eric," Bradley commanded. He jumped over the ticket barrier, his side arm out and ready. "Go," Bradley ordered. "I'll catch up."

"You better," Kevin said. "The last time you said that you disappeared."

"Don't worry, I'm right behind," Bradley replied. He ducked down behind the plastic barrier and took a couple shots as the rest of the group ran down to the platform. With his friends out of the way, Bradley opened fire on the aliens coming down the stairs. The ones that reached the bottom halted abruptly, as if their eyes weren't adjusting to the dark light.

Bradley took off after his friends. He could hear the Armazoids coming after him, but it only sounded like a few. He didn't want to think about where the rest of the horde had gone.

He found the group waiting for him on the platform, but he didn't hesitate. "They're right behind me," he said quietly but urgently. "Follow me." He jumped off the platform onto the tracks, he turned to help Kate down. They ducked under the side of the platform. It was pitch black. They hadn't hid a moment too soon. They heard the heavy feet and breathing of the Armazoids as they came down onto the platform, but after a few moments, they couldn't hear anything.

Bradley held his breath. Had the Armazoids left or were they just being quiet? He put his fingers to his lips, cautioning the group to maintain their silence. They waited a few minutes and then heard some grunts and retreating footsteps. The group heaved a collective sigh of relief.

"Damn!" Bradley gasped. "That was close." He got a flashlight out of his equipment and flicked the powerful beam on, illuminating the dark subway tunnel. He started walking down it, knowing they couldn't go back the way they came. "You two okay?" he asked, turning to the girls.

Kate didn't reply for a few seconds, shock making her eyes wide and empty. She shook herself. "I guess so. What the hell is going on?"

Bradley didn't know what to say. He shrugged and kept walking. "I have no idea. One minute we were walking down a street and the next it all just hit us."

"Where's Mr. Knightsbridge?" Kate asked.

"He got in the way," Kevin replied, smirking.

"So you left him?" Lisa asked.

"No, we told him to get to safety," Bradley replied. "And get out of our way."

"Oh, I see," Kate said. "Good move."

The station behind them rumbled. The group looked back.

"Come on, let's get out of here," Bradley insisted.

The group continued trekking up the tunnel. The sound of the breeze flying in from the platform echoed around the shadows that flitted around the dark tunnel.

Chapter 11

Washington, D.C. is under martial law. US troops and National Guard were everywhere. William Synder, the president's chief of staff, never would have imagined that his career would take such as drastic turn when he woke up that morning.

He stood on the front lawns of the White House, waiting for the president's helicopter to land. People were clambering outside the high, wrought-iron fence, desperate for answers on the invasion in New York. Police struggled to keep the people back. He squinted his eyes, looking into the distance as the blue Sea King helicopter thrummed over the city, slowly descending toward him. The huge blades began slowing down, and a military pilot stepped out of the helicopter and ran to swing the back door open. First-term president Christopher Henderson stepped out and walked briskly toward Synder.

"Good morning sir, shall I bring you up to date with the situation in New York?" Synder yelled over the engine as it shut down.

"Yes. What the hell is going on?" President Christopher Henderson asked. "Have our generals mobilized the troops in the city as I ordered? Have they set up a perimeter around the main police headquarters? What news from the mayor?"

"Yes sir, the troops are mobilized and a perimeter is set up," Synder replied. "But apparently the roads are jammed with trashed vehicles so they are clearing a one-way route to the Queensboro Bridge where a command post has been set up to aid survivors." He hesitated. "We've lost contact with the mayor's office."

"Dear God," Henderson muttered.

"Sir," Synder said, "We think its best if we discuss the crisis in the emergency bunker, I have the vice president down there as well, currently we are on DEFCON Three."

The two of them walked into the White House, Synder led the president to the elevator that would descend to the protected underground bunker. Synder swiped his ID card and the elevator quickly dropped.

"Have any other nations reported these creatures?" Henderson asked.

"No sir, just Manhattan is infested with these things so far as we know of."

The elevator came to a stop. Henderson and Synder entered the emergency briefing room, lined with glowing screens. Some TVs were tuned to the news and were showing the Queen's command center, the background smoky from the destruction around it.

Henderson sat at the head of the table and looked out at General Reeves and the Vice President Karen Hayes.

"Okay, bring me up to speed," President Henderson demanded.

Reeves walked to a digital board that showed Manhattan.

"Sir, my men have set up a unit around the main police headquarters here, and at the hospital just down the road here. People are turning up left, right and center. The only way out is across the Queensboro Bridge, here," the general said, pointing.

President Henderson rubbed his face. "Is that the only way out of the city? What about the New Jersey tunnel?"

"We have had to seal the tunnel off in case the alien invaders tried to get through to New Jersey or Newark," he replied. "We have set up a ton of Semtex on the Queensboro Bridge, ready to blow it up if the invaders try and break through the barricade we have on it."

"What about any of the other bridges?" President Henderson asked.

"No, sir. All the other bridges have been destroyed to prevent invasions of any other town. We have only one way out for evacuation: The Queensboro Bridge."

"What about JFK airport?" President Henderson asked.

"The airports—JFK, La Guardia, and Newark—have been closed," Hayes said. "In fact, all US airspace above the area has been closed, and all incoming flights have been redirected away from the New York and the Washington area."

"Have we heard from any alien leader?" President Henderson asked.

"Not yet, sir," General Reeves replied. "Nothing at all from these things."

"Well, we have to plan for the worst. We don't know how many more of these things there are, so I want your people ready for immediate action," President Henderson ordered. "I understand we are on DEFCON Three."

"Yes sir," General Reeves stated, "That is why..." He hesitated.

"Why what?" Henderson demanded.

The general took a deep breath. "Currently on standby at Edwards Air Force Base, I have six F-16s ready to go to New York and drop Hades bombs on the island General Reeves said.

"Any chance of a nuclear strike on Manhattan?" Henderson then asked.

"We have discussed that," Hayes said, standing up. She walked over to another screen and brought up a map of New York state. A red dot indicted the position of Manhattan.

"If we hit Manhattan with a nuclear strike," she said, "the casualties would be in the hundreds of thousands."

She drew a red circle around Manhattan that encompassed half the state and a lot of the Atlantic Ocean. "Then we have the nuclear fallout," Hayes said. "The death toll would probably rise to the millions."

"So nuclear is the last means of defense," Henderson concluded.

"Yes sir," Hayes replied.

"Ok, have the F-16s ready for immediate deployment on my order," President Henderson said. "Things are going to get nasty down there."

General Reeves stood up. "Yes, sir."

The president stayed seated, head in hands. "What am I going to say? The whole world is waiting for me," the president said.

"We have your speech prepared, sir," Synder reassured him.

"Okay. I'm going to my office. Let me know if any of their leaders make contact with us," he instructed. He walked out of the briefing room, miserably resolved to bomb Manhattan and tell his people that the nation was in peril.

Chapter 12

Bradley had almost gotten used to his heart pounding with fear. He stared at what the flashlight illuminated, unable to see anything beyond it. The stones beneath their feet crunched as they saw the lights from the next station slowly start to come into view. A parked-up subway train was at the platform, blocking the way.

"Going under?" Eric asked. Lisa whimpered.

"No," Bradley said confidently. "Through." He walked up to the back of the train, cautiously climbed the metal stairs and looked into the cab—not a soul in sight. He gently pulled the door open and was rewarded with a long, horrendous squeal of rusty metal hinges. It echoed down the tunnel, and everyone froze in a cringe.

Bradley slowly entered the carriage, its ground littered with newspapers and shopping bags left by desperate people trying to escape. He heard the rest of the group troop up behind him as he moved to the carriage doors to get to the platform. He placed his hands on the carriage doors and tried to pull them open, but they didn't budge.

"They're stuck," he said.

Kevin came up and pushed the "open door" button. Miraculously, the train still had power, and the doors slowly slid open. He smirked at Bradley.

"Good man," Bradley said.

The group cautiously walked onto the platform, Bradley ready with his sidearm at the front and Max guarding the back. He led them around the corner of the station and then put his fingers to his lips, showing his friends that they should quietly ascend the static escalator to get to ground level.

At the top, Bradley flicked off his flashlight and stowed it in his jacket. There was enough light coming from the end of the tunnel. There was a lot of paper on the ground—ticket stubs, newspapers, brown lunch bags—and it was all eerily blowing in the wind, creating small vortexes of trash that kept swirling in the corner of Bradley's eye.

They passed the ticket machines, some with orange tickets still waiting for their purchaser to remove them from the slot. Kevin walked over to one ticket and pulled it out, looking at the destination.

"Times Square," Kevin said. "What a waste!"

He threw it to the ground and pulled his own side arm, tag teaming with Bradley as they reached the station entrance. Outside the underground tunnel and its echoes, it was way too quiet. Broken shop windows stared at them, and the streets were smoking with crashed vehicles. Bradley let his breath out as he leant against the wall of the subway station entrance.

"Where now?" Max asked.

Bradley looked around the quiet sidewalks. "I remember this place," he said. "We drove through here when we were on our way to the bus station. I think it's that way." He walked down the street a little way until he spotted the shiny track that the city's new tram system followed.

He followed the tracks, and his group followed him.

"Do you think our driver will still be there?" Max asked.

"Only one way to find out," Bradley replied.

The huge new bus station loomed into view. The group quickly climbed the steps, feeling a false sense of security when inside the building. Bradley looked into the ticket windows as they passed. Blood spattered the windows and the cash registers were open and empty. There was no sign of any people, dead or alive. They reached the bus terminals, there was more destruction—and bodies. Two silver buses stood smashed into one another and the blood from one driver dripped over the advertisement banner on the side.

"Jesus!" Kate gasped.

"Don't look," Bradley said to her. He scanned the buses, looking for the one they had taken to get to New York. Spying it, he jogged over, slowing when he saw the door was wide open.

Bradley slowly crept along the side of the bus. He felt his back rub against the side and he took a deep breath as he approached the door. He swung his body around and looked into the bus. The large, stumpy body of their dead driver lounged in the seat, slash and burn marks from the Armazoids on his face and torso. Thick, dark blood congealed on the floor under him.

"Shit!" Bradley whispered. He had to check if the bus was still functional. He climbed the stairs and avoided stepping in anything sticky and red. The silence freaked him out. He found the key on the floor next to the steering column and picked it up. When he tried to turn the bus on though, nothing happened. He shook his head and slowly walked back to the group as they stood by the terminal building, waiting for him.

"Anything?" Kevin asked.

"Sorry," Bradley said. "The bus won't turn on."

"Great, that's the only bus in this place that isn't smashed!" Kate said. "Now what?"

Bradley took a second to think. "Let's just get to that police station," he replied. "There must be a safe way out of the city that way. The authorities must have some kind of evacuation plan."

Pounding feet threw them into a confusion. One of the girls screamed, and Bradley whipped out his sidearm. A group of Armazoids burst out of the station into the bus parking lot.

Unaware of anyone else around him, Bradley aimed and fired, taking down one alien after another.

Kevin's voice slowly came through Bradley's fierce concentration. "Bradley! We can get on the tram!"

Bradley shook himself out of his focus and turned to see his friends all running toward a tram with open doors, just like the one they had taken earlier that day to get into the city. He sprinted toward it, and as soon as he jumped in, Kate pushed the button to close the doors, and Kevin flipped the switch to make the tram move. Power surged through the vehicle. He pushed the control lever forward and the tram moved out of the station, leaving the angry aliens on the platform.

Bradley let out a sigh of relief and stayed on the ground, panting. Eric looked at Colin, who was still breathing heavily from their run to the tram.

"You tired?" he asked.

"Yeah," Colin replied.

"Get used to it," Eric said. "The day isn't over yet."

The tram moved quickly along the shiny track. Bradley got up to look at the destroyed city as they passed. Smoke, fires, and lifeless bodies seemed to be everywhere he looked. He closed his eyes and rested his forehead on the cool glass of the window.

Kate's voice broke into his reverie. "Uh, Bradley? You might want to take a look behind us."

Bradley's head shot up and he turned to face the back of the vehicle. Behind them, another tram was bearing down on them. As he watched, an Armazoid leaned out and took a wild shot at their tram with his ray gun.

"Speed it up, Kev, we got company," he called.

Kevin gasped and slammed the control lever to full throttle. The tram quickly picked up speed, but still the alien tram was gaining.

Another ray gun blast screamed past them. They seemed to be aiming high—

"Holy shit!" Bradley gasped. "They're aiming for our cable!"

Lisa crumpled to the ground, crying. Kate put her arms around her shoulders, but she was crying too.

Colin stroked his chin thoughtfully. "So if they hit our cable, we don't have power anymore. But at least we're not hurt." His face drained of color. "Until they ram into us..."

Eric turned and looked coldly at Colin. "You don't say," he replied sarcastically.

More wild shots flew around their tram.

"These demons don't give up, do they?" Bradley yelled.

"No, they don't," Kevin replied tersely, eyes focused on the track ahead, he hit the left turn switch in front of him. They rounded a corner and started descending a steep hill, speed climbing past 90 miles per hour. Luckily, this meant it was harder for the Armazoids to get their guns out of their tram to shoot. No quite so lucky was that Kevin could see red lights flashing at the bottom of the hill—it was the end of the line they have switched to. His eyes opened as they sped towards the flashing buffers.

Kevin pulled the red lever for the brakes. He watched as the brakes have failed. There is no way to stop. Bradley turned to see the bottom of the hill—and the end of the tracks—fast approaching. He looked around for a set of emergency brakes, knowing they wouldn't survive the crash at the end if they didn't lose more speed.

He turned to the group. "Okay, does anyone see emergency brakes anywhere? We gotta get this thing to slow down."

Max and Eric started walking around. The girls stayed on the ground. Colin pointed outside. "Bradley, I think there are manual brakes on the wheels..."

Bradley didn't think twice. He pulled the emergency "door open" button and lay down on his stomach, hooking his foot around the seat leg closest to the door. Max and Eric ran over, each grabbing a foot to make sure he didn't lose his balance and tumble out. The wind from the open doors buffeted everyone, making the girls and Colin scream.

As soon as Bradley stuck his head out, his breath got sucked away. He gasped, trying to breath. They were just going too fast. If he could just reach below and hit a manual brake... He stretched down, reaching for the red lever that controlled the set of wheels closest to him. Just a little farther and there, he could push it down.

There was a loud *clank-clank-clank* as the brakes fought to catch on the speeding wheels. Max and Eric pulled Bradley back in and closed the door. The tram was shuddering violently, but it was definitely slowing. Bradley looked up to see the bumpers and red lights at the end of the track. He looked behind to see the Armazoids halfway down the hill.

"Okay, everyone get to the back," Bradley yelled. *"Now!"*

The front of the tram slammed into the metal buffer, the windshield shattering into pieces. Bradley held his head down and braced himself as the engines crumpled up into the inside of the tram to the insides of the tram and the walls became a contracting accordion. Then it was quiet.

Bradley slowly opened his eyes and looked up as he listened to the hissing sound of the tram's engine. Sparks flew out the front of the tram. Fire burned from the brakes he had thrown. Bradley slowly staggered up, knowing they had to move. Shattered glass lay everywhere. He pulled the lever to open the back door then turned around to help Kate to her feet. Everyone looked okay but very shaken.

Bradley looked up the tracks to see the Armazoids' tram almost on top of them.

"Let's move!" he yelled, throwing Colin down the back stairs and pushing Lisa only a little softer. The group scrambled away from the smoking remains of their tram, Bradley the last to exit. They ran down the sidewalk to talk cover beside an adjacent building as the chasing tram rammed the other tram. Because the Armazoids hadn't slowed their tram at all, their entire carriage crumpled, killing them all instantly.

Bradley ducked his head as debris from the explosion sprinkled down on his group. When the dust cleared, he slowly got up and walked toward the scene of the crash, looking for any movement. He looked down the tram.

"All clear."

Colin sat down with a big sigh. "So we can rest?"

"We can't here," Bradley said. "That noise might have alerted anything nearby."

"We'll rest in a while," Kevin said.

The group slowly got up from the benches and looked around the deserted place as the smell of electrical fires from the two smashed up trams lingered.

***

Kate kept pace with Bradley while the others straggled behind, Kevin bringing up the rear. The path in the alley was up a gentle slope. Bradley felt the pull on his leg muscles as he held onto his handgun and scanned the area ahead for any of the Armazoids. He was getting tired.

Seeing a crossroads ahead, Bradley jogged forward to peer around the edge. He saw two shadowy figures slowly coming their way. Bradley clenched his fist up in the air and motioned for everyone to take cover. Kate gasped and jumped at the same time, pressing herself against the alley wall. Bradley stood dead still as the two dark shadows slowly got bigger. Kate looked over Bradley's shoulder and watched the two aliens walk down the alley past the group. Bradley's finger slowly crept along the soft metal towards the trigger of the handgun. The two Armazoids walked off into the depths of the alley.

Bradley sighed and turned around to look at Kate, fragile and shaking, as she leaned against the wall. She placed her hand on her head. Bradley walked up to her, sliding the handgun back into his side pouch. "You okay?" he asked.

Kate nodded her head. "Tired," she said. "And a stitch, plus a headache on the way."

"Okay," Bradley said. "We'll find a place to sit down soon. We can't do it here."

"Why not?" Colin asked.

"Too close," Bradley said. "They might arrive and surround us."

The group slowly turned around the corner and walked out into one of the main roads. Bradley had his sidearm out again, ready to pull the trigger at the first sign of any Armazoids. They left the alleyway and walked onto a main street. Six police cars were smashed into one another in front of them, but that's not what caught Bradley's attention. Behind the pile up, across with wide avenue, he noticed a small red cross on the top of a large building.

"That's a hospital," Eric said.

"Yes, that is," Bradley replied.

"Do you think there will be anyone in there?" Kate asked.

"Only one way to find out," Bradley replied. He walked out of the alleyway, still wary of the Armazoids. He crossed the road, walking around the smashed-up police patrol cars.

"Any weapons?" Max asked.

Bradley looked into one car, seeing nothing. "Nothing," he said. "We have enough to last us, anyway."

The group continued across the deserted road towards the hospital entrance. The breeze in the air felt spooky and the entrance to the hospital seemed to get further away as they approached the ambulance bay. One ambulance was there, smashed up onto the concrete guard rails in the middle of the bay. The red emergency lights were slowly starting to die away as the battery was drained of all its energy. Kevin

129

slowly walked up to the front of it, staring in the windshield through to the back of the vehicle. A stretcher hung out the back of the vehicle from where the paramedics had obviously tried to save a patient.

Kevin looked away as Bradley walked up to the set of automatic doors, reloading his handgun. The doors slowly slid open, but everything else was eerily silent.

"Keep together," Bradley demanded. "Come on, Colin."

"I'm right behind you," Colin replied.

Bradley slowly walked up the corridors stepping over pools of blood and vomit from the mayhem.

"Come on," Bradley snapped.

"Where are we going?" Lisa asked.

"To look for survivors," Bradley replied. "And supplies. We're all dehydrated."

"Should we split up?" Colin asked.

Bradley stopped and looked at Colin. "Okay, Colin. You go that way and we will all go this way."

"I am not going by myself!" Colin protested.

"Well then shut up and follow." Bradley turned back around and led them on.

They walked down several empty hallways, the silence making everyone jumpy. The rooms were empty of doctors, nurses, and patients.

"Do you think they've evacuated?" Kevin asked.

"I wouldn't have thought so, Kev. No time. Look how fast the things moved over the city," Bradley replied.

Bradley feared what could be around the corner. He walked down one hallway, following signs for the hospital cafeteria. He stopped on a landing with two elevators.

"Up or down?" he asked.

"Up," Eric said. "People might be hiding upstairs."

"Good thinking," Bradley said, smiling. "Not like you."

"I have my moments," Eric said, smiling back.

The group slowly walked towards the huge silver doors, but Bradley froze when he realized the light above one of them was moving, illuminating the number three, and then the number two, and then—

The chime from the elevator arriving dinged through their ears.

"Not up or down," Bradley said, grabbing Kate's arm. Bradley looked around frantically. "This way," he whispered. He pulled Kate by the arm over to the walkway, everyone else scrambling to take cover where they could. He turned around watching the two shiny doors slowly slide back. Two Armazoids walked out of the lift and headed into the hospital.

Bradley turned around, pointing towards the sign that indicated the cafeteria was down the hall. "Go," he whispered. Kate looked him in the eye then nodded, herding the group down the hallway. Bradley stayed, sidearm ready, watching the Armazoids disappear down a hallway in the opposite direction.

He found his friends in the kitchen of the large cafeteria, presumably because they didn't like to be out in the open. Bradley looked around at the mess left by those who had fled. Food lined the counters, ready to be served. Several pots were still bubbling on the stove. Kevin had opened an industrial-sized fridge and was distributing water bottles. He met Bradley's eye and nodded.

"Shouldn't we be moving?" Kate asked.

"No, let's let the ones downstairs clear out," Bradley said.

131

"How far is the police station?" Eric asked.

Bradley pulled out the map Roger had given him, marked with their route. He tapped it thoughtfully, figuring out where they were and how they had gotten there. "We came down here, so…" He found the hospital logo and traced his finger over to the police logo, a small white badge within a blue circle. "Okay. We are here. The main HQ is about three and a half miles away, but we will have to keep to the side streets, so we are looking about a two-hour walk." He looked around at his friends. "So drink up. This will be the last stop for a while."

"Can't we run it?" Max asked.

"No," Bradley said, eyeing the bedraggled girls and Colin. "We take it easy and only run if we have to."

Bradley leaned against the counter, looking down at the map. He turned his head and looked at Kevin. "Do you think Mr. Knightsbridge got to the police station?" he asked.

"I don't want to answer that," Kevin said.

"Yeah, I suppose," Bradley said. "At least that assignment won't be due on Monday."

"What assignement?" Eric asked.

"The one…never mind."

Bradley folded the small map away and placed it in his pocket then pulled out his cell phone. He shook his head.

"Still no network?" Max asked.

"Nothing," Bradley said. "It must come and go."

"Well, people must be struggling to get through to people."

Kevin nodded. "My mum, for example."

"Mine too," Bradley said as he slipped the phone back into his pocket. He looked over at Kate, who was lounging against the counter, sipping her water. Even after all they had been through, she still looked like a model. She looked over at him.

One of the cafeteria doors opened, clanging against the wall from the force of the push behind it. Bradley spun around, gesturing for everyone to duck down. But it was too late. Two Armazoids were staring at them through the opening in the kitchen wall where the workers dished food onto the people's trays. Bradley grabbed his gun, mirroring the Armazoids as they reached for their ray guns.

"Down," Bradley yelled.

Kate and Lisa, stunned by the abruptness of it all, finally dove to floor. Bradley ducked below the window as the rays from the Armazoids weapons fired overhead.

"Jesus Christ!" Eric yelled "Fecking things!"

Kevin, walking low, joined Bradley under the opening. He had a handgun in each hand. With a nod, they stood up at the same time and opened fire at the two aliens. They dropped

"Move," Bradley yelled.

"Where?" Eric cried, panicked.

"Anywhere!" Bradley replied.

He led the way out of the cafeteria the same way they came, Kevin and the rest of the group following. He looked down at the two dead Armazoids as they walked past them towards the exit. Bradley kept his eyes peeled as they came to the bottom of the walkway. He looked down the corridor towards the way he had come a short while ago, signaling the group to stay still. The pounding of feet warned them of the group of Armazoids right before they came into view.

"This way," Bradley yelled, pushing Max in front of him. Max stumbled, then took off running, followed by the others. Kevin held back.

"Just go, I'll catch up, Kev."

"Promise?"

"Of course." With that reply, Kevin took off, leaving his best friend in the face of an oncoming horde of Armazoids.

Bradley swung around, kneeling down. He opened fire at the long line of Armazoids running towards him. The corridor was narrow, only allowing space for two aliens to run next to each other. He glanced down the hallway his friends had taken. Kevin was at the far end, opening an exit door and ushering the group through. He looked back at Bradley.

"Come on!" he yelled.

Bradley knew he had to provide more of a distraction, especially before the Armazoids wised up and shot him down with their ray guns. He swung around, sprinting up another long corridor, trying not to slip on the floor. He reached a t-junction corridor that seemed to hold supplies, extra canisters of oxygen and gurneys lining the walls. He saw Armazoids coming from all directions.

Without hesitating, Bradley picked up a canister and slammed it onto a gurney, pausing briefly to fire at the closest line of charging aliens. He strapped the canister to the back of the bed using the straps for unruly patients to secure it in place. Then he hopped on the front of the bed, crouching down on his knees. Turning, he shot off the end of the canister, releasing the compressed oxygen and making the bed turn into a missile, shooting straight down the hall at the oncoming aliens.

Bradley laughed as he held on to the side rails, adrenaline powering through his body. He watched as the group of oncoming Armazoids.

"Shit." One said.

They turned around and started running away. He shot at their running backs with his depleting ammunition. The trolley bed sped through the hospital corridor, heading right toward the main lobby, and then right through the main glass doors. The glass shattered, covering Bradley in tiny, sharp fragments. He gasped, shaking his head to clear gas from his eyelashes and hair. He opened his eyes just as the hospital's steps came into view. He felt the trolley lift off the ground.

"Oh my God!" he yelped.

He jumped off the bed into the flowerbeds lining the stairs, landing on a prickly bush and crushing it. He lay there for a second, breathing heavily. Then he sat up to watch the bed continue down the street, careening wildly now that is was significantly lighter. It eventually stopped when it crashed into a military tank.

The tank's turret was pointing towards the city, away from the hospital. The huge machine was wrapped around a broken lamppost. Bradley tore his gaze from the wrecked tank and looked back at the hospital. He had lost the Armazoids for the time being, but he couldn't stay in the same place for too long.

Bradley shook his head trying to refocus on the current situation. He staggered out of the bush, walking cautiously over to the tank. He clambered up and looked in through the hatch. Sparking wires showed where the Armazoids had destroyed the controls, but there were no bodies. Bradley wondered what had happened to the soldiers who had been driving it.

He froze as he heard approaching footsteps, then whirled around, both guns drawn. He looked at the startled faces of Kevin, Eric, Max, Kate, and Lisa. He breathed a huge sigh of relief and holstered his firearm.

"You okay?" Kevin asked cautiously.

Bradley didn't want to answer the question. He nodded curtly, then looked around. "Where's Colin?" he asked.

Colin slowly emerged from around the side of the tank. "Right here," he said.

"Don't do that again," Bradley said.

"Sorry," Colin replied.

Kevin turned again to look at Bradley. "Sorry. Didn't mean to make you jump. We saw that gurney fly out of the main doors," Kevin said. "Kate here thought you were a goner."

"Not yet," he replied.

"Come on. Let's move," Bradley said as the group. They headed toward the nearest alleyway. Eric caught up to Bradley, pulling his arm.

"It was totally deserted, that hospital, wasn't it?" Eric said.

"Yes," Bradley said. "I don't think anyone else is left alive there."

Chapter 13

Mrs. Harrison pulled her automobile into her driveway. She relaxed into the cream leather seats before opening her door and getting out into the muggy late morning air. The people in the streets on her drive home hadn't seemed to be acting normally. She looked at her next-door neighbors as they bundled huge bags of supplies into their house. The elderly man looked over and waved quickly, and then continued to unload bags from his car trunk.

"You okay, Oscar?" she called over to him. "Haven't seen you and Mary for a while."

Oscar stormed over to the car window. "Oh yes, we're fine. Just back from the store—it's a mad house! And nowhere can you find any weapons. That gun club Bradley goes to is completely sold out!" He paused and looked at her blank expression. "You okay? You got everything? Need a weapon? I've got a few to spare. Look." He pulled out two handguns from his pockets.

Mrs. Harrison gasped. "Why? What's happened?"

Oscar's eyes opened wide in disbelief. "Don't you know? It's been all over the news."

She shook her head, confused.

"I think you had better go and look at the television," Oscar said. "I hope to see you again soon. We are staying inside in case it gets any worse."

Oscar turned around and ran over to his open garage. Mrs. Harrison watched as he began to pull out planks of wood. After retrieving his hammer, he held up the planks against the front window of his historically registered Victorian home. She cringed as he pounded nails into the plank to hold in place over the window.

She ran inside, checking her cell phone as she went— no service. That in itself was very peculiar. She shut her front door and walked into the living room, pushing the power button. The screen flashed to life, broadcasting a sub-title screen that took up the lower quarter of the screen: *Alien invasion in New York City.*

"Oh my God!" She gasped.

A frazzled, gray-haired newscaster popped up on the screen. "If you are just joining us, we are here to bring you bring you up to speed on the invasion of Manhattan Island. The numbers of reported dead are increasing by the second, making this the worst attack on American soil ever. We don't know the exact figures yet, but we know that thousands are dead, and hundreds of thousands are missing. We are now going live to an evacuation point in Queens which has been setup by the US Military and the National Guard."

Mrs. Harrison stumbled over to the couch, her heart pounding. She heard a car pull up in her driveway and ran over to the window, relieved to see her husband walking quickly up the path. She opened the door for him.

"Thank God you're ok. I was so worried. I've just heard the news," she said.

"I know, I know. Are you okay? Have you heard from Bradley?" he asked.

"No. I've tried getting to him, but the phone lines are jammed," she said in a frantic voice.

"Okay, okay. Try mine," he said. "It's got a stronger signal."

Mrs. Harrison looked at her husband's phone and saw the signal was operational. She flicked through the phone book and selected Bradley's name, fingers clumsy with fear. She placed the phone to her ear and listened to the gentle vibration as she waited, mentally begging for Bradley to pick up from the Queens evacuation point.

***

Bradley and the group walked down the alley behind a row of apartments, the path lined with garbage bins and trash. Feeling his phone vibrate, he tensed, then stopped and reached down, pulling out the phone.

"Okay Kevin, keep an eye that way; Max, that way," Bradley said. "Let's see how long this call will last with the shoddy reception."

"Who is it?" Max asked. "Ms. Hogan?"

"Not that bad," Bradley replied. "My dad."

"Oh," Max said.

Bradley kneeled down behind a garbage and can and answered the phone. "Hello," he said quietly. "I'm still alive."

His mom's voice rang back shrill and worried. "Oh God, Bradley! Thank God you are okay. We've just seen the news. Tell me you are out of the city."

Bradley looked around at his surroundings. "Actually, we are right in the center of the city, stuck up an alleyway." Then he cringed, thinking what his mom must be thinking. He didn't have to guess.

"Oh my God, oh my God." Her heavy breathing into the phone made him feel sick. "How have you survived so long? Tell me all that's happened."

Bradley released his breath. "Well," he said, "we were merrily walking in an outdoor market when—*bam*. These aliens came out of nowhere. We ran into a casino, chased by them. We pulled an injured woman out of a car, which exploded really soon after that, but we made it out. We left Mr. Knightsbridge—well, he left us. Kevin found a restaurant where we hid for a bit, but the things found us and burst in, after Eric tried fending them off with a pretend chainsaw. I sent them packing with my handgun and they ran. So did I, but in the opposite direction, trying to lead them away. We were separated, but I saved them when they were trapped in a warehouse. We found a weapon shop and seriously armed up. We went down into a subway station where we found Kate, Lisa, and Colin, this made the day even worse. When we came up out of the subway, we tried to escape to the bus station. We even found our bus, but the driver was dead. We jumped on board a tram, still being chased by another tram full of those things, ran through a hospital and stopped for a drink. I took a ride on an oxygen-propelled bed and now we are here talking to you. All in all, not a bad day out in the Big Apple."

Mrs. Harrison struggled to take in her son's nonchalant attitude and the gravity of what he was telling her. "Uhhhh—"

"Yeah, long day," Bradley said. "Still, we have far more shit to come."

"Bradley, this is Dad," Mr. Harrison said. "Can you hear me okay?"

"Oh, hi Dad," he said. "Yes, I can, just about."

"Hi, Mr. Harrison!" Eric yelled cheerfully.

Bradley closed his eyes. Eric's voice echoed around the empty alleyway.

"Keep your voice down," Kevin ordered.

"Hello Mr. Harrison," Eric whispered into the phone.

Bradley closed his eyes, trying not to make a comment to Eric.

"Bradley, listen to me. Have you got any sort of weapon to defend yourself with?" Mr. Harrison asked.

Bradley looked down at all his weapons. "Yes, a few," he replied.

Kevin grinned, looking down at his own arsenal.

"Okay. Have you heard from Ms. Hogan?" his dad asked.

"Yeah, she is at the police station."

"Try to get there ASAP," his dad ordered. "And for God's sake, be careful."

Bradley heard a beep. He looked down at his phone—the signal was gone.

"Bradley," Mr. Harrison said, almost shouting into the phone. "Bradley?"

Mrs. Harrison looked up at him and started crying. They were sitting in the living room in front of a TV showing the news, but the volume was muted. Mr. Harrison put the phone down and unmuted the volume as the president of the United States walked up to a podium.

"To my fellow Americans, and the world," Henderson began. "As you now know, New York City's Manhattan Island was invaded at approximately 11:45 a.m. EST by an intelligent species not found on this planet or any we know of. We have had no luck in communicating with the life forms. I am asking for all people throughout the country to

141

remain calm. Listen to your law enforcement personnel and continue to monitor your news stations. All flights across the country have been temporarily suspended, and all international air travel towards the US has been diverted or sent back to its country of departure. Once again, I ask you to remain calm, and I will keep you updated on the situation in New York as I get more information. Thank you."

Press cameras flashed one after the other. "Mr. President!" a journalist yelled, seeking more answers. But President Henderson walked off-screen, followed by two Secret Service men.

Mr. Harrison switched off the television and walked back over to the couch, putting an arm around his wife. "He's gonna be okay," he said. "He's gonna be okay."

The floor beneath their feat started to rumble. Mrs. Harrison shot to her feet, panicking. The china cupboard bumped open and they both watched as it fell in slow motion to the ground and shattered.

Mr. Harrison went outside. Looking to his left down his street, he could see a long line of military vehicles rumbling their way down the main street. Mrs. Harrison joined him on the front step, cowering behind him. The line of vehicles disappeared, heading toward Manhattan.

"Come on," Mr. Harrison said. "Let's get inside." He gently pushed his wife back inside and dead bolted the front door. Mrs. Harrison looked out of the window, the afternoon sun shining through and illuminating her worried face.

"He'll be okay," Mr. Harrison said again. "I promise."

Chapter 14

President Henderson's security detail sealed the emergency briefing room behind him. He sat down at his desk, trying to concentrate on the paperwork in front of him that detailed the logistics of evacuating Manhattan, the expected cost of damages, and the growing numbers of dead Americans. He stared blankly at a column of figures, unable to focus on anything. Absently, he loosened his red tie and threw it onto another chair. A knock on his door shook him from his reverie.

"Come in," Henderson said.

Two of his generals walked into the office, their uniforms crisp and clean.

"Sir, we have made contact," one general said.

President Henderson stood up, oblivious of the paperwork that fluttered to the ground. The generals led him to a room with a large screen taking up one wall, a desk with three chairs opposite it set up with microphones. He sat down in the middle chair as one general worked the remote to turn the TV on and tune it to the proper station.

One of the aliens appeared the screen, wearing an unfamiliar uniform. The space around him was completely black, not allowing the president or his generals to get a sense for where the alien was located.

"Is this thing on?" Circo asked, tapping the screen. "Piece of crap."

"Yes, sir," another Armazoid said in the background.

"What?" Circo said looking into the lens "Oh shit."

The humans on the screen looked very nervous. "Hello," he said, his voice trembling. "My name is Christopher Henderson. I am the president of the United States of America." The President took a deep breath. "What are your demands from us?"

Circo inwardly smiled at the president's obvious discomfort. "Well, thank you for your time," he said sarcastically. "Now we have your attention, let's get some things straight. If you are president of this planet, you should know what happened to one of our ships that crash landed here a few months ago."

The President was clearly startled. He could be seen talking with a couple other men in green uniforms. They were shaking their heads. The president turned back to the screen.

"We do not know of any alien spacecraft landing here—we would have returned it to you. I give you my word on that."

Circo looked at President Henderson. "Well, you have got three Earth hours to find out where it is. Otherwise we will be forced to intensify our attack on this dump you call home." Circo smiled. "Cheerio." He switched off the screen and laughed.

"Shit!" President Henderson said. "Right. This is serious. I want every single world president, prime minister, and leader asked about this, and I want some answers."

"Maybe a ship crashed in a country that is closed to the world...North Korea?" Synder asked.

"Possible," Henderson replied. "We won't know until we ask them."

Chapter 15

Bradley slipped his phone back into his pocket and everyone took a five-minute breather. He kept looking over his shoulder towards the tank.

"They okay?" Kevin asked.

"They're okay. Just my mom panicking," Bradley said.

"Are you surprised?" Kate said. "I mean…"

"Yeah. Anyway, let's move before those things catch up," Bradley ordered. "Come on. Stay close."

The group moved forward, Bradley and Kevin on point. Their alley came out onto a main road, but their path was partially blocked by a police car that had crashed into a telephone pole, blocking the alley entrance. Kevin moved forward to investigate while the rest of the group held back in the relatively hidden alley.

"Is it drivable?" Kate asked quietly.

Through the driver's side window, Kevin could see the digital gauges flickering and sparks coming from the ignition. "No. If we start that up, we could blow the whole thing." But then something else caught his eye.

Kevin flicked out his baton and slammed it through the back-passenger window. Bradley jumped, startled, and cursed.

"What are you doing?" Bradley hissed. He watched as Kevin reached in and pulled out a small black box, some dark, congealed blood stuck to its screen. Kevin wiped it away with a corner of his pocket and looked over at Bradley.

"That's a television," he said.

Kevin switched on the small portable television and fiddled with the tuner, staring at the static. The group gathered around the unexpected connection to the rest of the world. Finally, Kevin got a grainy, black-and-white picture of a female reporter to fill the screen. She was on a main road that led to a bridge, and the road was full of military vehicles escorting buses and cars across the bridge. They could just barely make out what she was saying.

"—the exit to the Queensboro Bridge where thousands, maybe hundreds of thousands are trying to evacuate the city. The US military have had to clear a route to the bridge from the main police station, which has been overrun with people who are injured, shocked, and confused. The New Jersey tunnel has been sealed. The only way out of the city now is by the Queensboro Bridge. I repeat, the Queensboro Bridge is the only way out of the city. Authorities ask that all civilians still in Manhattan should go to the police station or the Queensboro Bridge as soon as possible. There is less than twenty-four hours before the military takes decisive action.

We'll now go to an aerial view of the police headquarters—"

The screen flickered and battery sign flicked on and off.

"Oh shit, no," Kevin said. The small screen went blank. Kevin shook the set. He watched the small green light go red and then off. "Battery's gone," he said, chucking it away.

"Okay, we haven't got a hope in hell of getting off the island if we go to the police station, because everyone and their mother is probably headed there right now. So we should just get to the bridge," Bradley said with more confidence than he felt.

Bradley took out his city map and laid it out on the hood of the police car. "The bridge should be about five miles north from here. I don't want to be around when the military takes decisive action. They might drop a nuclear bomb to eliminate the aliens."

"I suggest we head up the coast of the island staying out of sight and we should be out of here within a few hours, maybe earlier."

"Got it. I like it," Eric said.

Kate slowly got up, Bradley noticing that she was favoring her left arm. He looked more carefully. Was that blood staining the shoulder?

"Kate, what happened to your arm?" he asked. He walked up to her and slowly pulled her hand away that was covering her shoulder. Dark blood stained her shirt, which had a jagged rip on the shoulder.

"Why didn't you tell me?" Concern made his tone harsher than he meant it to be.

"With everything that's happening, I, I didn't want to bother you." She looked down. "I did it when we left the hospital, cut myself on something."

Bradley let his breath out. "Okay, don't worry. I'll soon have that fixed up," he said. "In fact, I bet this police car has a first aid kit."

At the hint, Kevin walked over and rifled through the glove compartment, then found one under the passenger seat. He brought the small white box over to Bradley, who had made Kate sit on the ground.

Bradley opened the kit and took out an alcohol swab, some gauze and antiseptic, and a butterfly Band-Aid.

Kate pulled her shirt of her shoulder, revealing a small but deep cut that was still weeping blood. Bradley gently wiped the alcohol swab over it, but Kate winced and gave a small whimper.

"That will stop any infection," Bradley said softly.

"Ouch." She moaned again.

Bradley smiled devilishly, trying to lighten the mood. "Shall I kiss it better for you?"

Kate gave him a small weak smile as he put the antiseptic onto the gauze, then placed the gauze over the cut. She held it in place as he opened the Band-Aid and placed it over the gauze, keeping everything in place.

He looked down at her, her face a picture of concentration, and smiled. Kate glanced up at him and saw him looking at her.

"What?" Kate asked.

He grinned wider. "Nothing." He turned his attention back to his handiwork. "There we go. That should tide you over until we get out of here."

"If we ever do." Kate sighed.

"We will," Bradley said. "I promise."

He got up slowly, stretching, and reached a hand to Kate. He knew they'd stayed in one place too long—they were lucky to have found an alley hidden by the crashed police car. Out of the corner of his eye, he saw a red blanket under the cop car twitch. He froze. Kate saw where he was looking and froze too, see the blanket move slightly.

"Kev," Bradley whispered.

Kevin didn't hear him as he stood guarding the area around them. Bradley reached down and chucked a small pebble at him.

Kevin swung around. "What?"

Bradley gestured with his head to the blanket. Kevin nodded and slowly walked over; gun trained on the blanket. Bradley slowly reached down and then pulled the blanket off with a sudden jerk, jumping back. Kate looked in amazement at a small black cat as it hissed at the group and ran out from under the police car, back into the alleyway.

Kevin laughed. "You thought it was one of them, didn't you?"

Bradley just shook his head in relief and looked back out to the main road. Through the police car window, he could see something...looking right at him.

He immediately jumped back in fear as an Armazoid smiled at him through the cracked cop cars, then straightened up to look at the group hiding behind the car.

"Oh, crap," Bradley mumbled. He drew his handgun before the Armazoid could think twice and fired it directly into the alien's forehead. As the alien fell, he could see more of them coming their direction.

Max pulled out his sub machine gun and pulled out the extender, making it easier to hold onto. He stared through the scope, shooting at a few running Armazoids. Eric joined him, firing his sidearm—and usually missing.

"Go," Eric yelled. "We'll cover you." He pulled the trigger, missing again.

Bradley gave him a look. "I think I'll stay here, thanks."

Bradley sent Kate, Lisa, and Colin off with Kevin and Max to guard them. Then he turned and started taking pot

151

shots at the chasing Armazoids. Eric was using the top of the police car as a brace for his gun, shooting everything and laughing. He had clearly moved past his panic.

"Oh yes," Eric yelled. "I want this."

Bradley glanced back and saw the group had moved far enough away. "Come on, Eric," Bradley yelled.

Eric continued laughing maniacally.

"Eric! We gotta go!" Bradley took off running.

Eric stopped. "Oh, sorry." He sprinted after Bradley. They caught up to the group, who had slowed down to wait for them.

"Come on!" Bradley yelled. "Don't slow down."

Kevin hesitated at a crossroads—it was quiet to the right, and there was a shopping mall. "This way," he yelled.

They ran up the quiet road as the Armazoids charged at them. Kevin ran up the steps towards the entrance of the small shopping mall. The doors were locked.

"Oh, come on," Kevin yelled.

"Move," Bradley ordered. He aimed his handgun at the door and blew away the lock. Kevin grabbed the handle and held it open while the group piled in. He was just about to go in when Bradley stopped him.

"Where's Colin?" Bradley asked.

They looked back to see Colin running with the Armazoids close behind. His knee was bloody where he had clearly tripped.

"Come on, dick," Bradley yelled.

Colin flew through the door, and Kevin and Bradley slammed the door shut, holding it against the barraging Armazoids. He held onto the handle as the Armazoids grabbed it struggling to pull the door open.

"These monsters don't give up," Eric said, joining his friends in trying to keep the door closed.

"You don't say," Bradley replied, panting for breath. He looked up as a rusty shutter slowly started rolling down over the door. The glass door slowly opened as the group of Armazoids struggled to get in before the shutter closed. "Push, push," Bradley yelled.

Finally, the aliens were forced away by the shutter, and the fight for the door ended. Bradley looked back to see Kate standing by the shutter control panel.

"Good thinking, Kate," he praised.

The group turned to look at their surroundings. The deserted mall was four stories and was capped by a huge dome light that shed faint light into the empty stores. They noticed the light classical music playing for the first time. It was an eerie reminder of normalcy in very unusual times.

"Look at the size of this place!" Kevin said.

Bradley scanned the empty shops as he walked forward. Kevin went straight for a game shop, and Bradley followed. Only the air conditioner was humming. The register was open, bills littering the ground and fluttering in the cool air blowing in from a vent overhead.

"Hmm," Bradley said, shrugging. "No one around. Let's hope they have a good insurance company." He leaned over the counter, pulling out the dollar bills and stuffing them into his drawstring bag. Kevin joined him at the counter.

"Good one," he said and grabbed the dollar bills as well before he looked over at the line of new games. He picked up a small game box and put it in his bag.

"What's that?" Bradley asked.

"Fight Buster Three. It's new."

"Oh good. I'll have one too," Bradley replied. "Will give me something to do when I get home tonight." He reached over and picked out the game from under the counter.

"If," Kevin said sardonically.

"We will," Bradley replied. "We will." He looked around the shop. "Any more? Take your pick," he joked.

They glanced out at the two girls sitting down on the benches that circled a fountain directly beneath the dome skylight. They were quiet and slumped, but still beautiful.

"I have no idea what must be going through their minds," Bradley said to Kevin.

"I know," Kevin replied. "Shit scared and wondering if it's going to stop."

Bradley nodded.

"How far is this police station from here, now?" Kevin asked.

"It should be about three miles from here, but we stick with the bridge first. If we can't get to the bridge, then the cop shop."

Bradley and Kevin walked out of the shop. Bradley noticed with relief that the Armazoids had stopped hammering on the shutter. Instead, he heard a strange tapping. It seemed to echo around the whole mall.

"What is that?" he muttered.

Kevin looked up. "Uh, Bradley…"

Bradley glanced up at the glass dome. Armazoids were trying to break in, so far away it seemed like taps on a door. There seemed to be a few cracks in the glass already.

"They won't get in," Eric said. "No way. That's double glaced."

The glass shattered, and the girls screamed as glass, some chunks fairly large, rained down.

"Arm up, boys," Eric said excitedly.

"Best thing I've heard you say all day," Bradley replied. A coil of rope *whapped* to the ground, followed by several others. The Armazoids started repelling down.

"Shit!" Kevin yelled.

Kate had stumbled to the side when the glass first started falling, but Lisa had fallen into the fountain and was sitting, shocked and drenched, glass and water still sprinkling her. An Armazoid landed near hear and started forward.

"Lisa!" Kevin yelled. "You okay? You gotta move!"

Lisa focused on him, and then the Armazoid approaching her. "No, I am not okay," she said, her eyes glinting fiercely. "I am not taking shit from these aliens anymore!" She swung around, slamming her foot into the Armazoid that was almost on top of her.

"Oh, you bitch," the Armazoid squeaked.

Lisa gave it a roundhouse to the head and it fell, unconscious. Kevin whistled in appreciation.

Bradley searched furiously for a safe place for Kate, Lisa, and Colin while he and the guys handled the aliens. He finally spotted an elevator, a transparent one that allowed a view of the mall as shoppers rode it.

"This way," he yelled, pulling Kate over to it and gesturing for Colin and Lisa to follow. He hit the down call button and tapped his foot impatiently, looking back to see that the aliens were grouping in the middle of the room as Max, Eric, and Kevin picked them off from behind potted plants and benches.

The elevator dinged and the two glass doors opened.

"Come on, in!" He pushed Kate in, Lisa and Colin right behind. "Just hold the door closed button," he demanded.

The doors slowly closed and the elevator remained motionless. Bradley could see the fear in Kate's eyes as she looked at him.

"Don't worry," he yelled. He turned around and looked at the Armazoids as they advanced on his friends' positions. "Here we go," he whispered.

He pulled out two sidearms and started shooting, running back towards the action to get cleaner shots. Armazoids still climbing down their ropes fell with horrific screams as Bradley shot them out of the air, their limp dead bodies falling with loud *thumps* to the tile floor. Soon the ground was wet with green blood.

Bradley's onslaught drew the attention of the Armazoids that had been going after the others, allowing them a short respite. Eric had taken cover behind the doors of a shop, and with Bradley drawing the aliens' attention, he took a closer look at his surroundings. He was in the doorway of a sports shop, a display of bowling balls in its front window.

A thunder of footsteps getting closer caught his attention, and he turned to see a squad of Armazoids charging toward him. Not hesitating, he stepped into the shop and reached for the largest bowling ball, a swirling dark green sixteen-pounder. He took a deep breath and started running toward the Armazoids. When the aliens saw what he was holding, their eyes widened in alarm and confusion. They skidded to a halt and tried to backtrack, stumbling over each other. Eric wound up and let the ball go barreling toward them. The huge, green ball rolled into the Armazoids, knocking them down.

"Strike!" Eric yelled, laughing.

Kevin had made his own discovery. In a small supply closet near the bench where he had taken cover, there was a large stash of fireworks. Boxes of the incendiaries were stacked one on top of the other. He rubbed his hands together and picked a box up. Things were about to get very interesting.

Bradley had his hands full. The Armazoids had decided he was the biggest threat and were mobbing him, too close for single shots to be of any use. Bradley had his baton out, whacking any green thing that came within reach, but he was tired. His muscles ached and he wondered what his friends were doing.

"Bradley!" Kevin yelled. "Max, Eric, get over here!"

Panting, Bradley looked over at Kevin, who had propped up several dozen firework rockets on a few of the benches surrounding the fountain. Max and Eric started sprinting along the slippery floor towards Kevin and Bradley. Bradley fought on just long enough to make sure Max and Eric had reached safety, then pulled out his gun and shot down two aliens at point blank range to clear a path for him to the bench.

"Light the fuses!" he shouted, running to cover with the Armazoids close behind. Kevin lit the ten-second fuses, and Bradley just barely jumped the bench when they went off, right in the aliens' faces.

Smoke, sparks, and flames filled the building as incredibly loud explosions broke every store window on the first floor. The boys huddled on the ground, hands pressed tightly over their ears and breathing through their shirt collars.

Bradley slowly opened his eyes after the explosions had finished. Dense smoke filled the room, and he coughed. "You guys okay?" he asked, giving Kevin a shove.

Kevin shook his head and nodded, standing up slowly. Max and Eric squinted through the smoke, leaning on the bench. Bradley started coughing but was soon running over to the elevator to check on Kate, Lisa, and Colin. Miraculously, the glass doors hadn't broken, and Kate let go of the 'close door' button. The doors dinged open and the boys rushed inside, bringing the smoke with them.

Kate started coughing, and Bradley hit the button for the top floor—they needed to get out and above the smoke. The elevator thrummed to life and lifted them up. They couldn't see any sign of moving Armazoids in the thick haze.

When they reached the top floor, still smoky, they found a door to the roof and piled up the stairs, gasping when they reached the clean air and bright sunlight above. They had a beautiful view of the river, and a brisk breeze made the heat bearable for a few minutes.

Bradley zoned in on a yellow sightseeing binoculars. He fished a quarter out of his draw strong bag, putting it in the slit to take the covers of the lenses. Looking through it, the helicopters flying over Queens were magnified. He could see the military camp that had been set up to defend the other side of the Queensboro Bridge, ensuring safety for those who had crossed.

"Do you see a boat we can jack?" Kevin asked.

Bradley scanned the rivers—there were no boats in sight. "Nope."

"Could we swim?" Eric asked.

"Don't be stupid," Bradley replied. "You can't even swim."

"I can too!" Eric protested.

"It may be the only thing we can do," Kate interjected.

"No, it's too far. Besides, we'd be easy targets in the water. We stand a better chance of making our way through the city towards that bridge," Bradley replied. "Now, come on, let's move. There aren't any aliens around us—for now."

The group exited down a fire escape and made their way down to a path that followed the river. Bradley hoped that the aliens would stick to the more populated parts of the city. He found himself wishing a submarine would emerge from the deep river to pick them up and take them away. Looking across the water, he could almost believe nothing was wrong. Waves lapped the shore, the sun glinting off the water in sparkling explosions of light. Seagulls cawed raucously. Everything seemed normal on the other side.

And then he remembered his smoke-roughened throat, his weak muscles, and his battered body. He sighed.

"Dear, dear, dear," Eric moaned, stopping to stretch his back.

"What's the matter with you?" Bradley asked.

"Tired," Eric replied.

"I feel ya, bro," Kevin agreed.

Bradley willed himself to ignore his fatigue and focus on his surroundings. With everyone so tired, they were more vulnerable than ever. He kept one sidearm in his hand, safety off, just in case.

A small footpath diverged from theirs and snaked up to the left, leading to small building. A gate blocked entry, but the padlock that normally held it shut was cut open. Bradley approached it.

"Why do you think someone cut the padlock?" Bradley asked.

"Beats me," Colin said.

Bradley led the group through the gate and up the path. It was only a two-story building, and the front door was unlocked. They walked through the rooms, looking for survivors, but the building was strangely empty, silent except for the still-thrumming air conditioning units. They made their way up to the roof, where Bradley found a sniper rifle set up and aimed toward the city.

Kate whimpered behind him. Bradley whipped around and found the sniper, a bullet through his head, lying on the ground, dead eyes staring. His blood made a dark, thick pool around his skull.

Kate started to gag. "I'm gonna be sick," she muttered, then ran to the side of the building

Bradley went over to Kate as she sat down and began to cry.

"Hey, hey," he said gently, putting an arm around her. "I promise you I will get you back home," he said. "Promise."

Kate wiped her tears away. Max picked up the snipe rifle, hefting it in his hand.

"You better take it, Max. Your top shot at the club," Bradley said, standing.

"Oh, yes," Max joked. "Am I still buying you that drink?"

"Yes," Bradley said, smiling. "A deal is a deal."

Kevin pulled off his jacket and laid it over the dead soldier's face after taking off his dog tags. "Rest in peace," he murmured.

Everyone turned toward the city as a sudden rumbling sound came from the distance.

"What's that?" Kevin asked.

Max looked through the sniper scope to get a better view. He breathed out in relief as he gently smiled. "Eye up, people, we're skipping this dump," he said. "Look what the cat just dragged in!"

He handed the scope to Bradley, who looked down the street. A huge camo tank was barreling down the street, running over everything in its way. Five military Jeeps followed behind.

"Okay guys, we're out of here," Bradley ordered.

He was turning to get off the roof when a loud roaring sound made him turn back around. A blue streak slammed into the tank. Men started screaming.

"Oh, for God's sake!" Bradley moaned. "No, no, no." He dove to the floor, followed by Kevin. "Get down, everyone!"

"What's going on?" Eric asked.

"Just get down," Max demanded. He pulled Eric and Kate and Lisa to the ground together.

Bradley peeked over the wall. The tank was a charred shell and Armazoids had materialized out of nowhere, attacking the Jeeps.

"Jesus Christ!" Bradley said, not believing their chance at escape was so close yet so far. "Kev, Max, arm up. We've got a battle."

Each boy pulled out his preferred weapon and aimed. The close combat would make it hard, but they had to do something. Aliens were swarming their troops!

"Fire!" Bradley yelled. He squeezed the trigger of his weapon and watched as the attacking Armazoids fell to the

161

floor and the soldiers took cover, shooting from behind Jeeps and even using the tank as a shield.

Cartridges clattered to the ground as the boys shot continuously. They were making a big impact on the number of attacking Armazoids. The bursts of shots from the enemies' ray guns began to be less and less frequent.

"They are dying out," Kate yelled.

"Yeah," Bradley replied, shouting. "But not quick enough."

"I'm out," Max yelled.

"Think fast." Bradley threw a magazine over to Max. Max re-loaded the rifle as he stared back through the lens again. He started pulling the trigger again, a cool breeze off the river ruffling his hair.

Bradley allowed himself a quick breather. All he could smell was gunpowder and his own sweat. He felt the sweat run off his head and he wiped it away. He looked through his scope when a low thrumming filled the air.

An Apache helicopter approached the destroyed military convoy. It hovered above, getting its weapons ready to finish the Armazoids off. The turbulence from the blades buffeted the kids on the roof.

"This is our chance to be rescued!" Lisa yelled over the propeller noise.

Bradley hesitated, then shook his head. "I have a bad feeling about this."

"Come on, it's clear," Kate yelled, eager to get away.

Bradley looked out at the Apache helicopter as it cast its shadow down on the military personnel. He could see the young helicopter pilot looking down as a sudden *whoosh* came filled his eardrums, and a blue beam slammed into the helicopter. Smoke billowed out of the cockpit and the rotors slowly stopped spinning, tilting the machine over as it plummeted to the ground. A huge fireball engulfed the area, incinerating everything in range.

Bradley shielded his face from the burst of intense heat, then looked down onto a scene of destruction worse than before. All the vehicles were burning, and soldiers were running around trying to put out the fires that consumed their own bodies. Their screams ripped through the empty streets.

Another slight humming came from the distance, quickly growing louder and louder. Bradley squinted, trying to see through the thick smoke and hoping the oncoming machine was a friend.

"A helicopter?" Kate asked.

"It sure is," Bradley replied. He looked on in disbelief as a US Naval Sea King helicopter burst through the smoke.

The group cheered, waving their arms as the huge warship hovered above. The force from the blades blew the smoke and fires away as it landed in the middle of the street.

"Come on," Bradley yelled. "Let's get the hell out of here."

"I agree," Eric said.

They ran down the metal stairs to the ground level of the building, bursting out the front doors and heading towards the helicopter. Soldiers were already helping the surviving soldiers from the convoy onto the helicopter. The group breathed through their shirts to filter out some of the heavy smoke.

"This way," a soldier yelled. They ran over to him, coughing and staying together.

"Anyone injured in this group?" the soldier yelled over the engines. "Any one injured?"

163

"Her arm has a small cut," Bradley yelled back, gesturing to Kate. "But we're fine."

"Good, can I have your name?" the soldier asked. He recorded each kid's name on an A4 piece of paper. Then he looked back up at them.

"Right. What we're gonna do is drop you off at the police station. It's about a two-minute flight here. You'll be able to follow the evacuation route over the Queensboro Bridge from there." He gestured toward the helicopter, indicating the students should board.

The group clambered on and one soldier showed them how to strap themselves into the sides. The helicopter took off, loaded with survivors from the attack on the convoy. Bradley laid his head against the wall and closed his eyes, exhausted.

As he felt the helicopter drop, he opened his eyes. They were descending toward a huge white H spray painted to the side of the police station. Bradley sighed in relief when they touched down, no Armazoids in sight. The side door swung back, and everyone began unclipping themselves to disembark. Because the students weren't injured, they waited until the most serious casualties had been rushed off to receive medical help before climbing down.

Bradley turned to the soldier who had helped them. "Thank you." The soldier nodded and they shook hands. A moment later, Bradley watched as the huge helicopter lifted off the ground and headed back into the city, looking for any more survivors.

The group slowly trudged toward the main entrance of the police station, maneuvering around military vehicles, civilians, and soldiers.

"I thought we were never gonna get away," he said to Kevin. "But now we are here."

Kevin nodded, then frowned. "I bet my mom is shitting herself."

"My mom may have said something to her," Bradley said.

Kevin shrugged. "Can't wait till we hit that bar tonight."

Bradley laughed as they walked under the huge NYPD logo above the station entrance. He was stopped by one of the guards there.

"You'll need to take off the weapons vest. Only authorized personnel can have weapons in the safe zone, and soldiers still defending civilians in the city are in need of arms."

Bradley hesitated, then shrugged and took of the vest with its side arms, rifle, and ammo. The other boys did the same. The soldier nodded thankfully and handed the weapons off to another soldier. Bradley turned away and led the group inside the station. It was crammed with families, businesspeople, and beggars, most of them sitting on the ground, too tired or scared to talk. His eyes searched the room for a familiar face.

Ms. Hogan's voice penetrated the dull thrum of voices in the station. "Colin!"

Colin zeroed in on the location of his teacher's voice, finding her standing in the doorway of an office with a half-smoked cigarette in one hand. He ran over to her.

"Oh my God," she said, hugging him tightly. "Is, is that you?"

Colin hugged her back. Bradley and Kevin rolled their eyes, walking over to join them. They found the rest of their class in the office, seated in small groups around the room. Even Mr. Knightsbridge was there, looking extremely relieved to see them.

Kevin walked over to him. "Hey, Mr. K, how are you?" Kevin asked. "How was your trip through Manhattan?"

"I am good, thank you for saving me," he said, looking down in embarrassment.

"Is anyone else missing?" asked Bradley.

"Now that you seven have returned safely, everyone is accounted for."

Bradley nodded, satisfied. "And what about our EMP essay?"

Mr. Knightsbridge hesitated, confused, until realization dawned, and a smile broke across his features. "Bradley, you've got an A on that assignment."

"Nice! Now...how do we get out of here?"

Ms. Hogan held up a paper with the number 112 on it. "We've been assigned this number. When a bus comes and this number is on the notice board next to it, we can board. It'll take us across the Queensboro Bridge to another bus terminal where they have more buses to take people home." Her hand trembled as it lifted the cigarette to her mouth. "At least, that's what we've been told."

Bradley gave her a thumbs up. "Sounds good to me! Now, where's the closest restroom?" At Mr. Knightsbridge direction, the four boys headed out into the hall again and waited to have a turn in the men's room. At the sink, Bradley splashed water on his face, the runoff a dark brown from the gunpowder and grime that had stuck to his sweat. He dried off with a paper towel, feeling much better.

"Oh man." He said.

He smiled as he looked over at his friends, their hair messed up from the brief wash. "You guys clean up real good," he said, hitting Kevin lightly on the shoulder.

They returned to the office that housed their class, grateful for the break before they had to move again.

***

Bradley looked at the clock on the wall for the hundredth time and groaned. "We've been waiting for our number to be called like forever."

Kevin shrugged.

An officer entered the room and spoke briefly with Ms. Hogan. She nodded enthusiastically as the officer tipped his hat and left.

Bradley stood up. "Time to go?" he asked excitedly.

Ms. Hogan ignored him. "Alright, class, we are allowed to board bus five. Let's proceed in an orderly fashion to the bus in front of the station. Mr. Knightsbridge, is on the first bus with group one, we are the one behind."

Mr. Knightsbridge nodded humbly, going to the back of the students that were standing up.

"Does she think we're in kindergarten?" Kevin muttered to Bradley.

"Seriously," Bradley replied.

There was a line of buses, and a line of people sprouted from each door. Ms. Hogan led the way to the second one, slowly maneuvering her large group through the crowds.

They filed onto the bus, Kevin and Bradley sitting next to each other with Eric and Max in the seat ahead of them. Ms. Hogan sat in the front seat behind the driver with Colin, and Kate and Lisa sat down right behind them. Mr.

Knightsbridge in the one ahead as it sped off. Two soldiers sat in the seats opposite, one standing up to count people and ensure there were no empty seats. Satisfied, he signaled to the driver, who closed his doors and started his engine. The convoy of buses moved slowly down the road, guarded by military Jeeps and tanks at intervals along the street.

Bradley leaned back in his seat and sighed. "Tomorrow I'm raiding my savings account if the bank is still there. I'm going to Barry's and buying as much ammo as I can. I still have a bad feeling about this."

"I agree," Kevin said. "It is only going to get worse. I still don't know how we are still alive," Kevin stated.

"Well, all those martial arts and shooting lessons paid off," Bradley replied.

The boys fell silent, staring out the window at the smashed vehicles that had been shoved aside to clear the evacuation route. It would not be long now till they arrived in Queens.

Suddenly there was a commotion at the front of the bus. One of the soldier's stood up, screaming, "Incoming!" A moment later, a gleam slammed into the side of the bus. People screamed as the bus lost control, some falling into the aisle. The left wheel flattened into the road. Bradley clutched the headrest of the seat ahead of him, eyes wide. The bus screeched to a stop right before smashing into a brick apartment building. The lights flickered then shut off.

"What happened?" one person asked.

"We got hit by something," another passenger replied.

"No shit." Bradley replied under his breath

Bradley shook his head as he pulled the hidden handgun out from behind his trousers.

Kevin looked at him. "I thought you had to…"

"I forgot," Bradley replied giving Kevin the wink.

The bus doors flew open and two Armazoids climbed in, firing at the soldiers in the front and killing them instantly. Everyone was shocked into silence.

Bradley couldn't get a clear shot—he was too far back. He could only watch as the Armazoids roughly grabbed Ms. Hogan, Kate, and Lisa, and shoved them down the bus steps.

"Hey!" Ms. Hogan yelled, "What do you want with us?"

The bus that Mr. Knightsbridge was in is way ahead. He is unaware of what has just happened.

"No," Bradley said quietly. He jumped out of his seat as the aliens pulled Kate, Lisa, and Ms. Hogan away from the bus.

"Eric, Max, Kev, move it," he ordered. He held onto his firearm as he jumped over the people on the floor of the bus, stumbling out into the evening. Bradley could see Kate, Lisa, and Ms. Hogan being bundled into one of the parked military jeeps that the Armazoids had hijacked.

"Shit!" he gasped. "Come on." He opened fire on the green jeep as the Armazoids got in and started up the engine, roaring away.

"Bradley, here!" Kevin shouted from behind him. Bradley turned to see the guys piling into a patrol car.

"Wait!" Colin had left the bus and was running toward them.

Bradley didn't hear Colin shout. He had followed right behind him, and in the confusion had gotten in the back with Max and Eric.

"Bradley, Colin is in here!" Eric whined.

Bradley looked into the mirror to see Colin. "What?" he said. "How did you get in here?"

169

"Just got in," Colin replied. "Through the door."

Eric tapped Colin on the head.

"Don't be cheeky." He said

"Great!" Bradley said, focusing on the road again. "Stuck with you again!" He was catching up to the Jeep.

In his rearview mirror, the alien in the driver's seat saw the NYPD car slowly catching up with them, red and blue lights going on and off.

"Shit!"

The girls sat in the back, trembling and silent. Kate watched as the driver pulled out a small radio and quietly spoke into it. The other crawled over them to the back, where he punched through the glass and climbed onto the top where a machine gun was mounted.

A hail of bullets came from the top as the Armazoid aimed at the police car. Kate looked back frantically, knowing it was Bradley and his friends in danger. The police car swerved to avoid them, its bullet-proof windshield cracking when one-too-many bullets hit it. Kate screamed.

Suddenly the barrage on the car stopped, and sparks were raining down on them. Kate could still hear the machine gun thrumming and looked out the window to see the Armazoid had focused his fire on the huge Times Square digital clock. The bullets slammed into the huge board, creating sparks that fell around their Jeep. As they passed, the huge board began to fall to the ground right behind them.

"Oh shit!" Bradley yelled. He watched the military jeep turn left on a side road as the board continued falling towards the ground. The sky above them went dark as they sped under the plunging board. Bradley closed his eyes as they sped through, the board just clipping their trunk and sending them into a spin. Bradley retook control of the car managing to keep the speed up along the street.

"That was close," Eric stated.

"Too close," Colin exclaimed.

"Shut up, Colin," Eric said.

"No, you shut up," Colin yelled. Bradley took a deep breath, then turned the car around and resumed the chase. "Both of you shut up," he yelled. "Is everyone ok?" he asked more calmly.

"We're fine," Max replied.

"Right," he ordered. "Let's get these bastards." He rammed the accelerator down to full again. As they caught up again, the Armazoid manning the machine gun widened his eyes in surprise, then grinned. He spun the machine gun around, looking at them through the scope. He pressed the trigger and nothing happened. A look of frustration crossed his face as he struggled to reload the unfamiliar weapon.

"Kevin," Bradley yelped. "Take him out."

"What with?" Kevin asked.

"Right, uh—check the glove compartment!"

Kevin frantically sifted through the garbage in the glove compartment, but quickly found a handgun. He wound down his window and leaned out, sighting on the guard who was focused on his task. He slowly pulled the trigger and watched as the Armazoid fell, rolling off the roof of the Jeep and slamming into the ground.

"Yeah!" Kevin yelled "Eat that."

Bradley looked up as the green jeep turned onto the highway leading up and around Manhattan. He looked ahead at the green military jeep as Kevin held onto his handgun, Bradley looked at his hands trembling as he grasped the weapon and looked dead out at the car. "Hey," he went.

Kevin turned his head to the left looking at Bradley as he continued holding on to the handgun.

"It's ok," Bradley said. "We'll be out of here soon."

"Yeah," Kevin replied. "We almost were."

"Agh," Bradley said. "Never mind, think of the excitement." He started to catch up with the jeep as one of the other Armazoids clambered onto the heavy machine gun again. It swung it around pointing it towards the police cruiser again.

"Oh, shit! Here we go again," Bradley moaned. He swerved the car to the left, trying to dodge the bullets as they pierced the metal work. Eric, Max and Colin ducked down as the ricocheting echoed around the car.

"Shoot back, shoot back, shoot, shoot!" Bradley yelled.

Kevin wound the window down and leaned out of it. He stared through the scope taking pot shots at the Armazoid on the weapon as the last of the golden bullets launched out of it.

"Shit!" The Armazoid yelled. It clambered back into the jeep and sat down. It looked over its shoulder at Kate and Lisa as they huddled up against one another. "Look at you," it snapped.

Kate and Lisa didn't reply. Ms. Hogan still stayed quiet in the back seat as they looked forward out the front of the jeep to see one of the city's trucks. Kate, Lisa, and Ms. Hogan stared at the double decker vehicle as it carried one of the new city trams on it. Bradley looked at the front and back tram as they were poised over the end of each floor of the vehicle.

"Jesus Christ!" Ms. Hogan groaned.

The jeep swung to the left as Bradley stayed close behind. He looked forward; his eyes open wide with fear as he looked into the mirror as he saw the Empire State Building. He looked at the tall, huge building as it stood out in the middle of Manhattan Island. Bradley looked forward again at the tall truck as it hauled the trams along the highway. The sirens wailed as the green military jeep was now out of sight.

"Shit!" Bradley gasped. "Where are they?"

Bradley looked up at the truck and caught a glimpse of one of the Armazoids as it stepped through the tram on the bottom floor of the truck.

"What the hell are they doing?" Kevin asked.

Bradley stayed quiet as Kevin held onto the sidearm. He looked up as one of the Armazoids shot out the front glass window of the tram cab. It swiped its sidearm pointing down onto the car. The green rays fired out of the weapon slamming into the asphalt road.

"Shit!" Bradley yelled, ducking behind the steering wheel.

"Shoot, back, shoot back, shoot, shoot," Bradley yelled.

Kevin wound the window down and crawled out, holding onto the sidearm. He stared through the sights and squeezed the old weapon trigger in. The bullets fired out of the weapon. The tiny grains of dust blew into his face as Bradley kept behind the truck weaving the car from left to right trying get note of the jeep. "Where are they?" he mumbled. He looked up again as the two Armazoids shot out the metal chain holding the tram onto the bottom deck of the truck. "Ohhhh shit!" he went.

He hit the brakes hard as the front two carriages of the tram rolled out onto the road. The strong metal wheels turned up the asphalt road as it dangled over the back of the truck. Bradley struggled to keep away from it.

"Jesus! Fuck!" Kevin yelled.

Bradley watched the front of the truck start to swerve in and out of the smashed-up cars causing the tram to sway all over the place. The front cab slammed into the side of the car forcing it over to the right.

"Ohhhh my god!" Colin yelled "We're all gonna die!"

Eric looked down at Colin. "Don't worry," he said.

Bradley looked at Kevin as he continued dodging the loose tram as it scraped along the highway road. The tiny bits of asphalt kicked up onto the wind screen. The Armazoid at the front of the huge truck shot down at the huge clamps holding the tram in place. Bradley slammed the brakes on, skidding the car to the right, grasping onto the wheel as the tram rolled off the bottom of the truck into the streets.

"Shitting hell!" Kevin yelled.

Bradley looked forward again as the top of the loader started to lower, the back cab pointed at Bradley.

"Oh, here we go again," Kevin said.

Bradley looked up at the truck. The two Armazoids clambered through towards the middle carriages. They looked at the huge rubber joints as they held the carriages close together. One Armazoid pointed its ray gun down onto the carriage joints as the last of the sun's light beamed in through the window of the once new tram. The bolts burnt away as Bradley tried to see what the Armazoids were doing. He saw the flames from the rays as they continued shooting down onto the bolts of the vehicle. The rusty chain fell away front the front of the tram as the rubber started to tear.

"Oh, they are not about to do that." Kevin said.

"OHHHHHH, yes they are!" Bradley yelled.

The rubber tore, the front of the tram rolled off the truck, onto the highway. Bradley swung the car to the left. He felt the back screech as he looked into the rear-view mirror as the new tram rolled along the highway.

"OWWWWWWWWWWWWWWWWWWWWWW," Kevin yelled, leaning out of the window and watching the front of the tram disappear into the distance of the long highway. "Shitting hell!" he yelled.

Bradley focused ahead at the back of the truck as the next carriage rolled off the truck onto the highway. It tumbled onto the road, glass shattering everywhere.

"To the right!" Eric yelled

Bradley swing to the right.

"To the left!" Eric yelled

Bradley swung to the left.

"Eric?" Bradley asked looking into the rear-view mirror

"Sorry." Eric said closing his mouth.

"Thank you." He replied

Bradley sped past the last carriage looking up at the truck as the top was still lowered down. He swung the vehicle to the left catching a glimpse of the jeep ahead of them. But it what is was further ahead that caught his attention. He saw a roadblock that had been set up by the Armazoids.

"Look out!" Kevin yelled.

Bradley looked as the last of the tram rolled of the truck. He had to think quickly.

"I've got an idea," he said, looking ahead as the green jeep was let through the blockade. "Ok, Kevin, how many rounds you got left?"

Kevin looked down at his weapon. "Three," he said.

"Ok, take three single slow shots at the cab" Bradley said. "Distract him."

"Got it," Kevin replied "Why?"

"Trust me," Bradley replied.

Kevin leaned out of the window and took pot shots at the cab. As the Armazoid ducked down it lost sight of the roadblock.

"Christ!" It yelled.

"Hold on boys," Bradley went. "We're going flying." He eased the accelerator, falling behind the transport vehicle. The Armazoid looked up again and saw the roadblock close to him. He won't have time to stop.

"Holy shit!" it yelled and slammed the brakes on.

Bradley saw the bright red lights come on. He rammed the accelerator down. The G-force pushed him into the back of the seat. He clung to the steering wheel.

"Oh my God," Colin spoke as if it were his last words.

"Agree," Eric replied. "For once, with you."

Smoke bellowed out from the wheels as the truck came to a stop. The Armazoid looked into the rear-view mirror as Bradley held onto the steering wheel. Bradley felt the G-force pushing his body back into the seat as they rolled onto the back of the truck. The car travelled through the air, launching over the roadblock. Kevin looked down as the two front wheels slammed back down onto the asphalt highway. The suspension bounced back up as Eric's seat belt locked, stopping him from flying forward.

"Ouch!" He moaned.

"Phew!" Kevin said, looking at Bradley.

"I bet you never thought of that, did you?" asked Bradley.

"No, I didn't," Kevin admitted.

"I did," Colin said.

"Really?" Eric replied.

"Ok I didn't," he said after.

Bradley watched as the green jeep swung off the highway. He pulled of the highway himself, pulling the car around onto the road below. He looked at the empty streets, as he sped south, back down towards Manhattan. He looked up again as the car started to jolt. He looked down at the fuel gauge seeing the needle go into the red. "Shit!" he gasped. He looked up as the green jeep swung to the right into a car park. "Hang on," he said and ripped the handbrake up, swinging the car into the empty car park. Old plastic and paper bags were blowing everywhere in the light breeze.

"There," Kevin yelled.

Bradley watched as Kate, Lisa, and Ms. Hogan were bundled into the outdoor shopping center. The automatic doors sealed closed as the engine on the patrol car cut out.

"Shit!" Bradley said.

The car rolled to a stop by the green jeep. He slowly got out looking at the automatic doors as the sparks rained down from the sensor after the Armazoid had shot at it. "Shit!" he said again.

He looked into the dull, dark shopping center. The only light seen was that of the sparks.

"We going in?" Kevin asked.

"What do you think?" Bradley said. He stared up at the shopping center name as the smoke hissed out of the patrol car engine. He walked back over to the driver's seat, reached in, and pulled out the radio, it was connected to the car.

"Anyone near the Ravensgate Center, get here. It may be your last chance out of the city," he said and chucked the radio back into the car as he reached into his inside pocket. He flicked out his baton as the rest of the group did the same. Bradley looked at them as he crept up to the automatic glass doors and then looked over his shoulder into the car park. Not a soul was in sight.

"Let's go then," he said.

Bradley looked through the glass doors as the sensors had stopped sparking. He slipped his baton into his pocket and grabbed hold of the door. He slowly slid the tight doors open. "Come on," he said and shimmied through, looking down all the empty aisles. Not a soul or Armazoid was in sight. "Kate," he whispered "Lisa."

He watched as Max and Kevin entered the shop holding onto their flick out truncheons.

"Where are they?" Kevin asked.

Bradley scanned the empty store, looking at the open freezers and the frozen food sprawled everywhere. Just then he heard a scuffle. Bradley looked over his shoulder to see Eric stuck between the two glass doors. Colin was looking at him. "Oh, for God's sake, get him out," Bradley whispered pointing his baton at Eric.

"Coming in Eric?" Kevin asked.

Bradley looked down all the long aisles of the huge building. "Ok," he said, turning to the group. "Kevin, you're with me. Max, Colin, Eric, you three go that way."

"Understood," Max replied to the order he was just given.

Bradley slowly crept down the aisles of the shopping center holding onto the rubber material.

"Kate?" Bradley whispered, scared to talk. "Lisa?"

Kevin looked over his shoulder. He felt the freezing cold air from the freezers blow onto him as he stepped on the broken glass on the floor. The crack echoed around, and he froze in his tracks, looking at Bradley. "Sorry," he mumbled.

Bradley shook his head smiling as he continued walking forward and grasped the baton. He heard a faint scream coming from somewhere further in the store. "This way," he whispered, "move it."

Bradley and Kevin crept along through the aisles and stopped to see Max and Eric on the other side. Bradley signaled the two along as Kevin stuck behind him. They turned the corner only to see Kate, Lisa, and Ms. Hogan kneeling down on the floor, looking at one another.

"Shit!" Bradley went. He ran over to Kate and Lisa holding on to the baton as Kevin, Colin, Max, and Eric followed close behind. He dived down to the floor. "Hey, you ok?" he gasped. Kate didn't say a word as she trembled with fear.

"Hey," he said, "Can you hear me, what did they do to you?"

Kate slowly looked to her right as Bradley knelt beside her. There was a sudden sound of clicking coming from all around him. He slowly stood up and closed his eyes. He turned around and saw the whole group completely surrounded by the Armazoids. "Shit!" he went. He dropped his weapon and looked up as one of the Armazoids slowly walked up to him holding onto its sidearm. He felt his heart pounding in his chest as the rubber suit squeaked as it walked closer to him. Bradley's adrenaline rushed through his system as the Armazoid stopped and looked at him. The Armazoid swiped his sidearm, whipping it over his face. Bradley fell back onto the floor and looked up at the Armazoid with an expression of anger and pain.

"Please," Kate yelled. "What do you want?"

The Armazoid looked down at Bradley as he slowly leaned back up again, the red mark bruising the side of his face as the pain started to die away. Bradley spat the phlegm out of his throat as he sat down and looked at the alien.

"What do we do with them?" one Armazoid asked.

The first Armazoid looked down at the small group.

"Take these three," it ordered, "But kill the rest."

Kate, Lisa, and Ms. Hogan all looked at one another as Bradley looked up at the Armazoid. The sweat ran down his head as the two girls and teacher were carted away.

"Take them back to the ship," the Armazoid ordered.

"To the ship?" Eric mumbled.

"Yes, we have a ship," the Armazoid replied

Bradley looked up at the Armazoid as these were probably the last few minutes he has left on the planet.

"Any last words?" the Armazoid asked.

Bradley looked up at the Armazoid. "Yes," he said.

"What?" the Armazoid snapped.

Bradley jumped up and head butted him. The Armazoid tumbled back onto the floor, looking at Bradley as it swiped its weapon from the side pouch. The power built up in it as Kate, Lisa, and Ms. Hogan were led out the back door of the shopping center. Bradley looked at Kate as she was being led away, when the floor slowly started to rumble beneath them. The Armazoid looked down at him as the vibrations in the floor increased.

"The hell?" the Armazoid said.

Bradley slowly got up and moved next to Eric as a sudden crash was heard coming from one of the side entrances. He looked at the huge shelves of food as they started tumbling into one another like dominoes. "Move," Bradley screamed. He grabbed hold of Eric by the scruff of his shirt collar and pulled him out the way of the tumbling freezers. Bradley and Eric looked up as one of the NYPD

SWAT vans skidded into the center. The back finished skidding around as the back doors swung open. Two young Chinese men jumped out holding onto old AK47 assault rifles. They ripped off their face masks and looked at Bradley.

"Move your asses," one yelled.

"Agreed," he said.

"Let them have it!" a man yelled.

Bradley watched as a bomb was chucked into the middle of the floor. The timer is set.

"Shit." Bradley gasped.

 Bradley got up quickly picking up the flick out baton. "Come on move," he yelled. "Move, move, move."

"Hey," a voice yelled.

Bradley swung his head to the left. He jumped up grabbing onto the AK47 assault rifle. "Cheers!" he yelled. "Get that van out of here. It's our only transport the car is out of gas."

"Got it," the man yelled.

Bradley held onto the weapon as the round magazine clipped into place below the weapon. The two back wheels spun; the fridges collapsed onto one another blocking his way to the exit. He looked down at the timer on the bomb. He only had fifty-five seconds.

"Shit!" he gasped. "EVERYBODY OUT."

Bradley looked around as the Armazoids attacked out from all corners. He opened fire on them as Kevin led Max, Eric, and Colin out. Bradley watched as the last bullet fired out of the weapon. "Shit!" he mumbled.

He watched as one of the Armazoids swiped his laser. He flicked his baton out, clinging to the rubber end. "Come on then," he yelled.

The Armazoid sped towards Bradley who swung the baton around and slammed it into the shiny laser as his heart pounded. The Armazoid tumbled to the floor. Bradley looked at the timer as it continued ticking. He listened to the sound of the AK47 gunfire as it echoed around the store.

He spun around and ran through the shop, looking for Kate and Lisa.

"Kate?" he yelled. "Lisa?"

He looked around. "Shit!" he cried. "Where the fuck are they?"

He had only about thirty seconds left. He swung his head to the left and looked down one of the aisles at the huge glass window. That was the way he had to go. He sprinted along the aisles, looking into the freezers stacked with food.

"Help!" a voice screamed.

Bradley skidded to a stop. He looked back after the scream. Bradley stared at one of the Armazoids as he was laying on the ground of the store.

"Help me, please." he pleaded.

"Shit." Bradley sighed.

Bradley ran back down the aisle of the store. Bradley helped the Armazoid of the ground. He looked at his eyes as he ripped the laser out of the side pouch throwing it away.

"Thank you." he said.

Bradley kneeled down hauling the Armazoid up over his shoulder.

"Thank you so much!" he groveled.

"Don't thank me, now thank me later." Bradley said, "Before I kill you."

Bradley ran through the superstore with the Armazoid over his shoulders as he felt his heart pounding in his tired chest as the timer hit zero on the Semtex bomb. The eruption pulse ripped through the store. Bradley felt the floor vibrating as the fireball ripped up the aisles. He looked to see a small crack starting to form in the huge glass window in front of him. He threw the flick out baton through the air and watched as the weapon careened through the warming air and the metal bolt slammed into the window, cracking it. Bradley took a shallow breath as he arrived at the window.

"Cover your eyes!" he yelled.

Bradley squinted his eyes and dived through the window still grasping to the Armazoid on his shoulders. Bradley slammed into the concrete sidewalk, picking up the baton at the same time. He ran through the car park as the force from the eruption threw him forward through the cool afternoon air. A few seconds passed after the explosion ripped over his head.

"Bradley," Kevin yelled.

Bradley opened his eyes a few seconds later as he was picked up off the ground.

"Shit, man! You ok?" Kevin asked.

Bradley didn't answer. He looked around the car park.

"Where's …?" he asked.

"Sorry," Max said. "They've gone."

"SHIT! FUCK! NO!" he yelled.

Kevin looked to see the Armazoid on the ground starting to get up. He swiped the handgun from the pouch.

"Wait, no!" Bradley screamed.

Bradley pushed the handgun away from the Armazoid as Kevin squeezed the trigger.

"DAMN!" Kevin yelled, "Look he could kill us."

"He may be able to help us." Bradley replied.

Bradley looked back to see the Armazoid running.

"Don't you dare!" Bradley yelled with anger.

Bradley ran through the car park of the store. He watched as the Armazoid looked back at him as he sprinted after him.

"Come here!" Bradley yelled "Ya little shit!"

Bradley tackled the Armazoid down onto the ground.

"Please!" the Armazoid gasped.

"Get up!" Bradley ordered.

Bradley reached down slamming his hand onto the collar of the suit and dragged him towards the awaiting van looking at the group of armed men.

"On." He demanded, "Now, move it."

"Let's get out of here." Kevin stated.

The young man pulled the doors shut as the driver started up the engine to the van.

"How did you know we were here?" Kevin asked.

"Radio. You put a call out for help," he said. "Name's Cheng and this is Garcious."

Bradley looked out of the rear window as they slowly drove along through the empty car park and the burning building got smaller and smaller.

"How did you boys survive?" Cheng asked.

"Trial and error," Kevin replied.

"And a lot of error," Bradley said.

The van continued along through the streets, heading south towards Chinatown. The smoke from the burning shopping center slowly disappeared.

Chapter 16

Lieutenant Kipling stormed down the concrete steps of the crowded police station, looking at the groups of frightened people as they staggered along, escorted by his troops, after the attack on the bus.

He approached three men who had been on security detail for the evacuation bus convoy. "What happened?" he asked, teeth gritted.

There was a short silence.

"Sir, down there, about half a mile away," one soldier said nervously, not making eye contact, "a couple of the things broke through one of the barricades and attacked bus five. They kidnapped three women and escaped in a Jeep. They were shortly followed by five boys from the same bus who took over a patrol car."

Kipling didn't say a word at first. "Right," he said. "Damn brave! Where did they go?"

"They are most likely dead, sir. They were heading toward Central Park, where the concentration of the aliens seems thickest."

Kipling took a few seconds to think. "We need to double the security detail on all evacuation convoys," he commanded.

"But, sir, that will slow us down," the soldier said. "The area is struggling enough as it is."

"The area will struggle more if people don't trust the evacuation route and attempt to escape on their own. We will keep them safe!" Kipling ordered. "You are dismissed."

The soldiers ran off in different directions.

"Jesus Christ!" Kipling said to himself, walking back to the police station. He took another deep breath, looking back at all the frightened people as they stood waiting for vehicles to come and take them out of the stricken city.

A soldier approached. "Sir, there's a call for you."

Kipling nodded and walked briskly up the stairs towards his makeshift headquarters on a back office. Two soldiers saluted, and one pointed at the laptop on the desk. Kipling sat down and saw in disbelief that President Henderson was looking back at him from the screen.

"Mr. President, sir," he gasped.

"Thank you, Lieutenant Kipling," President Henderson said. "Bring me up to speed on the situation there, please."

Kipling paused to sort through his thoughts. "We have an effective evacuation system in place. Due to an attack on an evacuation convoy, we have just doubled the security detail for each convoy, which will slow the evacuation process but will maintain people's trust in the system and keep them alive."

The president nodded in approval. "Have any of these creatures broken out of the zone?" Henderson asked, putting his pen to his mouth.

"Not that I am aware of," Kipling said. "All bridges out of the Manhattan area have been destroyed. The only way out by land is via the Queensboro Bridge."

Henderson paused thoughtfully, then muttered, "We just can't risk it." He straightened up and said more clearly, "Do everything you can to protect that bridge and proceed with evacuations as quickly as possible. I am ordering the bombing of Manhattan Island at twenty hundred hours in order to prevent the spread of these aliens."

Kipling looked at his watch. "Sir, that only gives us three hours," he said. "We won't have time to complete the evacuation by then. We need at least ten hours to—"

"I'm sorry, but I cannot risk the lives of any more people," President Henderson interrupted, his face growing hard. "Take care, soldier."

President Henderson cut the connection, and Kipling sat back, letting out a deep breath he didn't realize he had been holding. "God have mercy on our souls."

***

President Henderson swiveled around in his chair. He placed his face in his hands and then looked at three men dressed in military uniforms. "I've just seen New York," he said. "Are the F-16s still on standby?"

"Yes, they are, sir," General Reeves stated.

"Get them in the air and tell them to keep well out of sight," President Henderson ordered. "If the Hades bombs don't work, we will have no choice but to revert to a nuclear strike"

Chapter 17

The vehicle screeched to a halt and the one remaining Armazoid hustled the girls out of the back seat, pushing them over to a hover vehicle that was hidden in bushes of the park near the road. As soon as they were secured to their seats, the Armazoid took off, flying low over the ground for a few minutes before stopping suddenly. The alien got out released the bonds on their wrists, then pushed them out.

Kate, Lisa, and Ms. Hogan all looked at one another wondering what the hell was going on. The Armazoid's eyes glittered as he focused on the group of three. Kate gasped as she looked down at her body starting to glow a light green.

"What the...?" Ms. Hogan gasped.

The group slowly started to shrink in size, one after the other. Kate looked up at huge leaves that drifted down from distant trees, casting huge black shadows over them. The Armazoid pushed them toward a cave they hadn't noticed when they were their normal size. They walked into its depths for several minutes, the only light coming from the alien's head light until a prick of light came into view ahead.

The light grew into the alien spaceship. Kate stopped in awe and looked at the huge ship parked right underneath Central Park.

The group progressed down a short ramp towards the bridge leading over to the ship. Two Armazoid guards stood at the entrance and moved aside to allow the girls to cross it. The Armazoid led them to a large elevator but made them put gas masks on before entering the large lift.

The two girls felt the heavy masks stick to their heads. Ms. Hogan didn't know what to say or think as they walked onto the huge elevator. The Armazoid pushed the tiny down button down on the control box. Kate jumped as the screeching of brakes echoed around them and the huge lift slowly started to descend into the depth of the huge ship. Kate stood trembling, not knowing what she was about to experience next.

The lift slowed down and stopped on arriving at the lower level. The huge shutters slowly started to open. Kate stared at the six Armazoids, and they stared back at her. Their escort pushed them out of the elevator and began talking with the others in a strange language of clicks and slurs.

Finally, one alien pushed Kate, Lisa, and Ms. Hogan to a waiting vehicle at the side of the hall. Kate tried to keep her emotions to herself as the Armazoid got into the driver's seat and started up the engine. The vehicle started to drift along the shiny floor.

"Where are you taking us?" Kate asked.

The Armazoid didn't answer as they continued along through the ship. After a little while Kate felt the vehicle slowly come to a stop. The Armazoid got out of his seat and gestured for the women to follow him.

Kate quickly stepped down onto the shiny flooring followed by Lisa and Ms. Hogan, and they walked along a narrow aisle. The small group headed towards a set of metallic automatic doors. It was guarded by a mounted machine gun armed by a tough-looking alien. Kate cowered beneath his gaze.

The group walked into the prison cell holding block and Kate was surprised to see all the small cells with captured people in them. *Their masks are off so it must be ok to breathe inside.*

"What are you doing to these people?" she asked. Again, she was ignored.

Kate followed Lisa and Ms. Hogan across the silver floor towards an empty holding cell. The shiny blue door hissed open, and their guard shoved them in. The door sealed shut behind them. A machine rattled on the ceiling, and Kate thought it must be purifying the air in the cell. She threw her mask onto the floor as the Armazoid walked away.

"We are so screwed," Lisa said, sitting back against a wall. She rested her head into her arms, dejected. Ms. Hogan sat down next to her and rubbed her shoulder. Kate looked through the cell's clear walls to the other prisoners. She wondered how these human survivors had reached the same fate as she. Now they were all equal and their lives had come to a halt.

"We're screwed," she said, echoing Lisa. "We are most definitely screwed."

Chapter 18

Mr. Knightsbridge sat staring through his window of the bus. He saw the military personnel standing guard at the entrance to the Queens Command Center and then the Manhattan skyline in the background. It was clouded with smoke and debris, a nightmare wreck of what it once was. He sighed, the horror for the time being is over. He looked at Amelia. She seemed melancholy and distant, reflecting on what had taken place. He slowly got up and walked down the narrow aisle of the bus, followed by Amelia. He stepped down onto the road and looked out over the river at two tanks pointing their turrets over the city skyline. Gusts of smoke blew into the once fantastic city.

"You okay?" Amelia whispered into his ear.

But before he could respond to her comfort one of the US soldiers walked onto the bus.

"Where is your tutor?" He asked.

A student pointed towards the couple as they stood by the river. The students watched as the soldier walked over to him. They knew it was bad news. Watching in sorrow, Mr. Knightsbridge fell to the ground. Head between his knees, they knew what has been said to him. Mr. Knightsbridge let his breath out and looked over at the bus, the students were gawking over at him and Amelia. "Let's just get the students out of here." He checked a slip of paper given to him by an officer. "We need to catch the 241 train to New Haven."

His class plodding along behind him, they entered the frantic train station. The bus that had dropped them off sped away, back toward the ruined island. Ready to evacuate more people.

Inside the station, a long line of trains lined every track, headed toward major cities along the eastern seaboard. Mr. Knightsbridge found the right train and got in line. Finally, it was their turn to board, and get out of the city.

"Okay, people," he quietly said trying to be strong. "Let's go home."

The students quickly found seats, and soon every gap and corridor on the train was full. The doors sealed closed and the driver started up the engines, ready to roll out of the station to the next evacuation zone. Outside, cars sped along the highway in one direction as military tanks continued to roll in the other direction. The train rolled along the tracks heading away from New York City. The long skyline slowly disappeared from sight as Mr. Knightsbridge lay back in his seat and closed his eyes thinking about Ms. Hogan and how Bradley saved his life.

Chapter 19

Bradley looked out of the window of the NYPD SWAT van as it pulled into Chinatown. The area was completely deserted of both people and aliens.

"What are we doing here?" Colin asked.

"Yeah, what are we doing here?" Eric asked.

Bradley didn't answer. He had no answers. All he had was his flick-out baton.

The van stopped by an alley and Cheng stood up, grabbing the Armazoid by an arm and hoisting him up. Thrusting open the back doors, Cheng jumped down and pulled the alien after him. Gracious was right behind him, locking the vehicle shut.

"This way," Cheng ordered. "Before anything sees us."

The group turned up the alley. Bradley tried to block the strong smell of burning Chinese food from his nose by taking shallow breaths through his mouth. Cheng led them through a gate at the end of the alley.

Bradley closed the gate and closed his eyes as the long squeak from the rusty hinges and bolts screamed out at him. He pulled the bolt across. Cheng was banging on a door up ahead, and Kevin waited for him halfway.

"Brad," Kevin whispered.

Bradley continued looking down at the bolt.

"Brad," Kevin said again.

"Who…? What…?" Bradley asked, shaking his head.

"You okay, man?" Kevin asked.

Bradley released his breath. "No, I'm not," he said in a dull voice. They trudged up to the door where an aged man was opening it at Cheng's insistent pounding. He ushered the group inside and shut the door with a clang.

They were in some type of employee cafeteria. Table and plastic chairs lined the walls, some overturned in an echo of the flurry of activity when the attacks first started. The old man led them through the room quickly, moving to a hallway lined with offices. The sounds from the outside slowly disappeared as they headed deeper into the building. Bradley looked into the empty offices as they continued heading along the dark corridors. The group reached the top of the stairs, and Cheng paused, silhouetted against the office windows behind him.

"Everyone, I've forgotten to introduce Marco," Cheng said, gesturing to the old man with one hand while keeping a firm grip on the Armazoid with the other. "Marco, this is Bradley, Kevin, Max, Colin, and Eric."

Marco slowly turned around and then turned to Cheng.

"Where did you find these guys? I'm surprised they're still alive. It's a war zone out there," he exclaimed.

"We were driving along the main street looking around for survivors when a call came over the radio about being near Ravensgate Shopping Center. So, we headed there and found them," Cheng replied.

"Why were you there?" Marco asked. "That's uptown."

Bradley took a deep breath. "Our friends have been kidnapped by those things."

Marco gasped. "I didn't realize they took prisoners."

"Well, apparently they do." Bradley looked down and kicked his foot against the ground, but quickly looked up again. "So, what is the plan?"

"Well, I say we introduce you to the rest of team and then interrogate that thing over there and find out what he knows," said Cheng.

"The...team?" Bradley asked, confused.

"Yeah, they're waiting up here. But first, there's one other thing I want to show you."

The group arrived outside of two wide double doors, which Garcious pushed and held open. They stepped out onto a balcony that overlooked an enormous room.

Below them, large crates and boxes.

"What do you do here?" Eric asked.

"Business," Marco said.

"What sort of business?" he asked.

"Just some very good business," Marco replied. "And if we survive this, I think I am going to be doing a lot more business, trust me my boy.

"I've always wanted another kick at the enemy," Marco said. "I can't sit around waiting for our wonderful Government to drop a nuke on us. Might as well go out fighting, that's my way."

"What?" Eric asked, confused.

Marco stood up straight and snapped his heels. "General Marco Bentley," he said, saluting smartly. "I was in Vietnam once for a short term, then onto the Gulf."

"Great," Bradley said. "Just what we need."

Cheng chuckled and led them to another room down the hall. When the doors opened, dim light flooded into the dark hallway, and the aroma of coffee filtered out. Men of various ages and races were standing around a small kitchen area, smoking or talking quietly with one another. They came to attention when Marco entered the room.

"Listen up," Marco said. "We have a problem. AJ, CJ here."

Two young black men stepped forward.

"This is Bradley, and these are his friends," Marco said. He pointed to the man on the left. "That's AJ, and that," pointing at the other man, "is CJ."

Bradley shook their hands.

Marco turned back to the rest of the assembled men. "Bradley here has had two of his friends kidnapped and he wants them back."

"What friends?" CJ asked.

"Two girls," Bradley said. "Plus a teacher. We were being evacuated by bus when the vehicle came under attack."

"Damn, man," CJ gasped. "We better interrogate that thing before we make any solid plans, but we will try to help you get your friends back, I want to get back at these things, my ma and girl were out shopping for my vacation next week, I lost contact with them a while ago so, I have nothing to lose, I'm in."

"It's either that or wait till the government nukes us," a Chinese man said with a chuckle. Other men laughed as well trying to lift the anxiety.

Bradley watched as a chair was brought forward towards the Armazoid. It looked terrified.

Marco brought a combat knife out of a side sheath. He began to play with it, digging muck out of his nails. The edge is gleaming in the fluorescent lights, flashbacks from Vietnam and The Gulf ran through his brain. "So come on," Marco spoke, "Mr. Alien, why you here, tell us what you know."

It whimpered. "My name's Arkalon."

Marco laughed lightly and leaned closer towards him. "I don't care about your name, why are you here at Earth, why did you charming things pay us a visit on this wonderful Summer's day?"

Arkalon took a short breath. "Okay. We were assigned to investigate a planet not known to you. We were infiltrated," Arkalon said.

"Infiltrated?" Bradley asked. "By who?"

"It is a planet called Sygonia, a planet that was not even known to us, the light from this planet isn't due to reach this planet for another six point nine million years." Arkalon said. "We discovered that they had infiltrated us. Even after interrogating the infiltrator we couldn't find out why they were here. It was like it had been removed from their heads."

Arkalon took another deep breath, staring at the threatening group around him.

"Sygonia managed to gain access to us by using one of us," Arkalon said. "Somehow they managed to transform into one of us. After finding the infiltrator, we went to investigate their planet and discovered a complex. So we sent a strike force to investigate, but the Dropship we sent must have been damaged, because on its return to the mothership, we believe it crash landed on this planet. We know it has valuable data on it that we need to defeat the Sygonians if war was to happen in the future."

Marco, realizing this alien was spilling all the beans without much force, stepped back. "What kind of data?"

"Who they are, their firepower, their government structure, their population," Arkalon replied. "I don't know; I wasn't on the reconnaissance mission."

"Jesus!" Bradley gasped.

"So why all the destruction on this planet?" Marco demanded, seeming to realize that he was still talking to an invader that had killed hundreds of people.

"We don't negotiate with our enemies," Arkalon said at once. "We're looking for our ship, and after we attempted to contact your leader and had no response or compliance, we invaded. Obtaining the data from that ship is essential." Arkalon stopped talking as a wave of coughs overtook him. He sagged into his seat.

"Have your people communicated with ours?" Marco asked.

"I don't know about that," he replied, "But you will have a bigger problem soon."

"Surprise me." Bradley replied.

Arkalon then spoke again.

"When we landed here, our long-range communications antenna was damaged. As soon as it is fixed, many more of our people will be here," Arkalon said. "In search of the missing data."

The group was collectively stunned into silence.

"Jesus." Marco said.

"So that means the complete Earth could be invaded?" Cheng asked.

"Yes," Arkalon said, he was breathing rapidly.

Bradley stepped forward. "Two of your people kidnapped three people of ours. Where are they?"

"In the holding cells back at our ship," Arkalon replied.

"That's where we go," Bradley said turning to Marco.

"You can't," Arkalon said, shaking his head, eyes still closed. "You'll never find it."

Bradley took a shallow breath. "You will show us the way. We're getting them back."

"They will kill me," Arkalon whispered. "If I'm not already dead."

"That's your problem," Bradley snapped and turned to Marco. "Marco, we need guns, and I mean lots of them!"

"Follow me, my boy," Marco replied.

Marco took Bradley back to the warehouse. Bradley stared up at all the crates stacked one on top of the other. Marco picked up an old black crowbar and pried off the wooden lid of a box. M16 machine guns gleamed up at the two men.

"Jesus Christ!" Bradley gasped. "My favorite gun!"

"Well," Marco said, "help yourself, kiddo."

Kevin walked over and looked into some other crates as Marco ripped them open. "MP5s," he said. "My favorite gun too!"

"Yep," Marco said. "Sixteen hundred a piece, but after today two grand a piece."

Kevin reached in and pulled a weapon out of the case.

"Take this," Marco said, handing Bradley a utility vest with pouches for the extra magazines. Bradley started loading them as the rest of the group armed up, readying for the assault on the ship.

"Oh yeah, I've just thought of something." Marco walked over to a set of unopened crates, Bradley following close behind. He watched in amazement as Marco pulled out what appeared to be a parachute.

"A parachute?" Bradley queried.

"Not just a parachute," Marco replied. "A parachute, floating devices, and a pocket for the radio and first aid." Marco said. "Also, an extra strap in case you have to mount up with someone."

Max watched as one of Marco's men pulled out a box of radios.

"I'm line one," Marco said,

"I'm line one too," Bradley said. "We can stay in contact. Use the ear and mouthpiece as well, you know what these things are like."

Bradley looked at a crate of small canvas kits. "Wait. What's this?" he asked.

"Binoculars," Marco said strapping it to his body. "Sold about a hundred of these babies so far."

"Who to?" Bradley asked.

"Just some people I know."

Bradley took up his radio as Arkalon called out to him.

"There is another thing," Arkalon said.

"Surprise us," Marco asked.

"Our ship has high levels of carbon monoxide," Arkalon said. "Too high for your species to survive, that is why we have this on our suits, because we cannot take in carbon dioxide."

Bradley turned to Marco. "Any gas masks in your cave of treasures?"

"Masks," Marco yelled.

One of his men lugged a crate over. Marco pried it open. "And all of you take an extra, just in case."

Bradley looked at the gas mask as he tuned is the radio. "Testing one, two, three," he said over it.

The men nodded as they tested theirs one after the other.

"I can't hear anyone," Eric said. "Hello, can anyone hear me?"

Marco slowly walked over to Eric and slowly pressed the on button, then tuned it to line one.

"Now try," he said hunching towards him.

Bradley looked at Eric. He started to load the shotgun he picked out from the crate.

"That goes there," he said, "And this one goes down there, and that goes in here."

Marco walked back over to Eric. He put his hand on his shoulder.

"Wrong way round." He said

"What?" Eric said.

Eric looked down at the shotgun.

"Oh shit," he said. "Try again."

Eric pulled the shells out of the shotgun.

"This goes that way." Eric said, "And that goes this way as well."

Marco looked at Eric, struggling to load the shotgun.

"You sure about him?" Marco asked Bradley.

Bradley looked at Eric as he struggled to load the shotgun. He shrugged his shoulders and looked over at Arkalon on the chair.

"We need a plan of their ship," Kevin said. "Do you think?"

"He will," Bradley said. "Trust me on that."

"When haven't I trusted you?" Kevin joked.

"Ha," Bradley laughed. Despite being loaded down with ammo, he felt much lighter. Having hope made a big difference.

He walked away, holding onto the M16 as he loaded the last few grenades into the pouches and tightened up the straps. He felt the strong material biting against his skin. Bradley left his friends to arm up and returned to the break room, taking a seat in front of Arkalon.

"We need a plan of your ship," Bradley demanded.

Arkalon sighed and reached into his pocket, pulling out a tiny disk. He handed it to Bradley. "If you push that small button on the top it will show you the whole ship."

Bradley put the small disk down on the table. He pushed the small blue button, hoping this wasn't some kind of explosive device. He watched as the hologram of the ship popped up in front of him.

Marco walked over and gasped. "Jesus, look at the size of it!"

Bradley and Marco stared at the hologram of the ship. It showed all the different corridors, including the holding cells at the back of the ship. The two leaders put their heads together and began to plan.

Ten minutes later they had a workable idea.

"Ok," Marco said. "Gather 'round and listen up."

"This is the Android, Hemorrhoid or whatever it is called. It is currently parked underneath Central Park. Have no idea how it got down there, but our friend here is willing to take us to it. The ship has a main elevator here. This is where we will be entering. We shall remain on the second floor as a few of Marco's sharp shooters take out are awaiting friends," Bradley said, wiping his forehead. "When the first lot has been taken out, we shall move on and take out the rest. Marco will stand by the elevator. Behind these crates and be out of sight." He paused and took a deep breath.

"Why is Marco staying there?" Max asked.

"Because when we get the girls out, we may need to get the elevator back quickly so he can keep an eye on it," Bradley replied. "There are a few parked vehicles at the elevator entrance. My friend here is going to drive. He will take us along this corridor to this part of the ship."

"What's that?" CJ asked.

"That is just behind the cell block."

Kevin stared onto the hologram as Bradley pointed at the holding cells.

"But that's away from the cell entrance." Kevin said.

"It's our only option. The main entrance is heavily guarded." Bradley replied. "We enter through a small ventilation shaft here as Max and a few others stay in the vehicle keeping an eye. This will take us right above the cells."

Bradley stopped for a second breath. "And now the assault." he said. "We remove the shaft entrance. When no one is looking we drop this flash grenade into the block and slide down the copper wire we are taking with us."

Kevin stepped forward. He took a closer look at the ship.

"When we enter the cell block, I and whoever is with me will take out any guards." Bradley said. "Eric, Kevin, you two pull back here taking out any of those things that may burst in, while we bust the girls out."

"What about Ms. Hogan?" Colin asked.

"We'll worry about her when we get to her." Bradley replied. "Oh yeah. Colin, can you use a gun?"

"No." Colin replied.

"Call yourself an American?" Bradley replied. "Max, give Colin a one to one on firearms please my dear friend."

Bradley looked at the men lined up as Max took Colin aside. "Any questions before I go on?" he asked.

The men stood silent. "Ok." he said. "Once we are out, we rendezvous back at the vehicle here with Max, and then we head back to the elevator. Then you get the hell out of there."

"What about the ship?" Max asked. "And where after that?"

"We get back to the bus. We drive as fast as we can to wherever they are evacuating and we get out of this city, because to be honest I don't think they are going to continue the evacuation."

"Why?" Kevin asked.

"Look at the state of that evacuation zone. They got through those soldiers. How the hell are they going to evacuate the rest of that police station and the rest of the people? There are hundreds there," Bradley said. "I personally think there will be a mushroom cloud soon."

The men started grinning and nodding their heads as Bradley wrapped it up.

"Shall we move then?" Bradley asked. "Anyone need to go take a nervous piss?"

The group stood silently.

"Right. Mount up," Marco yelled. "Where's my girl?" He walked into the back office, moving his desk out of the way while the guys gave each other confused looks. Bradley watched as he walked out of his office holding onto a heavy machine gun. The long line of golden bullets dangled by his side when he had locked them into place.

"What the...?" Bradley gasped.

"Right. Let's see who goes for me with this bitch," Marco said. "Let's move to the city bus parked outside, I knew that would come in handy."

Bradley held his M16 as he prepared to leave the warehouse and venture out into the city.

"Oh Bradley," Marco said, pulling him aside and handing him three charges.

"What are these?" he asked.

"C4," Marco said. "Push these three buttons up and hit this." Marco handed him the detonator. Bradley slowly slipped them into the pouches, ready to be used. He was ready.

The group of fifteen men walked down the alley to the city bus and piled in. The Armazoid could barely stand, but he looked resigned to his fate. As one of the men started the bus back up, Bradley leaned against the bus wall. He had never felt this tired before. Now he had to go to an alien ship, which had been shrunk in size, underneath Central Park and rescue Kate.

"Move it." Marco ordered Arkalon.

Arkalon strolled along with the armed group through the warehouse towards the exit. Eric was behind him.

"What's that?" Eric asked.

"What's what?" Arkalon replied.

"That." Eric said pointing at the filter.

"Oh that," Arkalon replied, "That filters out carbon dioxide, stops us from being poisoned."

Arkalon is pushed onto the bus.

"Come on sweetheart," Marco said, "Call yourself a soldier?"

Bradley took a seat towards the back of the bus.

"Let's hope we don't run into any of these things." Marco said.

"Agreed." Bradley replied.

***

The bus pulled out of Chinatown, the streets quiet and empty. There was not a police or military vehicle in sight.

Bradley was just starting to get comfortable when he saw something out the corner of his eye.

"Stop!" He yelled.

The bus stopped. The doors opened, he and Kevin joined Marco in circling a NYC News helicopter that had smashed to the ground in the middle of the street. Its blades dangled down uselessly, and hisses of smoke popped out from the engine. Bradley slowly walked up to it, looking into the smashed cockpit door window. All the electrical gauges fizzled where it had slammed into the ground. The pilot was dead.

"Anyone there?" Kevin asked.

Bradley took one last look at the mangled wreckage then shook his head. He turned around slowly, walking back towards the van.

"Wait." A weak female voice wafted out from the wreckage.

Bradley turned around to see a young lady news reporter followed by her camera man with a nametag that read "Jon."

"Hi," she said. "Sorry to startle you."

"Hi," Kevin said, smiling at her. Her blond hair was disheveled, clips having fallen out. As he watched, she reached into her pocket and pulled out a mirror to check her hair. She patted it and clipped the mirror shut.

"Oh, thank God there are people still alive," she said. "I thought everyone was dead in this part of the island."

"Quickly," Bradley ordered. "Move before anything hears us."

Kevin helped the cameraman back towards the van while Bradley stopped to look at a crashed military Jeep. He pulled the metal door open and looked at the back seat.

"Oh, nice," he said.

Kevin walked up to him. Bradley pulled out a couple of small, unused rocket launchers.

"We'll take these," he said. "May come in handy." He handed the launchers to Kevin.

"Give them to a few guys on the bus," Bradley ordered.

"Come on," Kevin said. "Let's get the hell out of here."

The young reporter got onto the bus. The group of men looked at the young woman as she stood in her light pink suit and skirt that barely reached mid-thigh. They stared at her bare legs. She cleared her throat uncomfortably.

Bradley helped the reporter along the bus to the back seats. She sat down onto the old tatty material and looked at Bradley. "So, I'm Laura. Are you people evacuating I hope?" she asked.

"Hi Laura, I'm Bradley," Bradley said. "We're actually going to Central Park." He paused. "Your friend had better get his camera ready because you two are going to get the story of a lifetime."

Chapter 20

The bus pulled up next to the park. Not a living soul was in sight. Bradley looked at Kevin with a smirk on his face.

"Here we go," he said in a quiet voice. Behind Kevin, Bradley suddenly recognized a cafe—the one where he had been only a few hours earlier, before any of this had happened. He saw a flicker of movement in the window.

"Wait here," he said.

"Why?" Kevin asked.

"I gotta check something out."

Bradley softly ran over to the cafe and pulled out his silenced handgun, nosing it through the door that hung slightly ajar. He caught a glimpse of a small shadow in the rear room. He slowly crept into the room towards the shadow, ready to pull the trigger if an Armazoid was lying in wait to attack him. He took a deep breath as the door slowly closed behind him with the breeze.

"Don't shoot," a voice whimpered.

Bradley's eyes adjusted to the faint light and saw Rico, the waiter who had been hitting on Ms. Hogan earlier that day.

Rico slowly got up and looked at Bradley, recognition crossing his face. "Hey, good to see you again my friend!" he said excitedly.

"You to," Bradley said. "Why aren't you at the police station?"

Rico slowly got up and brushed the dirt off his old white apron. "I couldn't leave. It was too risky! Those things could have, could have killed me!" Bradley opened the door for Rico and the two men left the cafe. Rico looked around in horror at the destruction, nose crinkling at the smell of smoke and gore.

"This the first time you been out since then?" Bradley asked.

"Yes," Rico said.

Marco came over, looking annoyed. "Who's this?"

"Marco, meet Rico," said Bradley, "Rico, Marco."

"Hi, Rico. You tagging along with us?" Marco asked.

"Yeah. Let's get to that evacuation zone," Rico urged.

"We're not going to the evacuation zone," Marco said.

"What?" Rico asked in a shocked voice.

"Ms. Hogan," Bradley gave Rico a suggestive nudge in the ribs, "Was kidnapped by these things. We're going to get her, and I think she is single."

"Ms. Hogan?" Rico repeated, still shocked at what Bradley has just told him.

"Our little friend here is going to help," Bradley said, indicating Arkalon with a wave of his hand.

Rico shook himself out of his shock. "Well then it's a good thing I am ex-service."

"That's the spirit." Marco said.

After retrieving some spare weapons for Rico from the bus, the ever-growing group set off through into Central Park. They stalked down deserted paths and waterless fountains, in tune to anything that might be dangerous. Arkalon trudged at the front, steadily making his way towards

212

the ship. The group continued along the path when they heard a shuffle coming from the dense shrubs. Bradley signaled the group to stop.

"What is it?" Eric asked.

Bradley looked into the shrubs as it continued shuffling from left to right getting worse. He edged his finger towards the trigger ready to use it. Bradley watched as Aussie, the hobo from the morning, fall out the shrubs.

"You!" Bradley gasped.

"What!" Aussie yelped "You're not taking me back there, those commies molested me!"

Marco stepped forward and put his hand on Bradley's shoulder.

"Step side please Bradley?" Marco asked.

Marco walked up to Aussie.

"Aussie my good man." He yelped, "How good to see you old chap."

Kevin looked at Bradley.

"So, he was telling the truth this morning." Kevin said to Bradley.

Bradley looked at Kevin as Marco spoke at Aussie.

"How you been man?" He asked.

"Bad." Aussie snapped, "Guess what happened this morning."

Marco smirked looking at Aussie.

"Let me guess you ran into some alien asshole?" He asked with a smile.

Aussie looked shocked.

"Yes." He gasped "How did you know!"

Aussie took sight of Arkalon.

"THERES ONE THERE!" He yelled pointing at Arkalon "Let me."

Aussie went for Arkalon.

"Woah Aussie, my good man" Marco said, "He's with us, take it easy."

"You guys molested me!" Aussie yelped "You hear me, you touched me!"

Bradley let his breath out looking into the sky as the white fluffy clouds passed overhead. Eager to get into the ship. He watched as Aussie continued trying to storm for Arkalon. Bradley slowly walked over to Aussie and Marco.

"Gentlemen?" He asked.

"You communist!" Aussie yelped.

"Gentlemen?" He asked again.

Bradley looked at Aussie.

"Aussie." Bradley ranted.

Aussie stopped.

"Are you ex-service like Marco?" He asked.

"You bet." Aussie yelped.

Bradley looked at Aussie again.

"Would you like to get back at these things?" He asked, "For molesting you?"

Aussie looked excited.

"Shall we move then?" He asked.

The group advanced further into the park, Arkalon eventually leading them up a tiny path toward a small crevasse in the ground.

"It's in there," he said. "I will need everyone to stand by me."

Bradley glared at Arkalon, sidearm cocked. "One false move and you are history."

The group of men walked up to Arkalon. Bradley looked down at Arkalon as his eyes gleamed. He felt confused, as he was about to enter a world where no human

214

had ever known to have been before. Arkalon's eyes stopped glittering. Bradley's heart started to pound as his body started to glow a light green.

"Oh my God!" Laura gasped. "Get the cam ready."

"You bet," Jon replied.

The whole group shone a light green. Bradley looked up into the night sky as the trees seemed to grow taller. He shook his head as the green glow disappeared from the group.

"What happened?" Eric said.

"We shrunk," Kevin said.

"How did you do that?" Bradley asked Arkalon.

"We just can." he replied.

Laura looked at Jon. "Camera on me," she said. "On three."

She lifted the microphone up to her mouth. "This is Laura Welshman reporting from Central Park. You are not going to believe what we have to say to you viewers this evening after this historic and horrific day for the United States of America."

Bradley turned around and looked at Laura as she spoke into the camera. He pulled out his handgun from his pocket and looked at the entrance to the cave.

"Come on," he ordered.

Marco followed Bradley towards the huge entrance that had seemed like such a small opening before. He stared upwards, not seeing the top of it in the darkness. "This must be some ship," he said.

Bradley turned on the handgun flashlight. As the group moved down the corridor, he searched the shadows for any rats or spiders they would have to deal with. After twenty minutes, a prick of light appeared and slowly grew into the behemoth ship. Bradley pulled out the small pair of binoculars from the survival kit. He zoomed in, straining to see the other side of the huge ship—he couldn't.

"Damn." he whispered.

Marco had his own binoculars out, scouting out the manpower. He whistled softly. "There are quite a few of the bastards guarding it."

"I remember something like this when I was in 'Nam," Aussie said. "I was patrolling when we came across a Vietcong camp. There were loads of the bastards."

"We're not in 'Nam now," Marco said, "but I remember as clear as crystal."

"They're mine." Aussie gritted his teeth in anticipation.

"Aussie, wait," Bradley cautioned. "If they know we are here it would compromise us."

Bradley looked again to see a few Armazoids guarding a bridge leading over to the ship.

"There's only a few there," Marco said. "We can take them." He signaled to two men with silenced M16s. "You two. Take 'em out," he ordered.

The two Chinese men crept forward, wielding their weapons. Luckily, their small size made every rock and pebble into a defensible position. They knelt down and took the shots. Bradley saw the Armazoids guarding the bridge fall lifeless.

Trying not to slip on the crumbly ground, Bradley led the team forward towards the bridge. He stopped when he noticed a set of red beams zooming across and above it. "What's that?" he asked Arkalon.

"That's electric," Arkalon replied. "If you go through them the alarm will go off inside the ship. You can only turn it off via the control box on the other side." He pointed a metal control box by the door of the ship.

"Oh," Kevin said, scratching his chin.

Bradley looked over to the other side of the ship at the metal control box. He turned around and looked up at the rock bulging out behind him.

"Marco," Bradley said. "Where's that rope?"

"Bradley, no!" Kevin adamantly shook his head.

"I've got to," he replied. "This planet depends on us. Today is going down in history."

He took the rope from Marco and tied a lasso. He took a deep breath and walked up to the edge of the ship. He looked down into the deep dark edge between the ship and cliff, but quickly returned his eyes to the control box, visualizing what he needed to do.

A voice behind him startled him. "Deep," Marco said.

"Damn, Marco," Bradley gasped. "I wish you wouldn't do that."

"Keep your eyes open boy," he whispered. "Can't always be here to protect you."

Bradley stepped back. He started swinging the rope around over his head. He chucked it, but the noose fell short and fell into the crater. Bradley felt sweat trickle down his neck, and he pulled the length back up. He glanced over his shoulder, tensing for any kind of alarm the rope might have caused. Nothing moved.

"And we try again," he muttered.

Bradley carefully swung, aimed, and let go—and the noose fell neatly over the small power box. Not allowing himself a moment to relax, he quickly pulled it tight and tied the other end around the rock behind him. Then, handing his M16 to Kevin, he clambered on and climbed forward, hand over hand, foot over foot, until he reached the other side, hands burning and muscles shaking. Trembling from fatigue, he reached out and opened the control box, hitting the red button to stop the electricity that guarded the bridge.

The red beams disappeared. He sat down with a huge breath of relief as the rest of the team ran across the bridge to join him by the elevator doors. Kevin handed the M16 over to him.

"Thank you," Bradley said as he stood up and put the M16 over his back.

Marco inspected the digital screen next to the elevator as Bradley addressed the group.

"Okay, you know what to do. Group one, head along with me. The rest stay with Marco," Bradley ordered.

"Gas masks," Marco ordered.

Everyone pulled out the masks and slipped them on, switching on the accompanying radio.

"For God's sake, do not take them off," Bradley insisted. "A few whiffs of carbon monoxide and you're history."

"What's carbon monoxide?" Eric asked, head tilted in confusion.

Max shook his head in disbelief. "Just don't take your mask off, please, for me."

Marco fiddled with the control panel. Marco pushed the button in. The brakes clunked off one after the other.

"Here we go," Bradley whispered. "Good luck, everybody."

He felt butterflies in his stomach as they slowly started to descend into the depth of the ship. The rollers slowly took the huge plate down into the ship.

Laura cleared her throat and looked into the camera. "You are not going to believe what we are currently doing," she said into the microphone. "We are slowly descending into the alien spacecraft that is currently beneath Central Park here in Manhattan."

The elevator continued dropping down into the depth of the ship. The huge plate started to slow down as it approached corridor A.

"Ready?" Marco asked.

Bradley pulled out the silenced handgun from his side pouch. He walked over to Kevin, who was sporting his MP5 machine gun. The elevator shuddered to a stop and the doors slowly opened. Bradley knelt down as the inside of the ship came into view.

"Let the silencers take out anything here" He ordered.

"Got it." Kevin replied.

The shutter opened. The Armazoids looked, they didn't have time to react. Bradley squeezed the trigger launching the bullet through their heads. Bradley took out the last with his handgun.

"Yeah!" Aussie yelled.

"Get them moved," Bradley demanded. "And Aussie, be quiet." He looked around and stared down the long corridors, the lights too bright after their time in the darkness of the cave and elevator. After the gun fight, the following silence was eerie.

Arkalon led team Alpha—Bradley, Kevin, Max, Eric, Rico, AJ, and CJ—over to a hover vehicle waiting by the elevator. Marco and the rest took cover behind large blue storage containers, ready to provide back up and to keep an exit open.

"Right, let's do this," Bradley said.

Arkalon had turned a sickly shade of green, knowing he would die as soon as another Armazoid spotted him. He turned on the engine as Bradley got into the seat next to him.

"Don't forget, one false move and I'll blow your damn brains out," Bradley said, clenching his fist.

Arkalon nodded and pulled away from the elevator. They had barely traveled five minutes when the floor began to rumble. Bradley looked back to see lights down the corridor getting closer.

"What is it?" he said in an abrupt voice.

"I've got to let these people pass," Arkalon said.

"Why?" Bradley asked, grasping his M16.

"You'll see," Arkalon said "Trust me on this, please."

Arkalon pulled over to the side. Bradley and the rest of the group slowly started to raise their heads and look out of the windows. The vehicle stared vibrating heavily.

"What the...?" Kevin gasped.

Bradley peeked up through the window. He watched in horror as a long line of Armazoid military vehicles rolled by.

"What the hell are they?" Eric asked.

"I don't know," Bradley said. "They look like tanks."

"They are," Arkalon replied to Bradley.

"What?" Bradley gasped. "Why?"

"It's coming," Arkalon said.

"What?" Bradley yelled over the loud vibrations "What's coming"

"You know, that signal that they're sending to our planet," Arkalon said. "They're planning to station the ship above the city so they can send it."

"Shit!" Bradley gasped. "Come on, we have got to get on with this."

The last of the Armazoid vehicles rolled away towards the large elevator.

"I'd better warn Marco," Bradley said. He flicked on his radio. "Marco," he said over the radio. "You've got a large convoy heading your way. For Christ's sake, stay out of sight."

"Roger that," Marco replied.

Marco turned looking at his group.

"You heard the man," he said, "Move them rears out the way."

Marco kneeled behind the blue containers by the elevator. He held on to his heavy machine gun, still trying to smell the napalm from Vietnam. The image of the trenches, the smell of the burning buildings as the shells from the machine guns flew over his head, still haunting him. He felt the ground starting to vibrate. He peeked between the sets of crates as the huge Armazoid vehicles came into view. He stared at the long turrets as they came down the long corridor. "Jesus Christ!" Marco gasped. "There's enough fire power there to blow the shit out of this island, our machines wouldn't stand a chance against them."

The Armazoids opened the elevator up. The shutters slowly rolled open, allowing the vehicles to roll on a couple at a time. Marco watched as the vehicles lined up one after the other. Two Armazoids rolled their machine onto the elevator. They watched as the shutter came down, slowly locking into place. The brakes released one after the other. The huge elevator rolled to the top of the shaft carrying the few Armazoid vehicles. The two Armazoids rolled off the elevator, running over the bridge onto the muddy ground. They sped through the cave heading towards the exit. Their tracks turned up the mud as they rolled out of the cave heading onto the pathway. The Armazoids looked around the empty park as their machines returned to their normal size. They glowed a light green as they headed off into the destroyed city.

Chapter 21

Holding onto his M16 rifle, Officer Adam Jones looked through the glass door of a New York lawyer's office. It was where he and his fellow comrades had been stationed all day to search for survivors and monitor any enemy movements. He turned around and walked back into the building.

"How long now?" He asked.

"Calm down," Bob said.

"Calm down?" Adam gasped. "We have to get out of here."

"Adam, listen to me," Jack said. "Go and have a rest. I'm sure we'll be able to get out when we need to."

"Well, let's go," Adam shrieked.

"Adam," Bob said soothingly, "Go and sit down."

Adam nodded and slowly walked through the building. He looked at the two soldiers as they stood at the rear of the building, holding their rifles. "You guys ok?" he asked.

"We're fine," one of them said.

Adam turned and walked over to the set of leather couches in the office's lobby. He placed his M16 down next to him and reached over to a side table that held a pitcher of water and a set of glasses. He poured himself a glass and glugged half of it down then thumped it back down on the table. He opened a glossy magazine, trying to take his mind of the attack. But something captured his attention. Adam stared at his glass of water, rippling unnaturally on the level table. He slowly picked up his M16.

"Hell!" he muttered.

He got up and walked through the offices to the front entrance.

"I thought I said sit down," Bob said.

"Quiet," Adam snapped.

He walked through the glass door to the sidewalk. The vibrations were stronger. Adam felt his heart pound as a long turret came into view from a side road. He didn't recognize the model as the shiny vehicle rolled out, heading towards the building.

"What the...?" he said.

Bob and John cursed, heading toward their rocket launchers stationed at the sides of the entrance. The two soldiers kneeled down on the ground, arming the launcher and looking through the scope at the alien vehicle as it continued to roll towards them. The rocket shot through the air and slammed into the vehicle—bull's eye. Adam squinted his eyes and looked through the smoke as it started to disperse.

The long turret of the Armazoid tanks came into view again.

"Holy shit!" Bob gasped.

He reloaded his launcher and took another shot at the vehicle, again to no affect. The soldiers watched in horror as the turret swiveled to line up with their building. A rocket fired from the launcher, blasting through the glass front of the law office and erupting inside. None of the soldiers or police survive.

"Ha!" The Armazoid yelled.

President Henderson sat in his office, debating whether or not to turn on the TV. He started at a loud knock on the door. It echoed around the empty room.

"Come in," Henderson ordered

Synder stormed in, his normally blank face contorted by shock. Henderson knew the situation had taken a turn for the worse.

"Sir, you are needed in the emergency briefing room immediately."

Henderson nodded and got to his feet, following Synder to the briefing room.

"Bring me up to speed," he demanded.

General Reeves stood up and flicked on the television. Henderson put his glasses on and stared in disbelief at the camera footage from a news helicopter that was focusing on the line of alien tanks.

"My God," Henderson gasped.

Henderson could hardly speak. He stared at the gleaming Armazoid vehicles as they rolled down the empty Manhattan streets.

"Where are they heading," Henderson asked quietly, still shocked.

General Reeves locked eyes with Henderson. "Straight towards the downtown police station."

Henderson closed his eyes. "What is the estimated time of arrival?"

"According to their speed sir, and their route," Reeves replied, "around fifty-five minutes."

"Sir," Admiral Johnson spoke in. "I have the anchorage in firing position sir may I add."

"How long would it take to send it across to New York?" Henderson asked, rubbing his head.

"Ten minutes, sir," Admiral Johnson replied. "It's your decision, but you have to make it soon."

Henderson looked at the television again, at the destruction caused by the alien tanks that could spread to the rest of his country. He couldn't think clearly—the pressure was too great.

"Sir," the commander said again. "You need to make a decision."

Henderson closed his eyes, shaking his head.

"Sir," Synder yelped.

Henderson took one last look up at the screen. "Let the F16s attack. If they fail..."

Synder looked at President Henderson, waiting for the order.

"DEFCON One."

Henderson slumped back in his chair as the commander lifted the phone of the hook.

***

Bradley looked up and down the corridor as Arkalon slowed the vehicle down. Holding on to his M16, he walked over to the wall of the ship and looked up at the lights as they beamed down onto the shiny floor. Arkalon pulled the vehicle over to the side of the corridor and stepped out, walking over to a vent beside where Bradley had stopped. The rest of the group took up a defensive semi-circle, facing away from Arkalon in case anything came down the tunnel. Arkalon reached into his pocket and pulled out a tiny screwdriver from his pocket, he began to work out the bolts of the vent. It was a large panel, and Bradley helped Arkalon lift it out of its frame.

"Remember what I said. They will be just below us. It's too dangerous to go straight down and in. It is very heavily guarded," said Arkalon

Max walked over to Bradley. "Ready?" he said.

"Yes," Bradley said, looking down at Arkalon. "CJ, AJ, and the rest stay here, but for God's sake, keep your heads down. Even if they come, stay out of sight, don't shoot unless you have to."

"Got it," CJ said. His group moved back to the hovercraft and ducked out of site between the seats.

Bradley pushed Arkalon into the vent. "In you go, sweetheart."

Arkalon slid into the slanted shaft, followed closely by Bradley, Kevin, Max, and Eric. Arkalon started crawling down the narrow ventilation shaft, and the boys did the same. After a few minutes, Arkalon stopped at another output vent that shone with light.

"It's just here," Arkalon whispered.

Bradley looked through the vent into a short corridor filled with glass cells, each housing three to five people.

"We're going to need more masks," he said. "How many we got"

The group dropped the extra masks onto the floor of the vent.

"I'll count them" Eric said

Bradley watched looked at Eric as he began to count the masks.

"Here we go" He said "One, two, three, four, five, six, nine, seven, no wait hang on start again, one, two three, four, five, no hang on, one, two."

"I think we've got enough." A man said.

"Ok." Eric replied.

"Just enough," Bradley whispered in relief. He gestured to Arkalon. "Pass that thingy."

Bradley started unscrewing the ventilation shaft gently, trying not to make a noise. He pulled the narrow metal plate out of the shaft and handed it to Kevin. He carefully stuck his head upside down out of the opening to get a better view. He saw Lisa open her eyes in shock, but he pulled his head back up when two of the guards approached Lisa's cell. He replaced the metal plate just in case the guards looked up.

Bradley considered the number of guards; he knew there was no way he could take them all out with a single weapon.

"We've got to go too full," he said.

"Well, let's go," Kevin said.

Bradley nodded. "Right. Kevin," he said, "you're with me. We'll take out the guards while Max and Eric watch the entrance. Don't stand in front of the door—stand to the sides and take out anyone else who comes in." He flicked on his radio. "AJ, you stay and keep an eye out up there. Things are about to get hot."

"Roger that," said AJ.

Bradley turned back to his friends. "Everyone clear?"

"Got it," Max said.

"Me, too," Eric said.

"Flash," Bradley asked, hand out to Max.

Max chucked Bradley a small flash grenade. Kevin got out a couple lengths of rope and secured them to the hope in the wall.

"Okay, you lot ready?" Bradley asked. "On my mark."
He grabbed a length of rope and held the metal plate, ready
to lift it up.

"Go," he whispered.

He ripped the steel plate away, putting it onto the
ground of the shaft, and ripped the flash pin out. The guards
looked up as the tiny grenade bounced along the floor.

"Eyes!" Bradley yelled, turning away.

The small flash grenade erupted. The Armazoids fell
back onto the ground from shock as the bright white light
blinded them.

"Go, go, go!" Bradley yelled.

Bradley grabbed hold of the rope. He slid down it,
feeling his hands burning as he landed on the ground. The
Armazoids were still on the ground, blinded, when Bradley
landed and took them out with his M16. Eric landed next to
him, followed closely by Arkalon, Max, and Kevin.

"Move, move!" Bradley yelled. He sprinted over to the
cell holding Kate and Lisa in. He ran over to them, hand
gestures staying to stay inside. Bradley couldn't hear them
through the glass of their cell and his own mask. He ran over
to the cellblock control panel at the end of the corridor as
described by Arkalon. Arkalon was already there, but he
wasn't doing anything.

As Bradley approached, Arkalon looked up. "Because I
have no duties in the prison, the alarm will go off as soon as I
touch this panel."

"But can you open the doors to the cells?"

"Yes, but it will take a few minutes."

"Then let's do this!"

Kevin ran up, just finished with putting gas masks
outside of each cell so that when the doors opened, the

prisoners could put them on. Arkalon reached for the control panel and started fiddling with controls. Immediately, an alarm wailed. Max and Eric, guarding the front entrance, readied for incoming backup guards.

"I can't wait. I can't wait to get at 'em," Eric yelled over the sirens.

Max looked down at his friend's shotgun. "Um, Eric," he said, pointing. "It's not loaded."

"What?" Eric said, looking down at the Winchester. "Oh shit." He started putting shells into the weapon as he flicked on his radio. "Hey, Marco, why did you un-load my gun?"

Marco's voice crackled back. "Do you really think I would give you a loaded weapon, boy?"

Rico immediately ran up to the cell holding Ms. Hogan. She mouthed his name and put her hand to the glass.

"I'm here for you," he said to her.

Bradley turned to Arkalon. "How much longer?"

Arkalon pushed one last button. "You can now open the cells one at a time." He slumped to the ground, exhausted from his injuries and betrayal.

"Kev, open Kate and Lisa's door." Kevin ran over and opened the glass door, and the three women ran out. One by one, the team opened doors, assisting with gas masks, until all prisoners were released. Kevin ran over to a young American Chinese soldier as he out his mask on.

"Thanks. Name's Lieutenant Jefferson," he said.

"No problem," Kevin said, "The more the merrier."

Jefferson ran over to a small room and picked up his rifle and ammunition.

"Ready, when you are," he said.

"Main entrance, now," Bradley yelled. "Move it." He led the way to the main entrance of the cellblock. As he approached the main door, however, blue rays suddenly rained down on it.

"Shit! Get back," Kevin yelled, pulling Bradley back.

Bradley peeked out and saw a heavy ray gun firing down on them. "Oh, don't worry about that," he said. He loaded a grenade into his launcher and slowly started to creep out from behind the door, looking through the scope at the ray gun. He squeezed the trigger of his weapon, launching the small grenade into the air. Flames erupted as Bradley ducked back behind the door.

"Move!" he yelled.

Kevin followed Bradley out of the cell. A long line of people were headed down the corridor.

"Bradley," AJ yelled over the radio. "We got contact."

"Two minutes." Bradley replied.

Bradley heard gunfire through the earpiece. He looked at Kevin as they started sprinting along the corridors and up a flight of stairs, back toward the Armazoid vehicle they had come on. He knew they were close when he heard the ray guns of the Armazoids. He skidded around a corner and came upon AJ ducking behind the cover of the vehicle as a circle of Armazoids slowly closed in.

"Fire," he yelled, taking down the attacking Armazoids. Kevin was right behind him, guns blazing.

Max and Eric hustled the frightened people toward the long hover craft. "Move, move!"

The group of frightened people ran to and loaded the vehicle, the last one jumping on just as Bradley felt the floor suddenly start to vibrate. He looked down the corridor he had just run from and saw more of the Armazoid tanks progressing towards them.

"Oh shit!" he moaned. "Not again!" He turned around and ran up to the alien vehicle, where Arkalon was sitting in the driver's seat, gasping for breath. He threw himself into the passenger seat.

"Come on, move," he yelled. "Move, move, move!"

Arkalon sealed the doors shut and rammed the accelerator down to full.

CJ turned around, looking at the group. His heart started to pound as he looked towards the back of the vehicle. He saw Marsha, his girlfriend, and his mom looking at him.

"CJ!" Marsha yelled in shock.

CJ ran down the vehicle towards them. He grabbed Marsha and pulled her to his chest. His mom close to her as well. Bradley turned around to see Armazoids in another hover gaining on them. Despite the frightened people, Bradley ran to the back of the vehicle, leveled his M16, and blew out the glass of the rear window. He squeezed the trigger, firing at the vehicles as they started to ram them. "Shit!" he gasped.

Bradley reloaded one of the grenades into the launcher. He could see the hatred in the eyes of the pursuing Armazoids. He smiled and pulled the trigger, releasing a grenade that exploded on impact with the chasing vehicle. Bradley watched as the machine rolled over with the explosion.

"Yeah," he yelled. "Proud to be an American!"

He suddenly lost his balance as the vehicle took a sharp right turn at top speed. He ran back to the front of the vehicle. A roadblock of Armazoid vehicles was on what had been their escape route. Arkalon rammed the accelerator down too full as the corridors behind slowly disappeared from sight.

"We've lost 'em," Kevin said after a few minutes.

"For now." Bradley replied. "How far are we now from the elevator?" he asked Arkalon.

"After that last unexpected turn, we are now about two miles from the exit," Arkalon replied. He braked to turn another corner and they entered a huge room full of green crates and tall cranes.

"What's this place?" Bradley asked looking out the front window.

"It's a storage facility," Arkalon replied. "Everything from weapons to food is stored here."

Some of the cranes were moving crates, but Bradley couldn't see their drivers. He hoped they were just robotic. Something caught his eye from the above. Through an open skylight in the roof of the vehicle, he saw one of the green containers suspended fifty feet above their vehicle, dangling from the claw of a crane.

"Ohhhhhhhhhh shit!" he gasped. "Go, Arkalon!"

Arkalon slammed the accelerator down a moment before the huge, green container thundered down from the air and slammed into the ground, exploding as it did so behind them. Kevin looked out the back window at the flames.

Containers started falling like hail from hell, bus-sized comets of death. Bradley watched as the containers landed all around them and thanked his lucky stars Arkalon seemed to be an adept driver. He grabbed onto the pull as they swung around one that had fallen in front of them. Kate and Lisa screamed as the flames gleamed close.

"Jesus, these guys are serious," Kevin said, his voice high in fear.

They finally reached the end of the storage facility, and Arkalon said they had about five minutes to the elevator.

Bradley nodded and flicked on his radio. "Marco, it's Bradley. We're coming up to you in about four minutes," he yelled over the radio.

"Okay, Bradley. We're okay—what the!" The line went silent, then, "What the hell? Jesus Christ! Open fire! Give it all you've got, boys."

"Marco?" Bradley asked.

There was no response from Marco.

"Shit!" Bradley gasped. "Come on, move, move, move!"

"I'm trying," Arkalon said "Please."

Bradley scanned the way ahead. Something caught his eye. He looked more closely to see a small gleam coming towards the vehicle.

"Holy shit!" he yelled. "Incoming."

He reached over and grabbed the wheel. He swung the vehicle to the right, hoping to get the rocket to skim the side or miss them. The rocket ran along the side of the vehicle, throwing it to one side.

"Shit!" Eric yelled.

The Armazoid vehicle flipped and skimmed the floor on its roof until it slowly came to a stop in the middle of the corridor. The smell of burned parts still hung around the inside of the vehicle, which luckily hadn't collapsed on itself.

Bradley slowly opened his eyes and looked around the overturned vehicle. "Ouch!" he moaned, rubbing his back.

"Quick thinking, Bradley," Kevin said, slowly getting up and walking along the roof of the vehicle, which was now the floor. "Anyone hurt?" he yelled as people began to stand up.

People nodded dumbly, holding hurt shoulders or cut arms, but nothing looked serious. AJ suddenly started up and pulled out his gun, shooting out of a broken window toward two advancing Armazoids.

Bradley turned around, knelt down and aimed. The two Armazoids were armed to the teeth, and were too far away for a good shot. Then the ground started to vibrate again. He looked over his shoulder to see the Armazoids from the roadblock catching up with them—in tanks.

"Oh double shit!" He took out two Armazoids in front, then headed toward the other side of the vehicle where Eric was comforting the rescued prisoners.

"I'll get these people out," Eric said.

"Good. Take Max and the rest with you. We'll make a stand here. Be careful, I think Marco is still under attack," Bradley said as he flicked on his radio.

"Marco?" he went. "Marco?"

The radio was dead.

"Shit!" Eric gasped.

"Come on, go" Bradley ordered. He peered around the side of their crashed vehicle at the oncoming enemy. He glanced over to see Eric leading the group away.

"Eric." Bradley said letting his breath out.

"Yeah." He replied looking back.

"Haven't you forgotten something?" Bradley asked.

"What's that?" He replied.

Bradley looked at the shotgun left on the roof of the vehicle.

"Shit." He said, "Sorry."

"Eric, when you approach that corner to the elevator, stay back until I and the rest get there," Bradley said. "Do you understand?"

"Yes, understood, I think." Eric replied, then turned away to continue leading the group away from the imminent battle.

Bradley looked back through the M16 sight onto the vehicles as they pulled up. "Don't fire till I give the word," Bradley ordered.

Kevin grasped his MP5, ready to use it. The Armazoids stepped out of their vehicles and headed towards the overturned vehicle.

"Come out with your hands raised," the Armazoid ordered. "Now, and we will not hurt you."

Bradley placed his hand on the trigger, ready to open fire. The Armazoids got closer and closer.

"Fire!" he screamed at the top of his voice.

The group opened fire onto the Armazoids, mowing them down.

Bradley looked around to ensure Eric and the group had disappeared and turned back to see a tank's turret lined up with their cover.

"Shit." Then much louder, "Incoming!"

Kevin and Bradley quickly ran from the vehicle. The laser powered up in the canon of the tank and launched.

"Down," Bradley yelled.

The laser slammed into the vehicle, which erupted into flames.

"Damn man," Kevin yelled, scrambling back to his feet. "What's with these things?"

"Enjoy yourself," Bradley replied. "I am."

Under cover from the smoke of the fire, Bradley and Kevin ran along the shiny corridor until they caught up with the group. They were almost to the last turn to the elevator. Bradley reloaded his M16 and ran ahead, peeking around the corner.

Dead Armazoids were sprawled everywhere. A few of the vehicles stood empty in the middle of the corridor. Bradley slowly walked around the dead Armazoids, trying to avoid pools of their sticky green blood.

"Marco?" Bradley whispered. "Marco? Where the hell are you?" He slowly crept up to the blue container where he had last seen his friend, tightly holding onto the M16.

Marco jumped up from behind the blue container. "Aggggh," he yelled. "Who wants a piece of me? You lot want to try it? You Viet Cong bastards…"

Bradley fell back, tripping over a dead alien. "Marco, it's me!" he yelled.

Marco stopped and looked at Bradley as he stood holding his M16. "Hey Brad," he said. "Good to see you again."

Bradley was relieved. "Marco, you shit," he said.

Marco laughed. "Let's see them, then," Marco asked. "Where are they?"

Bradley turned around and saw the group coming out from around the corner.

"We just found a few strays." He winked at Marco and indicated Kate with a nod of his head.

Everyone tensed at the sound of feet running up the corridor they had just come from. Bradley ran over to the control box and selected to top floor. "Move it!"

The shutter slowly opened and everyone ran in. Marco turned around and opened fire on the Armazoids as they ran towards the elevator, the shutter seeming to close in slow motion.

"Yaahhhh!" Marco screamed.

"Come on close, shitty thing," Bradley yelled. He knelt beneath Marco and fired his own sidearm.

Finally, the shutters shut, and the brakes clunked off. Everyone stood their panting.

"We kicked those commies' asses!" yelped Aussie.

Bradley felt relieved as the huge plate slowly started to roll up towards the top of the shaft. Laura was speaking into her microphone again, and Bradley wondered absently how the hell she had survived. Where had she even gone while all this was happening? He was too tired to care. They were almost out.

Suddenly there was an enormous explosion and the lift clattered to a halt. After two moments of complete silence, the elevator started dropping into a free-fall. The girls screamed as the emergency brakes came on, causing everyone still standing to fall to their knees.

"Shit! What happened?" Bradley asked.

"They blew the generator," Arkalon stated from his position on the floor.

"What? How do we get out?" Bradley gasped.

Arkalon pulled himself exhaustedly to his feet. "Follow me," he said. He ran to a far corner and lifted a small metal plate. Against the wall outside the elevator were ladder rungs bolted into the chute's wall. "We go down," he said.

"Down? Don't you mean up?" Max asked.

"It's a quicker way, trust me," Arkalon said. "And safer. Trust me."

Bradley turned and shrugged toward Marco. He looked down into the darkness.

"Down the hatch," Eric said brightly.

Bradley, followed by the rest of the group, slowly started to climb down the ladder.

"How far?" Bradley asked Arkalon.

"Not far at all," Arkalon replied. "Trust me."

"I don't," Bradley replied.

As they climbed, smoke began to clog the chute. People began coughing. Bradley could see Arkalon below him, opening a panel and slipping through. He glanced up to see how the rest of the group was fairing and saw red lights flashing on the underside of the elevator. Then he saw the emergency brakes slowly retracting.

"Move fast, people!" he yelled. He slid through the opening Arkalon had made and ended up in a small corridor, moving quickly to the side to accommodate more people. He heard screams in the tunnel as people realized the elevator was dropping towards them.

The last man, a rescued prisoner in his mid-fifties, got stuck in the shaft. His pant leg had caught on the ladder rung, and he couldn't pull it free. Bradley crawled over to pull him through.

"Come on!" He yelled.

Bradley pulled the man, but he didn't have time to get him in.

"Tell my wife-" He yelled.

The elevator slammed into him, yanking him out of the shaft and back into the chute.

Bradley closed his eyes as the sound of the screaming man echoed down the shaft and slowly faded away. A moment later, a huge crash was heard, and heat rushed up the shaft, causing Bradley to lurch back from the opening.

He turned around, frustration and determination and sadness flickering across his face. "Come on, move," he ordered.

They crawled along the narrow corridor for a few minutes in silence, then Arkalon crouched down and removed a panel, revealing a shaft.

"This way?" He asked.

He slid down. As Kevin went down, Bradley looked around. Only Eric was left.

"Coming Eric?" Bradley asked.

"Hang on, won't be a minute." Eric said, "That goes there, and this goes there, and that, no hang on, shit start again, that goes there and this goes there."

Eric looked at Marco and Bradley.

"Won't be a minute."

Eric continued to tie his shoelace.

"I'll see you down there," Marco said. "In about an hour's time."

Bradley slid down and landed in the middle of the group. He looked up into the vent.

"Eric!" He yelled. "Can you hurry up please?"

"Won't be a minute." Eric was heard, "That goes there, and this goes there."

Bradley looked at the silent group.

"What?" he asked, brushing himself off. "Why you all so quiet?"

Bradley looked up to see one of the Armazoids standing there, staring at the group, its ray gun pointed straight at them.

"Well, well, well," it said, "One more to the nice little group."

Bradley looked at Marco. "Shit."

"Well, well, well," the Armazoid said, circling around toward Bradley. "Isn't this nice. I can see a promotion heading my way."

"Yeah, you're really good at this," Bradley replied sarcastically.

The Armazoid looked at Bradley closely, trying to puzzle out the sarcasm. He turned abruptly to the rest of the group.

"Weapons down. Come on—now, he is getting a promotion."

Bradley heard some shuffling coming from the ventilation behind him. He let his breath out and looked at the Armazoid as he smiled at the group.

"One step to the right, please, Marco," Bradley asked, nudging him to the side.

"Right you are, my boy," Marco replied, going along with the push. "Why?"

"Trust me," Bradley replied lightly.

The Armazoid walked towards them, eyes narrowed.

"What?" he said. "What are you talking about?"

"Oh no, nothing," Bradley said, eyes wide in innocence, shaking his head. "You've got us, truly."

The Armazoid smiled, walking closer. He stopped right under the ventilation shaft. The shuffling sounds got louder until Eric came into view.

"Wooooa!" he yelled. "Can't stop, coming through!" Eric shot out of the vent and slammed into the Armazoid feet first. The Armazoid staggered, eyes rolling back in this head, then dropped to the ground holding its groin.

"Jesus Christ." The Armazoid groaned "What's wrong with you things?"

Eric got up and dusted of his pants. He looked down at the Armazoid groaning in pain holding its groin.

"I'm sorry about that." He said to the Armazoid.

Eric went to help the Armazoid up of the ground.

"Quick march soldier!" Marco yelled. "Let's move that rear."

Marco pulled Eric away.

"This way!" Arkalon yelled. He led them down the corridor, to their right there was a set of steps that lead down to a platform. It looked like a monorail station.

"What's this?" Asked Max.

"It's a monorail station." Arkalon replied.

"Where's the ticket machine?" Eric asked.

Marco looked down at Eric.

"It's over there." He said. "One adult one child."

"On my way." Eric replied.

Marco reached out pulling Eric back by the ear.

"Back you come boy."

Bradley looked up the tunnel and caught a glimpse of light approaching, it was one of the monorails.

"Hide," he ordered. "Marco, cover the stairs!"

"Sir!" Marco replied.

Bradley ran down the platform towards the end, spun around and lay down on the ground. He looked at the long line of lights as the monorail train rolled into the station and sighted the driver in his scope. The train looked almost entirely empty. Kevin got down next to him, aiming at the doors to shoot the few passengers as they exited. As the doors opened, Bradley shot the driver and Kevin shot the passengers. They all dropped lifeless. Max ran up and searched the train, calling out a "Clear!" when he found it empty.

Marco ran onto the monorail followed by the armed men and survivors. Bradley got comfortable in the driver seat. He glanced at the station entrance and saw Armazoids charging down the stairs.

"Ready or not, here we go!" Bradley yelled and pushed the lever to bring the train out of idle and begin acceleration.

"How far do we go?" Bradley asked Arkalon.

"Two stops from here."

Bradley sped along the tracks. He gave it full power, feeling his body pushed back into the chair at the continued acceleration. Bradley watched as the lights passed the front window.

"How far we got to go?" he asked Arkalon.

"Not this one." He replied. "The next."

"Got it."

The monorail approached the first station. It was swarming with Armazoids.

"Shit!" he gasped and powered the monorail through the station, heading back into the tunnels as laser rays bounced off the vehicle.

"Stand by for the next stop," he yelled back to the group.

Kevin stood up, holding onto the MP5. They approached the next station. Bradley applied the brakes just in time to stop before passing the platform of the next stop. The station is empty, no Armazoids on the platform, nothing. At the top of the platform steps, a stationary Armazoid weapon was poised at the top of the steps, ready to blow them away.

"Holy shit!" Bradley yelled. "Down!"

The Armazoid opened fire on the top of the monorail. The rays burnt through the clips holding it to the overhead line and it erupted into flames. Bradley felt the front carriage start to drop down.

"Brace!" He screamed.

He fell onto the control panel.

"Everyone down!" Kevin yelled.

The front of the monorail dropped down below into the ditch.

He realized Bradley wasn't there and ran back down the train.

Kevin ran down the carriage of the monorail as the nose dropped down into the ditch below the station. Lights flickered as he saw Bradley in the front.

"Bradley?" Kevin yelled.

Bradley looked up feeling the stick sticking into his stomach.

"Okay," he said, coughing. "Still alive."

"Come on," Kevin said. "I'll help you up."

Bradley slowly placed his foot onto the control box. He hauled his body off the shiny floor as Kevin reached down, put his arm out to help him and pulled him up. Bradley stood up, shook his head.

"Stay down," Kevin ordered.

Bradley knelt down by the rest of the group. "Bring me up to speed."

"That," Kevin said, gesturing to the huge gun. "We can't get past it."

"Can't we head along the tunnel and get off at the next station?" Max asked.

"No," Bradley replied, looking up at the Armazoid machine ray gun as he rubbed his head. "There are going to be those things at every platform." He thought for a moment. "Anyone got that launcher?"

"I do," Marco yelled. "Here we are, kid."

Bradley reloaded his M16 and looked up at the Armazoid gun as it continued hammering the monorail.

"Give me the launcher," a Chinese man demanded.

Marco handed the man the launcher. He armed it, ready to open fire onto the machine ray gun.

"Ready? If you've got the shot, take it," Bradley instructed.

"Got it," he replied to the order.

The man dived through the smoke and aimed, but then moved further into the open.

"He's gotta take the shot now or he's gonna be seen," Bradley muttered.

Suddenly the smoke shifted, giving the alien gunner a perfect view of the Chinese man and his launcher. He didn't have time to launch the weapon.

"No," Marco screamed as the man was blown to the floor, the launcher skidding away, still operable.

"Shit," Bradley gasped. "Cover me."

"What?" Kevin yelped "No!"

Bradley didn't reply to Kevin as he dived out onto the platform towards the launcher. The group opened fire onto the Armazoid, distracting it while Bradley quickly aimed and fired. The rocket whistled through the air and slammed into the weapon. Flames erupted killing the Armazoid in one.

"Come on!" Marco yelled. "Move them rears!"

The group ran up the stairs. "This way," Arkalon called.

Bradley ran along the corridor as Kevin ran behind, making sure they all stayed together. Bradley slowly raised his fist and stopped the group. He raised his M16 and slowly crept along the wall of the ship. The way ahead didn't feel right. Bradley peeked around the corner to see the other elevator with another one of the Armazoid vehicles there.

"Move," he yelled. He ran up to the vehicle. "Jump on, people," he ordered.

Then he suddenly stopped. He felt the ground beneath him lurch. "What's that?" he asked.

"They're starting up," Arkalon said. "Not long now."

"What do you mean?" Bradley asked.

"They are preparing to move the ship," Arkalon replied.

"Let's get out of here," Max said immediately.

"I agree," Lisa replied.

"Me, too," Colin said.

Bradley ran off the vehicle over to the control box. He selected the top floor, rubbing his hands. The huge shutter slowly started to roll up into the open position. Bradley looked down at his hands as he started to glow green.

"We're resizing," Arkalon replied.

Arkalon slowly moved the vehicle into the freight elevator, and the doors closed behind them, slowly closing the ship from view.

"Bye, bye," Colin said. "Fucking place."

"For once, Colin, I agree," Bradley said.

The brakes clunked off one after the other. Bradley sat down in the seat next to Lieutenant Jefferson. "Was this in the job description?" he asked.

"Yes, it was," he replied. "But I never thought I'd live to see this."

Bradley laughed. "I might sign up after this."

"I think we are going to need all the help we are going to get," Jefferson replied, "If any more of these things come."

"They won't," Bradley said. "They won't."

The elevator came to the top of the shaft. Bradley looked around the top of the huge ship. "Where is the edge?" he asked.

"This way," Arkalon ordered.

The group looked along the top of the huge ship. "Come on, come on," Bradley mumbled.

***

Arkalon put the brakes on, slowing down as they came to the ridge of the ship. Bradley stepped down from the vehicle ripping the mask of his face. "Oh, that's nice, fresh air," he said. He looked over the edge of the ship, down on to the city. "Where would you say we are?" he asked.

Kevin scanned the ground below him, trying not to stumble. "Careful," Bradley said.

"I'd say we are about a mile from that cop shop; maybe a bit more," Kevin replied.

"Good," Bradley replied, "Right. I need some more M16 ammo."

"What are you doing?" Kevin asked. "Why can't we jump now?"

Jefferson ran over. "How do we get down?" he asked.

Bradley looked around. He stared at the skyline of the city to see a small Black Hawk helicopter flying over the city. He swung his head around looking at Jefferson's assault vest. He looked at the small, yellow canister in the vest. "Thank you," he said reaching in pulling the flare out. He kneeled down and looked over his shoulder as the group stood quietly on the top of the ship. Bradley looked at Kevin as he ripped the white cord out of the yellow canister.

The helicopter pilot looked over at the top of the ship. He looked at the red smoke blowing up into the air. "Look," he said, turning towards the ship. He looked down onto the deck of the ship to see the group on the top. "We're going in," he said.

Bradley smiled as the helicopter flew towards the ship.

"Right, who's going in this?" Kevin asked.

"Em," Bradley replied. "Kate, Lisa, and Ms. Hogan are jumping the rest on that."

"I'll take Marsha," CJ yelled. "Mom can go with someone."

"I'm ok with that," Bradley said. "Can I have any spare M16 rounds, please?"

"Right," Kevin replied. "Wait. What about you? Why do you want more ammo?"

"I'm going back," Bradley said.

"WHAT?" Kevin freaked "NO YOU CAN'T WERE LUCKY TO HAVE MADE IT THIS FAR!"

"Do you remember what shit face said in the warehouse?" Bradley asked.

"What?" Eric asked, "What have I done now?"

"Oh God," Kevin said remembering.

"Yes," Bradley replied. "So, I'm going back with my friend here."

"I'm coming," Kevin insisted.

"No, you can't," Bradley snapped. "Listen to me, you need to get Rico, Kate, Lisa, and Ms. Hogan, and the others, back down to the ground."

"Look, let me come. Rico can take them down," Kevin replied, trying to persuade Bradley.

"No," Bradley yelled putting his hands on his shoulders looking at him in the eye. "Go, get them down and get to that cop shop and, for God's sake, stay off the main streets if those things are out in force now."

"Ok," Kevin replied in a subdued voice. He turned around as Max and Eric walked over.

"Are we off, then?" Eric asked.

"Not all of us," Kevin stated.

"Why? Who's staying?" Max asked.

Kevin looked at Bradley.

"Bradley?" Max said. "Why are you staying?"

"In a short while these people are going to relay our location to their home planet. If that signal is sent, we would be invaded by more of these things and I'm not having that," Bradley said, folding his arms.

"There will be other ships out there," Eric said.

"Even if there are any more out there looking for us. At least with the signal cut, it will buy us some more time to prepare for another attack," Bradley replied.

He nodded his head as the black hawk touched down on the deck. Jefferson helped the stricken people onto the machine.

"How many are left?" Kevin asked.

"Just me, Lisa, Ms. Hogan, and Rico," Kate yelled, "Plus Marsha and CJ's mom."

"Good" Bradley said. "Right. Who can double and give Kate and Lisa a chute each?"

"I can," a voice yelled.

Kate looked at one of the kits attached to the man. He handed it over to her.

"What is that?" she queried.

"It's a parachute," he replied.

"A what?" she yelled.

"A parachute. You're going to drop back down to Earth my darling," Bradley smiled at her.

"Oh, no, I'm not," she said.

"Oh yes, you are," Bradley said. "It's the only way."

"Aren't there escape chutes?" Eric asked.

"Yes, over there" Marco pointed "Go and release them for me, my man."

"Right you are." Eric replied.

Eric started walking off into nothing.

"Back you come boy." Marco said grabbing him by the ear.

Bradley turned around as Jefferson waved the helicopter off the stand. He watched as the helicopter flew over them. He looked up at the frightened people as they looked out of the open door.

"What's that?" Eric asked.

Bradley squinted in the evening orange sunlight to see a small, blue light traveling through the sky. Kate shut her eyes as the blue rocket slammed into the Black Hawk. Bradley watched in dread as the helicopter spun out of control and slammed into the skyscraper, slowly falling down the side.

"Bollocks!" Marco yelled.

The Black Hawk helicopter swung out of control spiraling to the ground. Screaming could be heard in his imagination. The machine disappeared below the ship. The last thing to be heard is a slight rumble from the explosion. Bradley stood in shock.

"Brad!" Marco yelled over.

Bradley didn't say a word as he stood in shock.

"Brad!" Marco said again.

Bradley stared into space.

"BRADLEY!" Marco yelled again, "Stay with me soldier!"

Bradley shook his head out of the dream. He stormed over to the group as they stood by the edge of the ship. The only way down know is to jump using Marco's survival kit he gave to him.

"I'll take Ms. Hogan!" Rico yelled. "I'll be ok."

Bradley nodded as the group continued taking off parachutes and handing them to the single droppers. Bradley looked at Kevin and the rest of his group. "Come here, boys?" he asked. He placed his arms around the group, hugging them. "We've come this far. For God's sake, don't fuck it up here."

"We'll be ok," Eric said.

Bradley kept his feelings to himself, struggling to hold them in. "Sorry if I've been a bit picky today," he said.

Kevin looked up at Bradley. "Bradley, you haven't been picky" Kevin said. "If it wasn't for you, we'd all be dead."

"Me, too," Eric said. "Don't even know what it means but I second it."

Bradley let the small group go, it was hard to do so but it had to be done. He looked at Kate and Lisa as they stood by Marco. He watched as Kate suddenly started to run over. She leapt into Bradley's arms. She placed her lips on his as Kevin watched in amazement. Eric smiled as she let Bradley go.

"I knew she always loved him." He said.

"Right," Bradley said in shock. "I'll see you boys later for that drink."

"What?" Kate gasped.

"I'll tell you later," Bradley replied, "Max don't forget you owe me."

251

CJ turned and looked at Marsha. "I'm not dropping, either." CJ said slowly.

"WHAT?" his mom gasped "HERE TAKE MINE!"

"I have to go with Bradley," CJ said. He reached into his pocket. His mom watched as he kneeled down on the deck of the ship. "Marsha," he quietly asked. Bradley looked over as he held onto the M16. CJ slowly opened a small ring box. Marsha placed her hands over her cheeks and looked down at the engagement ring.

"I'm sorry. This is the wrong place, but I was going to ask you when we would have been in The Bahamas next week. However, I think that has been cancelled for now," CJ said. There was a short pause. CJ tried to steady his nerves. "Marsha," CJ said slowly. "Will you make me the happiest man in the world? Will you marry me?" he asked.

Marsha nodded as she wiped a few tears away from her eyes. "Yes," she wept. "Yes, I will." CJ slowly pulled the silver engagement ring out and put it on Marsha's finger. He looked up at his mum.

"Oh my god!" she gasped. "My little boy's getting married." The group started clapping as CJ and Marsha kissed. It had to be done.

"Right. I've got to go," CJ finally said. He looked at Marsha and his mum as they both had solo parachutes on. "For fuck's sake be safe," he yelled.

"Right," Bradley yelled. "CJ, AJ, you're with me."

"I'm ready," AJ yelled.

"Me, too," Jefferson yelled. "I'm coming to"

Marco looked over at Bradley. "Marco," Bradley asked.

"Yeah boy?" he yelled.

"Be careful." Bradley ordered.

"What about Colin?" Max asked.

"He is with me," a voice yelled.

"And Ms. Hogan is with Rico?" Bradley asked.

"I got her," Rico replied.

The group prepared for the drop.

"Who's taking Aussie?" Marco asked. He looked at Aussie as he stood there, looking dazed.

"He can go by himself," Kevin replied as he handed Aussie the chute.

"What's going on, now?" Eric asked.

"Stand here," Marco ordered. "Stop chatting."

"What are we doing?" Eric asked again. "Inform me please."

He looked over the side of the ship as Marco hooked his arm around him. "Are we going to jump?" he asked.

"No, Eric," Marco said, "We're going to fly."

"Argh, cool," Eric joked "Which way?"

"That way," Marco said pointing down.

"Not that far," Eric replied. He looked over at Aussie as he looked down onto Manhattan. "You ok, Aussie?" Marco yelled.

"Yeah," Aussie replied. "Just like 'Nam."

"God, not another one!" Eric moaned.

"Hey," Marco snapped reaching over tapping him on the head, "Once a soldier always a soldier."

Bradley looked at the group as they prepared to drop. "Right. I'm off," Bradley said.

"Take it easy," Kevin said. "Oh, and I want you back. I think its Downtown Haven tonight."

"Damn right," Bradley replied. "Get to the police station and wait there or, if you can, Queensboro Bridge, but do not wait for me."

Bradley got into the Armazoid vehicle, followed by CJ, AJ, Jefferson, and Arkalon. He started up the engine as Arkalon stood holding onto the pole.

"Right," he said. "Let's get this done."

Bradley started up the engine to the vehicle. He slammed the accelerator down as Kevin turned around and watched it disappear along the top of the ship. He turned around again and looked at Lisa as she looked over the edge of the ship down onto the city, trembling with fear.

"You guys ready?" Kevin asked.

"Ready when you are!" Marco yelled "I cannot wait for this shit."

Kate looked down as Lisa stood trembling, almost being sick.

"Are you two ok?" Kevin asked, placing his hand on Lisa's arm.

"I, I, I am fine," she wept. "No, I'm not."

"Ready," Marco yelled. "On three. One, two… three."

Marco and the rest of the group leaped off the top of the ship.

"DI KA RAMA BUNGA!" Marco yelled.

Kevin listened to Marsha as she yelled at the top of her voice while ripping out her parachute cord. Kevin looked over the side of the ship as the red parachutes all opened up one after the other. It was a scene he would never forget. Lisa stood looking down at the ground as Kevin looked at her. "I knew you wouldn't," he said to her.

"How did you know?" she wept.

"I just knew," Kevin said. "Remember gym class a few years ago? You were too scared to jump of that vaulting box."

Lisa burst out crying.

"Right. You're gonna jump," Kevin ordered. "Remember -rip this cord out and it will release the chute and before you know it, you will be down on the ground with me again."

Lisa nodded as she wiped the tears away from her face.

"Ready?" Kevin said.

Lisa shook her head. "I can't."

"Ready- on three. You can do this, Lisa," Kevin yelled. "And when we get back to Haven it's us and Bradley in the bar."

Lisa gently nodded.

"Ok, ready," he yelled in her ear. "One, two…"

Kevin pushed Lisa off the top of the ship. He heard her scream as her chute opened out.

"Ha, ha," Kevin laughed. "I'm a bastard, aren't I?"

He looked at the chutes as they floated to the ground. He took a deep breath, and leapt off the side, pulling the ripcord. He felt his body slow down as the chute opened up. Slowly he descended towards the ground. He felt the cool evening air blowing into his face as the ground got closer and closer. "Oh, I love this," he said as he pulled his legs in, ready to land on the street. He looked at the sidewalk below. That is his target. He hunched his legs up slamming into the ground. There was a slight tweak of pain, but that went within a few seconds. Kevin rolled out of the parachute swiping the sidearm looking around. No Armazoids can be seen. The coast is clear for the time being. The smell of the burning vehicles came to his nose again. He looked down at the group as they stood by the entrance to an alleyway looking around for any Armazoids. Cars had been slammed in all directions by the Armazoid tanks. Kevin unplugged the chute from his body.

"You ok Kevin?" Marco asked.

"Yeah. Must do that again sometime," he laughed.

Kevin looked around.

"Where's Eric?"

Marco let his breath out turning his head. Kevin looked as well. He looked to see Eric, his shoot is stuck over one of the streetlamps, his legs kicking back and forth. One of the Chinese men was climbing up the streetlamp to release him. Lisa ran over to Kevin. She opened her hand and slapped him on the face. "Three, he says," she yelled. "We'll jump on three."

"I'm sorry," Kevin said.

"You could have killed me," Lisa yelled.

"But you survived, didn't you?" Kevin said. "Told you could do it, didn't I."

"Woah!" Eric yelled falling, "Ouch."

Marco looked up at the ship through his binoculars. He saw something moving. "What the...?" he said quietly. He stared up through the lenses as a small cannon rolled out from underneath the ship. It seemed to be pointing down towards the ground. He felt his heart pound wondering what the hell it was going to do. He heard Kevin and Lisa as they continued squabbling about the jump down. "Guys?" Marco asked.

Neither Kevin nor Lisa heard him. Marco looked at the ground as he held on to his binoculars.

"GUYS!" he yelled.

"WHAT?" Lisa and Kevin said simultaneously.

They both looked at Marco and then up at the ship.

"What is it?" Kevin asked, pulling the small set of binoculars out of the survival kit. He zoomed the lenses and looked up at the ship.

"The hell?" he exclaimed.

He looked up at the cannon and saw a light blue light building up on it.

"Oh, hell no," Marco said.

"Oh hell, yes," Kevin replied. He put the binoculars back into his pocket as the cannon fired down towards the ground.

"Come on," Marco yelled. "MOVE IT THAT WAY NOW!"

They looked at the long beam as it slammed into the ground by the group. It slowly started traveling towards them.

"Come on," he yelled.

Kevin pushed Lisa along as the intense heat from the ray burnt them.

"Shit, shit, and double shit!" Kevin said.

Marco ran ahead as the blue ray continued to follow them up the alleyway. Kevin passed Ms. Hogan as she ran along the alleyway with Rico. The ray incinerated anything in its path. The small grey dustbins melted down to the ground. Ms. Hogan stumbled over as the ray honed in on her. Rico looked at her as she lay on the floor and looked back as she felt the heat burn the back of her neck. Rico ran over to her. "Come on," he said, picking her up. He yelled in pain as the raging heat burned his back, but he hauled Ms. Hogan along the alley.

Kevin looked up as Rico hugged her. "Rico, will you marry me?" Ms. Hogan asked out of fear and stress.

"I'd love to," he replied. "Few months' time?"

Ms. Hogan looked at the burn on his back.

"Ouch," she said.

"It's nothing" Rico said. "Been in worse."

The group came to a stop halfway down the dirty alley. He watched as the energy disappeared back into the ship.

"Ok, take five," Marco panted.

"I'm getting too old for this." Rico said.

Marco looked at Rico.

"You're getting old?!" He yelled.

Kevin leant against the wall.

"You ok?" Marco asked.

"Yeah," Kevin replied struggling for breath. "How about you?" he asked Rico.

Rico looked up at him. "It's just a burn. I'll be ok. I've had worse."

Ms. Hogan looked at Rico. "I love you," she went quietly.

Kevin rolled his eyes. "Come on," he said. "We have to keep going before one of them things comes back."

The group continued along the dirty alleyway, looking up every now and them at the underneath of the ship in case any more of the spikes reappeared.

***

Arkalon pulled up at nondescript, white double doors. "It's here."

CJ stepped off, M16 at the ready, followed by Jefferson, who sported the C4 charges and detonator. AJ, CJ, and Bradley covered either side of the door.

"Open it, Arkalon," Bradley demanded.

Arkalon ran up to the door as Bradley knelt down, ready to go in.

"Right, let's get these planted, blow it, and get the fuck out of here," AJ said.

"I agree," Jefferson said, nodding.

Bradley watched as the two doors rolled open. "Move!"

He advanced through the opening doors holding his M16 machine gun, knowing he hadn't many magazines left to use. In the center of the room a huge generator hummed, electricity surging round it as a large satellite-type dish began to unfold and push through two hatches in the ceiling that were rolling back, revealing the afternoon sky.

"This is it?" Bradley asked.

"Yes," Arkalon replied. "Yes, that's it."

A sudden blast of rays had Bradley diving for the floor. They seemed to come out of nowhere.

A voice echoed through the room. "Human boy, how nice to meet you!" Circo stepped out from behind a shelf.

"Yeah, nice to meet you too, alien thing," Bradley yelled through the mask.

"Tell me," Circo said. "What brings you to this ship then?"

"We know why you're here," Bradley yelled. "You think one of your crafts crash landed here."

"Correct," Circo said.

"Why didn't you come here in peace? We may have been able to help you."

"We Armazoids don't work like that," Circo said. "Anyway, we tried contacting your leaders but had no luck."

Out of the corner of his eye, Bradley could see his AJ and CJ hiding behind another shelf, not noticed by the Armazoid leader. "Oh, so that's who you are?" Bradley said.

"What was that?" Circo yelled.

"Nothing," Bradley replied, struggling to yell through the gas mask.

"When are you transmitting?" Bradley yelled.

"Any minute now, and then this dump of planet will be ours for a short period of time and you humans will cease to exist."

Bradley signaled to the group. He held three fingers out slowly counting them down to one as he reached for the small C4 charges in the pouches on his belt.

"Fire!" he yelled.

The group dived out from the entrance and opened fire onto the Armazoids as they stood pointing their weapons down from the above. Bradley coughed as he set the M16 to full automatic fire. He only has a few magazines left. He squeezed the trigger and fired rounds from the weapon. He snuck beside the control box looking at a small set of steps leading along the side of the satellite generator.

"Aha!" he said, reloading the weapon.

He reached into his pocket and pulled out the charges as Jefferson, AJ, and CJ fired onto the shooting Armazoids.

"BRADLEY WE GOT YOU COVERED!" AJ yelled, "DO IT!"

Circo watched them on the camera as Bradley slipped down the side, laying small charges ready to blow the shit out of the machine.

"Come on take him out." Circo ordered. "If he blows that."

"Were trying." The Armazoid replied.

Bradley laid the last charge and slowly walked up the stairs, keeping his head down from the rays from the attacking Armazoids. He reached into his pocket and pulled the detonator out. He took one last look around as one of the Armazoids shot down at him. He dove to the ground, dropping the small detonator.

"Oh fuck!" He shrieked, "No, no, no, come on don't do this to me no."

Circo looked at Bradley as he struggled to pull it out of the tiny cracks in the floor. The Armazoids continued shooting at him from above. Bradley watched as the huge brakes clinked and clanked off. The huge metal plate slowly raised the satellite dish towards the top of the ship.

"Shit!" he gasped. "Come on, no."

He struggled with his fingers in trying to get the detonator as CJ, AJ, and Jefferson fired onto the shooting Armazoids.

Bradley looked up as the dish slowly got to the top of the ship. The huge fans started to open up, pointing into the air, ready to transmit the signal back to Armazoid billions of light years away. Bradley wrenched his fingers through the sharp metal slits as he tried to reach for the detonator. He struggled with all his might as Jefferson, followed by CJ and AJ, ran over. The Armazoid looked through his scope as AJ ran towards Bradley. He pulled the trigger and fired the ray through the air. The ray slammed into AJ's back.

"NOOOOOOOOO," CJ yelled.

AJ fell onto the floor, blood running from his body. The whiteness of his eyes gleamed as his body fell to the floor. Bradley ignored the scream from AJ, he knew what had just happened to him.

"Got it!" Bradley yelled, pulling the detonator out.

He looked up as the satellite reached the top of the ship and he pushed the small red button down, not wasting a second. The huge antenna finished unfolding. The group looked up as huge explosions rocketed through the shaft. The brakes on the satellite's metal lift exploded. CJ grieved over AJ as he lay on the ground dead, and as he looked up at the explosions and the fire raining down on the group.

"Down!" He yelled at the top of his voice.

Bradley took another look up to see the huge elevator dropping down. The doors were sealed shut.

"Oh shit, now, where?" Bradley asked.

"This way," Arkalon said, running down a small staircase underneath the satellite.

"CJ," Bradley yelled.

CJ stood looking at AJ. "I knew him all my life," he quietly said.

"CJ!" Bradley shrieked "COME ON THAT THING IS PLUNGING"

CJ turned around and ran over to Bradley as the huge satellite dish thundered down the shaft. Fire raged from all corners. Bradley felt the intense heat as they ran along the shiny corridor away from the fireball behind them. He heard the elevator slam into the ground. He peeked over his shoulder as the fireball chased them along the maintenance tunnel. He looked ahead again to see a set of open doors.

"Quickly," Arkalon yelled "It's not that far from here!"

Bradley ran through the door. Arkalon turned around, pushing the tiny buttons on the door. The doors slowly closed as the fireball slammed into it. CJ gained his breath back. He clenched his fist as Jefferson leant against the wall.

"Shit, fuck, shit!" CJ yelled.

"CJ," Bradley sympathized.

CJ slowly turned and looked at Bradley. "I'm sorry," he said remorsefully, nodding at Bradley.

"Let's get the fuck out of here," Bradley replied.

CJ nodded. Bradley looked at Jefferson. "You ok?" he asked.

"Yeah. Loving it," Jefferson replied "Just what I signed up for"

"Come on," Bradley said again. "Let's try and get out of here."

***

In an entirely different part of the ship, three Armazoids reviewed several radar screens.

"We got incoming," one yelled.

Another hit a button, alerting three Spacefighters on the launch pad to take off. One by one, the jets launched off the deck and flew over the Hudson toward the F-16s that had encroached on their airspace.

"Let's go," one Armazoid pilot said.

The three crafts approached the F-16s, not even attempting to be discrete. In a matter of moments and three laser blasts later, three charred hulls of what had previously been the US military's elite bomb plane crashed into the Hudson. On impact with the water, their payloads exploded, exploding water and debris into the air almost a mile high.

"Incoming from four o'clock." The radio blared to life, cutting short the victory laps of the Armazoid pilots. They pivoted to see the air force jets trying their best to get close to the huge spaceship.

"Let's get 'em," one Armazoid said.

This time they let the jets get off a couple rockets. The explosives bounced off the mother ship's hull, nut even scratching it. The pilots were incinerated before the surprise left their faces.

Kevin ran down the back alley, trailed by a lonely Colin. Marco was way ahead with his boys and most of the survivors. Rico and Ms. Hogan were most probably ahead as well—they hadn't stopped holding hands since she had been released from the holding cell.

Kevin kicked a piece of trash out of the way, lost in his thoughts. A sudden thrumming noise made him look up, and he stared in disbelief at one of the Armazoid Spacefighters hovering above the alleyway. Its propulsion systems blew cyclones of garbage in the narrow space.

"Oh fuck!" Kevin said. "MOVE." He pushed Colin along the alleyway as the blue rays started blasting out of the ship's cannon. Kevin leapt forward as the concrete from the buildings on either side tumbled to the ground, choking the air with a thick dust. He coughed as he helped Colin along.

Making it to the corner, they saw the police station to their right in the distance. People were running everywhere as Armazoid tanks and other vehicles rolled closer. Soldiers were standing their ground by the barricades.

He heard a sudden scream. He turned to see a young Asian girl with a backpack cowering behind a streetlamp as an Armazoid approach her, grinning. It raised its laser gun.

Kevin swiped his MP5 and looked through the sight. "Hey, you!"

The Armazoid turned and looked at Kevin, who shot him straight through the forehead of the suit it is wearing. It slowly collapsed to the ground.

"Thank you," the girl called out, running over.

"No problem," Kevin said. "Follow us!" They started running towards Marco's group ahead. Kevin could see Lisa, Eric, Max, and Kate, and he pushed himself to catch up.

Kevin ran up past Lisa. "Lisa, come on," he yelled as Marco gave Max a swat on the butt as he passed and laughed.

They were going to make it to the barricade ahead of the Armazoids!

He glanced back and couldn't see Lisa. He skidded to a halt, glancing at each face running by. Where was she? Kevin heard a scream and zeroed in on Lisa lying on the floor, looking back at the Armazoids as they got closer. She has fallen over and hurt her ankle.

"Shit!" he gasped.

Kevin sprinted toward her. She was holding her ankle and sobbing. Kevin landed down next to Lisa. He looked at her crying.

"Are you alright?" he yelled.

"I guess so." She replied, "I have twisted my ankle."

"Not to worry." Kevin said.

Without hesitating, he hoisted her over his shoulder and started running back toward the station.

After a few seconds, Lisa said, "I've been wanting to ask you something for a long time."

"Oh, yeah? What is that?" Kevin asked, panting.

It took Lisa a few seconds to get her confidence up. "Will you go out with me when we get home?" she asked. "I've always liked you."

Kevin panted for breath as he hauled her along, stumbling to the side when a laser gun blasted too close.

"I'd love to," he finally replied. "I was going to ask you, anyway."

"Really?" Lisa said. Kevin could hear the smile on her face even if he couldn't see it.

"No," Kevin joked. "But well, you never know. How about Bradley and Kate?"

"What do you think?" She replied.

Ahead of them, Max looked back just in time to see an Armazoid aiming towards Kevin. The Armazoid smiled.

"Perfect." He said.

He fired at Kevin's retreating back. Kevin suddenly froze with pain. Max looked on in horror. Eric gawking, mouth wide open with shock. Lisa gasped as Kevin came to a sudden stop. He felt the pain fly up through his back, Lisa fell to the ground when he collapsed. She knelt over his still body, the blood darkening his shirt and pooling beneath him.

Lisa huddled over him in shock, looking on absently as the Armazoids fired on the rest of the group—her friends.

"Shit!" Max yelled. He dropped to the ground, hiding behind two garbage bins on the side of the street. He could see Kevin in the middle of the street, blood running into the gutters, Lisa still as a statue over him.

"Leave him," a voice said from behind.

"Fuck no!" Max yelled. "He or Bradley wouldn't leave us if we were in this position. We are going to finish this together."

Max looked at Kevin, thinking furiously as laser rays continued slamming into the garbage cans, burning through them.

"Right," he ordered, looking at the group. "Cover me."

"Wait," Eric said. He handed Kevin a small yellow canister.

"Thanks." Kevin ripped the pin from the smoke grenade, allowing his MP5 to dangle by his side. "Ready?" he yelled.

The group nodded. Max launched the grenade out towards Kevin, a dense black smoke obscuring everything. He ran out, crouched down, as Eric and the group fired onto the Armazoids. Max felt the dense smoke entering his lungs but reached Lisa and Kevin unharmed.

"Come on," Max said, roughly grabbing Lisa's arm. "Move it."

Lisa stumbled up and limped towards the group behind the garbage cans. Rico ran towards her, helping her the last few steps.

Max looked down on Kevin, his eyes still barely open.

"Sa-sa... save Lisa," Kevin mumbled. "Tell Brad, Brad, he is a good." His eyes rolled up in his head and he lost consciousness.

"Oh no, you don't," Max yelled down to him. He strained to lift him, dropping him roughly when a blue beam shot through the smoke and melted the pavement next to them.

"Shit!" he gasped.

Lisa arrived at the bins with Rico and ducked down behind them. She looked through the opening, trying to make out what was happening in the slowly fading smoke. Eric was next to her, squinting in the same direction. A Spacefighter still hovered above them, but its attention had been diverted to shooting at other people. Eric smiled as Max ran out of the smoke, Kevin across his back.

"Yes!" Eric yelled.

"Come on. Go," Max yelled over at them. "Move it!"

Eric put his arm around Lisa helping her along the road as Max struggled with Kevin. Two US marines ran up to them.

"You guys okay?" one yelled with fear.

"No," Max said. "My friend has been shot by them things."

"Shit!" one marine said.

The two marines helped Max carry Kevin along to a waiting ambulance. They placed him on a gurney, Kevin's blood had already stained their uniforms. The two paramedics strapped him down and one took his pulse, shaking his head. "He's lost too much blood, and we don't have any to give him."

Max and Eric watched as the shooting started again from behind. The medics placed plastic patches onto his chest, connecting the machine to him, still trying to stop the blood. They shocked his body time and time again. The heart monitor showed a straight monophonic line. The medic pounded down on Kevin's chest as the machine continued to show a flat line. Nothing could be done.

"No," Max gasped.

The medics gently shook their heads. One put a comforting hand on Max's shoulder, but he shrugged it off, wiping a few tears away.

Marco walked over to the group. "You boys okay?" he asked. "Got these shits to deal with now." His eyes widened at the sight of Kevin, pale and without a heartbeat.

"What the-" He gasped, "Give me a, son of a bitch."

For a moment, Max couldn't hear the gunshots and the screams and the encroaching tanks. He just stared at his friend's lifeless body, still thinking Kevin was going to get up and start shooting those damn things.

Marco shook his arm, his words sounding distant. Finally, he heard him say, "Max, listen to me. Max? Come on, we got a job to do."

Max's mind focused and his eyes narrowed on the street ahead of him.

***

President Henderson looked up at the screen. He felt his body sweating with stress.

"Sir the attack from the F Sixteens has failed." Reeves said remorsefully "The alien invaders are now using air to air machines."

President Henderson didn't know what to say.

General Reeves sat up trying to capture President Henderson's attention.

"Sir," he said, "Them things are arriving at the Police HQ, are we going on DEFCON One"

Henderson looked down at the floor of the emergency briefing room.

"Sir!" William snapped trying to grab Henderson's attention

William kept his eyes on the President. He can see he isn't going to make a decision within the next couple of seconds.

"Sir." Reeves said

William looked at the President.

"SIR!" William screeched.

The room jumped to the yell from William.

"Do it." Henderson ordered in one.

President Henderson stormed out of the Emergency briefing Room as Admiral Johnson picked up the telephone on the table next to him. He held it to his ear.

Captain Kirk Wakeland stormed in the *Anchorage*'s command center. He looked at the submariners.

"Sir, we got orders," a comm crewman yelled to him, running up.

Wakeland looked down at the piece of paper offered to him. His heart rate increased reading the messages. He took a moment to gather himself before looking up at the expectant crew.

"Okay people. Manhattan."

The crew scrambled to stand up and salute. "Yes sir!"

"All hands-on deck" Wakeland ordered.

Moments later, the *Anchorage* blasted out of the cold ocean. The water rushed off its sides. The hatches on the top of the Anchorage opened up. Wakeland stared down at the screen in front of him.

"Fire," he said, his calm, clear voice not betraying a hint of the fear and responsibility he felt for following ordering a nuclear strike on New York City.

After entering in the clearance codes, the crewman replied, "Detonation T-10 minutes, sir."

***

Bradley looked up as they came to the end of the maintenance tunnel. He looked through a small vent leading up into a small room.

"Ready?" he asked. He clenched his fist and kicked the small tunnel cover off its hinges. He peeked his head out and looked around the empty room.

"What is this place?" CJ asked, jumping out.

"I don't know," Bradley quietly said.

"It's the control room." Arkalon said.

A screen filled one wall, displaying a blueprint of...the ship, Bradley suddenly realized.

"What the hell is that?" he asked. He clicked on the digital mouse next to him and pulled up what appeared to be a view of a US army satellite poised above the planet.

"Jefferson," Bradley called. Jefferson ran over to Bradley holding his rifle. "What do you make of this?" he asked.

Jefferson looked at the digital screen. "I have no idea," he replied.

"Click on that icon there," Arkalon said, gesturing to a black circle at the bottom of the screen.

The picture of the satellite slowly got bigger as the speakers next to the screen opened up from behind the monitor.

"This is BLAST," a voice came from the speakers. "BLAST was invented by the United States government as an alternate weapon of mass destruction. It can emit an electromagnetic pulse that cripples the electronic communication of a prescribed region of Planet Earth."

"Wow!" Bradley said. "Never knew of that!" He sat for a moment, pondering the situation. He suddenly jumped up. "That's it!" he said.

"What's it?" CJ asked.

"Well, if our BLAST could just send an EMP over our dearly beloved Manhattan city, our visitors will no longer exist."

"How?" CJ asked.

"Remember back at Marco's warehouse?" He said, "Carbon dioxide is poisonous to these things, that is why they are in those suits, the filter on the back filters it out."

CJ opened his eyes. He knew Bradley may have just finished off the Armazoids.

"Wait. How do we operate it?" CJ asked.

Bradley froze in his tracks. "Ah," he said. "Now that's going to take some thinking."

Arkalon slowly walked over to him. "You can use the computer," he said.

"What?" Bradley gasped.

"The computer?" Arkalon said. "We can control anything from here."

Bradley was shocked. "Holy shit! All this time your people had access to our weapons of mass destruction?"

"I'm afraid so," Arkalon replied.

"Well, let's do this," Bradley said. He sat down at the computer and rolled the mouse over to the satellite. The machine beeped.

"As easy as that?!" CJ asked.

"Yes," Bradley groaned. He pulled up the map of Manhattan on the computer screen. "Shock of a lifetime!" he said, dragging the mouse to create a rectangle over Manhattan. "Enough?" he asked CJ.

"Yep, that will do it," he replied "Hopefully."

Bradley pressed enter, and a countdown appeared on the screen, counting down in big, red numbers.

"Six minutes!" CJ gasped.

"Hopefully Kevin and the rest of them got to the police station," Bradley said, flicking on his radio.

***

Eric kneeled down by a police patrol car that was part of the barricade around the station. The Armazoid vehicles were getting closer and closer by the second.

Bradley's voice crackled over their headsets; the signal was weak. "Kevin?"

Eric looked at Max. The shooting started again as the vehicles and Armazoids got closer to them.

"For God's sake, answer me, you tit.," Bradley said.

Eric gently shook his head as Max flicked on his radio. The signal was weak.

"Kevin's tied up right now," Max said.

"Well, where is he?" Bradley demanded.

"He is helping Kate," Eric replied.

Bradley didn't have any time to argue. "Okay, listen very carefully."

Max was distracted as the Armazoid tanks stopped, aimed, and fired at a US tank that was just behind them.

"Incoming, move!" Max yelled. He dove to the side, pulling Eric with him, but the explosion still lifted them off the ground and threw them back down. Ears ringing, Max got onto his hands and knees.

"Ouch." He moaned, "Jesus Christ."

He looked up to see an Apache helicopter flying low and shooting the Armazoid tanks. He couldn't hear the explosions, but the heat from them washed over him.

"Max, Max," Bradley yelled into the radio. He could hear explosions and heavy breathing, but Max didn't respond. "Oh, fuck me, not again." He flicked his radio off.

"Let's get out of here," CJ said.

"But where to?" Bradley asked.

"There is a vehicle docking bay about half a mile from here," Arkalon said.

"Cool," Bradley said. "Let's see if this BLAST thing works first."

Hundreds of miles above them, BLAST was opening up huge blades, rotating to point toward Earth. The disks at the back begun to spin, one after the other, powering up the pulse as the new machine continued opening up.

Below, Eric and Max crouched behind the police car, hearing back and shooting at the oncoming Armazoids. Eric squeezed the trigger on his shotgun. The last shell fired out and slammed into one of the Armazoids as the vehicles slowly rolled towards the station.

"I'm out," Eric said, dropping his gun.

"Me too," Max replied.

"And me," Rico said.

Max and Eric looked at Marco as the last of the golden bullets fired out of his weapon.

"I'm out, too," he yelled, "Bastard!"

Exhausted and out of options, they dropped to the ground one by one. Eric closed his eyes wondering what death would be like. He just wanted to die quickly and get it over with.

The nuclear missile closed in on Manhattan just as BLAST finished powering up. The huge force of electricity fired out of the satellite over Manhattan. The satellite slowly banked in orbit, sending the pulse down and over Manhattan.

The EMP swept over Eric and the group over the Armazoids. Eric was shocked. He looked up at the Armazoids. They stopped looking at the group. They started to choke. They fell to the ground, clutching at their throats until they froze, deathly still. The Spacefighters fell from the sky one after the other, slamming into buildings.

The pulse travelled across Manhattan and swept through the nuclear missile. The avionics and gadgets inside fried one after the other. The back motor cut out and pointed down towards the ground. Eric and Max jumped as the rocket slammed into the middle of the street. They slowly got up and walked over to it. It was dead.

The area was quiet. Only the ship above remained, somehow unaffected by the pulse. Max slowly got up and walked over to one of the dead Armazoids. He saw the air filter on the back of its suit had stopped working. The aliens had suffocated.

"It's dead," he said. "It's dead."

***

Bradley looked up at the digital screen as BLAST fired its pulse over Manhattan.

"Done," he said.

"How do we know it's killed them?" CJ asked.

"Well, he's still alive," Bradley said, gesturing at Arkalon. "But maybe it's a different story outside. I think it's time to go."

"Let's go," CJ replied. "Come on Jefferson."

Bradley loaded the last magazine into his M16 and loaded one of the grenades into the launcher. They followed Arkalon towards the rear exit. He pushed the small red button that opened the shiny, silver doors. Bradley led the way down the stairs, hearing voices and clangs ahead. He peeked his head around the corner and looked in disbelief at one of the Armazoid tanks. He went back to the group. "It just gets better, doesn't it?"

"What's up?" Jefferson asked.

"There's one tank plus some of our friends, so anyone got a smoke grenade?"

Everyone in the group shook their heads.

"Okay, is there another exit?"

Arkalon shook his head. "It's too far."

Jefferson stepped forward. "Okay," he said. "On my signal, go."

He cocked his rifle back, ready to open fire.

"What?" Bradley said in a loud whisper. "You'll be killed."

"I'll take the risk," Jefferson replied. "It's what I signed up for to protect."

"Look—" Bradley started.

"Bradley," Jefferson said. "After today, you are more important than me. Now get moving, kid."

Bradley just watched as Jefferson crept along the wall.

"Okay," Jefferson yelled. "Go, go, go!"

Bradley, CJ, and Arkalon ran out of the small corridor as Jefferson rolled out. He opened fire on the tanks and Armazoids as the other three sprinted past into another corridor. A moment later, they heard an explosion. Jefferson was dead.

The floor started to vibrate as the Armazoid tank rolled in hot pursuit.

"Shit! Move!" Bradley yelled. He struggled to keep moving as his leg muscles started to burn from all of the running. Arkalon waited by a huge door frame, gesturing them to get to him. CJ and Bradley made it through the doorway, and Arkalon hit a huge red button, causing a set of shutters to begin closing over the entrance.

Bradley put his hands on his knees, panting.

"What's that?" he asked.

"It's a set of shutters," Arkalon replied. "Look."

The shutters sealed shut just as the tank rolled into view.

"Should buy us some time," CJ said. They turned to continue down the corridor when they heard the click of a weapon being cocked.

Bradley looked up to see a small flap open up on the side of the wall. Bradley and CJ's eyes opened in fear as they watched a black heavy machine gun slowly point down at them.

"Oh, fuck it!" Bradley yelped. He watched as the blue power surged up behind it, ready to shoot down on him. "Come on!"

The blue rays fired out the back of the weapon. Bradley grabbed Arkalon, pulling him to the floor. CJ was hit by the rays and fell to the ground, bleeding out from the burns.

"Go, go!" CJ said weakly. His eyes glazed over. "Tell Marsha, I ,I-"

Bradley felt his heart harden at the sight of his dead friend. His eyes narrowed. "Now I'm pissed." He turned the grenade launcher on the machine gun mounted on the wall and pulled the trigger. The explosion blew the gun off the wall.

"Ha," he said. He turned toward Arkalon to tell him to lead him to that docking bay when he heard the clicking sound again. He looked up, watching another machine gun come out of the side of the walls. "What?" he moaned.

Bradley pulled Arkalon along, reloading his grenade into the launcher. He spun around, firing it at the weapons that emerged from the walls. He reloaded the last grenade into the launcher and took out one of the chasing machine guns.

"In here," Arkalon yelled, opening a set of silver doors. Bradley fell through the doorway, rays slamming into the door as it sealed shut. Bradley slowly got up, leaving his M16 on the ground—he was out of ammunition.

"What is this place?" he asked Arkalon.

"This is the weapon storage room," Arkalon said.

"Perfect." He pulled the last C4 charge Marco had given him as he looked at the missiles lining the walls, ready to be used.

He reached down and pulled out the charge from his pocket. He kneeled down, looking over his shoulder as he knew he only had a short time to leave the ship. He switched on the charge, placing it against a wall with particularly large rockets. The sudden blaring of an alarm made him jump up.

"What's that?" he asked.

"The ship is getting ready to leave," Arkalon said. "You haven't got long."

"Come on," Bradley said. He and Arkalon ran out of the weapons room and over to the large, open elevator.

"This is it," Arkalon said.

Bradley turned to him. "Listen, come with me. You could provide our government with information on your people. I can say that you helped me, and nothing will happen to you."

Arkalon looked at Bradley. "No," he said firmly.

"Why?" Bradley asked. "You stand a better chance of living, as you said you will be dead when you get back to your own planet."

"No," Arkalon said again. "I'm sorry, I can't."

Bradley frowned.

"Now go!" Arkalon yelled. He pushed Bradley into the elevator then hit the button for the vehicle bay in the bottom of the spaceship. Bradley watched him run off as the doors shut. Something didn't seem right.

The brakes clunked off one after the other. He shook his head as he leaned against the power box as the lift slowly started to lower down into the depth of the ship. He felt the lift shunt to a quick stop. The silver shutter slowly opened, allowing him to get out. He walked into the huge bay and looked at all the parked Armazoids vehicles.

"Right. Let's leave this heap of shit," he said to himself.

He walked into the center of the bay and looked around at the huge shutter leading to the outside of the ship. He moved slowly, making sure there weren't any Armazoids hiding for him. He was about to open the door to the outside when a voice stopped him.

"Not so fast," Circo ordered.

Bradley knelt down on the floor, exhausted. The lights around the huge bay were switched on. Bradley looked around as Armazoids walked out of the shadows, surrounding him.

"So, Bradley," Circo asked over the tannoy. "Where you planning to escape my human friend?"

"Yes, I was," Bradley replied, too tired even to be sarcastic.

"Well done," Circo said. "Or, it would've been well done."

Bradley glanced at the lever to open the hangar door. He had to get there. He slowly started to move toward it but stopped when he felt something rub his leg, it is the flare gun Roger had given him at the weapon shop earlier that day. Without looking down, Bradley smiled. The Armazoids slowly advanced towards him.

"Don't make any sudden movements," one Armazoid ordered.

Bradley took a deep breath. He dropped to the floor. Reaching down to his leg, he swiped the flare gun and pointed it up into the air. He squeezed the trigger. The flash launched up into the air and exploded, blinding all the Armazoids. He only has a few seconds before they can see him again. Bradley ran towards the lever and pulled it. Immediately the door began to open. Bradley crouched by the opening, waiting for it to be big enough to jump over.

Suddenly an immense wave of heat hit him in the side.

"Agggh!" Bradley yelled. "God damn it." He clutched his side and fell, narrowly avoiding another laser beam.

Finally, the doors were wide enough, and Bradley threw himself out into the evening sky.

He slowly rotated himself in the sky, turning to face the ship. It seemed very far away now. He pulled out the C4 detonator and pushed it.

The explosion ripped along the through the ship blasting open all doors. The walls ripped into one another. The huge explosion ripped along some of the corridors of the ship.

Bradley looked at the huge ball of fire as tiny scraps of metal floated down past him. He turned around and looked down towards the ground as the Hudson River came into view. He grasped the red cord on his parachute, ripping it halfway out. The chute didn't open.

"Oh no," Bradley screamed, tugging and tugging on the cord. It wouldn't budge.

He continued tumbling towards the ground. He pushed the small metal cord back in as far as it would go, the river getting bigger and bigger.

"Come on," Bradley yelled. He ripped the cord on the chute a final time. The small parachute opened, pulling the large one out. He slowed down, floating towards the river. He braced himself for a wet landing. Bradley closed his eyes as he slammed into the water, gasping as the water filled his wounded side. He flipped to his back and pulled the toggle to inflate the life preserver that was attached to the parachute vest. He listened to the canisters hissing as the blue bands slowly came out the side. He let his head drop into the cool water of the Hudson, now a relief to his aching body. The small handgun dropped from his hands and slid into the river. Small bubbles exited the weapon as it slowly sank disappearing from site.

Bradley looked up at the tiny stars many millions of galaxies away, as they started to appear as the sky is getting darker. It had always been a dream of his to go and see one. But now it no longer was. He wanted to keep way away from them for as long as possible. The small waves rocked Bradley about. He slowly leaned up, feeling very woozy. He felt the wound stinging as he slowly started pulling himself to the pier a short swim ahead.

Bradley arrived at the wooden pier, he climbed onto the dock where the boats would be parked up. Coughing up the river water from his lungs. He slowly got up hoping to find anyone who could point him to the police station. He dropped the survival kit onto the ground. He walked, he pulled out a bandage from a pocket of his vest. Without looking at the wound, he lifted his shirt and wound the bandage around and around his torso. He gritted his teeth with the pain. The road started to vibrate. Bradley looked to see three US army tanks, escorted by a few Jeeps, rolling towards him.

"Perfect." He thought.

The jeep pulled up next to him.

"You okay, sir?" one soldier in a Jeep asked.

Bradley got into the Jeep, not mentioning his wound and simply requesting to go to the police station. He just wanted to make sure the group was okay and if they made it. Bradley rested his head and closed his eyes as they traveled over the uneven roads back to the police station.

Bradley thanked the soldiers for the ride and walked up the concrete steps. A long line of people waited to board buses to take them away from New York for good. No one knew what he had done to save them. That made him feel strange, like he was their invisible guardian angel. He slowly walked through the open doors, covered in dirt and soot and drenched through. He headed toward the office where his class had been put before. He saw Kate and Ms. Hogan in the doorway, both looking very worried.

Kate glanced his way and looked past him, then brought her gaze back to him in a double take. She blinked.

"Oh my God," she said quietly. Then, much louder, "Oh my God!"

Kate jumped up and ran to him.

"Bradley!" She fell into Bradley, hugging him around his shoulders. He groaned with pain as he hugged her back tightly. Lisa, Eric, and Max ran over for hugs and back slaps, everyone laughing and talking about nothing in their relief to see Bradley is okay.

"You guys okay?" Bradley asked, energy dwindling fast. He swayed on his feet.

"Just about," Kate replied. "Better now we know you're okay."

"You okay, dork?" Bradley said.

"I'm okay," Eric replied.

"Not you, Eric," Bradley said. "Him." He pointed at Colin, who had been hanging back.

"Oh," Colin said, flustered. "Yes, yes I'm okay." He looked down, embarrassed, then looked back up, meting Bradley's eye. "Bradley. Thank you."

Bradley slowly reached his hand out to shake Colin's. It was a grasp of friendship.

"You did well in that ship," Bradley said to Eric. "Looks like you can finally hit a target."

"Thanks," Eric replied, shrugging modestly. "I do what I can."

"And you Max," Bradley said. "You kicked the shit out of some of them."

"Ha," Max said. "Of course, I am buying you that drink, a deal is a deal."

"And you, Rico," Bradley said. "You were good as well. Glad you joined us."

Rico ducked his head in acknowledgment.

"Talking of service," Bradley said, "Where is the old sod?"

Marco walked into the office after going to the restroom.

"Right here, boy," he replied. "Give me a hug."

Marco and Bradley hugged one another, Bradley grimacing from the contact with his side. He could feel the blood still dripping out of the wound.

"Where's Aussie?" Max asked, looking around.

Marco smiled. "Let's say he found an empty hotel, and it had a bar."

"What?" Eric asked.

"Oh, I see," Bradley said, smirking. "Good for him. That will be us later."

"Bradley," Kate said. "You saved all our lives. If you hadn't been with us, we would all be dead."

"Ha," Bradley said. "Of course, anytime! Anyway, I want to hug Kevin. Where is he?"

The group went quiet quickly.

Bradley looked down at Max. "What?" he asked. He leaned against the wall, feeling dizzy.

"Bradley, listen," Kate said quietly. Bradley looked at her, and she reached out and held his hand. "There was an accident, a short while ago."

Bradley couldn't believe his ears. He shook his head in disbelief. "No," he said. "No, no, no." He slowly leaned forward placing his head in his hands. More blood began to seep from the wound on his side. "Aggh," he moaned.

"What?" Kate asked, concern darkening her face.

Bradley fell back on the floor. A red smear streaked the floor where his side rubbed against it.

Kate gasped and stood up. "Can we get some help in here?" she called to some paramedics walking through.

Bradley lay on the cold floor of the station, the faces of the group swimming in and out of focus.

"Bradley, come on, man," Max yelled. "Don't do this to us."

Bradley struggled to keep his eyes open as the two paramedics ran in. They loaded Bradley onto a stretcher to take him to the military medical center that had been set up in nearby tents. He realized he was crying. Kate was still holding his hand, but he couldn't hear her. He absently wondered if he was going to see Kevin in the afterlife. The blood on his side was sticky. Stretcher slammed through the entrance and skidded to a stop.

"What do we have?" a doctor demanded. Bright lights shone down.

"Injured male," another doctor said. "Lost a lot of blood."

Time went by slowly, or was it quickly? Bradley was linked up to a heart machine and a slow *beep, beep, beep* filled the room. As it slowed, Bradley found he couldn't keep his eyes open.

"We're losing him," he heard. There was a straight, long beep.

"No!" The doctor yelled. "Not you too."

The heart monitor stayed monophonic.

Author Stephen William Cheshire, from the UK. Born in London on the 29th November 1988, is a Foundation Degree graduate in Aviation from New College Nottingham in the UK. He then went on to do a BA Top Up in Travel & Tourism.

He loves to travel and uses all his travel experiences to put together his novels. Many of the scenes in his books come from when he has been abroad. Either sitting in a hotel or walking around a foreign city.

His life goal is to fly for a commercial airline.